"I don't need your help, and I'd appreciate it if you'd leave me the hell alone!" Trey snapped.

Jamie had drawn back, startled at his abrupt bark, but then she merely looked at him consideringly. "Jean will have lunch ready soon."

He stared at her. "What is it with you? Are you trying to kill me with kindness?"

He could have sworn he saw the corners of her mouth twitch, as if she was suppressing a smile. "Would it work?"

He was startled out of his determination to irritate her until she left. "Why? Why don't you just give up?"

"Stubborn?" she suggested placidly.

He shook his head in disbelief, staring at her. Her expression was soft and warm, conversely sending a chill down his spine.

"I owe you my father's life," she said softly.

But they both knew it went deeper than that.

Dear Reader,

It's March, and spring is just around the corner. To help you through the last of the chilly days and nights, we've got another lineup of terrific books just waiting to be read. Our American Hero this month is Linda Turner's *Cooper,* the next hot hero in her miniseries called "The Wild West." He's a man you won't want to miss.

The rest of the month is equally irresistible. Justine Davis is back with *Wicked Secrets,* a tale every bit as enticing as its title implies. Lee Magner's *Banished* makes it worth the wait since this talented author's last appearance. And then you'll find Beverly Barton's *Lover and Deceiver,* Cathryn Clare's *Sun and Shadow,* and Susan Mallery's debut for the line, *Tempting Faith.* Each one will have you turning the pages eagerly; this really is what romance is all about.

And in coming months, keep looking to Silhouette Intimate Moments for all the passion, all the excitement and all the reading pleasure you're seeking, because it's our promise to you that you'll find all that—and more—in our pages every month of the year.

Yours,

Leslie Wainger
Senior Editor and Editorial Coordinator

Please address questions and book requests to:
Reader Service
U.S.: P.O. Box 1325, Buffalo, NY 14269
Canadian: P.O. Box 1050, Niagara Falls, Ont. L2E 7G7

WICKED SECRETS

Justine Davis

Silhouette®
INTIMATE V MOMENTS®

Published by Silhouette Books New York

America's Publisher of Contemporary Romance

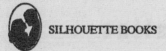

SILHOUETTE BOOKS

ISBN 0-373-07555-3

WICKED SECRETS

Copyright © 1994 by Janice Davis Smith

Printed in U.S.A.

JUSTINE DAVIS

lives in San Clemente, California. Her interests outside of writing are sailing, doing needlework, horseback riding and driving her restored 1967 Corvette roadster—top down, of course.

A policewoman, Justine says that years ago a young man she worked with encouraged her to try for a promotion to a position that was, at that time, occupied only by men. "I succeeded, became wrapped up in my new job, and that man moved away, never, I thought, to be heard from again. Ten years later he appeared out of the woods of Washington state, saying he'd never forgotten me and would I please marry him? With that history, how could I write anything but romance?"

To the Orange County Chapter, RWA—
always there, in good times and bad,
and an incredibly talented bunch.
I'm proud to belong to the powerhouse!

Prologue

There is always a wicked secret,
a private reason...

— *W. H. Auden*

Gunfire again. It echoed over the ringing in his ears, over the gasping of his lungs for breath.

Had they shot some other poor fool, thinking they'd pinned him down once more? Or did the trigger-happy idiots have some innocent jungle animal to their credit now?

They were passing him now, too close. He huddled in the mud beneath the huge fronds of a brilliantly green fern, wondering what creatures were eyeing him as a morning meal. Four legs or less, he hoped; it had been one with a hundred or so that had put him in the hands of Lucero to begin with, with a bite he'd barely even felt. Appropriate, he thought vaguely. The thick, scraggly mustache that split Lucero's swarthy face distinctly resembled that damned centipede.

Trey Logan smothered a despairing laugh as the footsteps grew more distant. God, he was losing it. At this rate,

Lucero's men wouldn't have to hunt much longer; they'd just have to sit and wait until he broke and ran through this damned jungle screaming at the top of his lungs.

With exquisite care he shifted position, trying to ease the fierce throbbing in his leg. He knew it wouldn't do much good; the ugly wound was too new, too fresh . . . and probably infected. No gangrene yet, but if he had to spend much more time in this jungle, constantly moving, it wouldn't be long. He remembered the legend of the ranger who'd been caught alone behind the lines in the Pacific, in World War II. The man had stepped on a mine that had misfired, only mangling his foot instead of killing him. The wound had festered, then begun to rot. And the ranger, knowing he had to survive to pass on vital information about troop movements, had cut off his own foot. And made it out with his news.

Trey shuddered. Well, he wasn't a ranger anymore. And he had no such information. And no one waiting for it. Or him. No one would miss him if he never made it out of here. His death wouldn't even make a ripple in anyone's life, except maybe a small one for Hank, who would have to replace him.

As the sounds of the patrol's passage faded away, he tried to take comfort in the knowledge that at least he had accomplished his objective. He had gotten Hank's brother out alive. He'd completed the mission.

Readily will I display the intestinal fortitude required to fight on to the ranger objective and complete the mission, though I be the lone survivor.

The words, the last *R* of the R-A-N-G-E-R creed, floated up through the haze of pain as clearly as if he still wore the uniform. Move farther, faster, and fight harder. Well, he wasn't doing that very well right now. *If you did still wear the uniform, Logan, they'd take it away after this. You're fit only for an army like Lucero's.*

Lucero. Gen. Rodolfo Lucero.

Somewhere deep inside him, beneath the pain, beneath the grim knowledge that any breath could be his last, a tiny ember of determination flickered, then caught. He drew his legs up under him, jaw clenching and sweat pouring from him as he fought to ignore the ripping agony that shot through his left thigh. His newfound resolution wavered. He closed his eyes, locking the pain away, picturing Lucero's evil, grinning face and what he would do to it when the time came. Just as he had so many times before, when the man's vicious laugh had been echoing in his ears as the pain he was inflicting racked Trey's body.

Slowly, silently, he began to move.

Chapter 1

"What's going on?" Jamie McCall asked, eyeing the army green van blocking the long, curved driveway, and gaping a bit at the Arnold Schwarzenegger clone who was carrying long pieces of shining metal tubing she couldn't identify into the house. "Are we being invaded?"

"How's the prettiest little girl in California?"

Jamie turned to smile at her tall, gray-haired father. "Losing it, Daddy. Goliath didn't even wink at me."

She said it teasingly, with no trace of rancor. Jamie McCall was under no illusions about her own appearance; she found it decidedly average, and no amount of fatherly doting or fatuous flattery from aspiring young men would change her mind. Especially when she knew those young men had one—if not two—eyes on her father's rather stratospheric financial ranking in affluent Orange County. Even her father's sometimes annoying protectiveness hadn't hidden that fact from her.

"That," her father said seriously, "is because he is married to a woman who, from what I've seen, could break him in half."

Jamie laughed. "Then it's just as well they found each other, isn't it?" She eyed her father curiously. "So what is it now, Daddy? The ultimate Erector set?"

A smile creased the older man's aristocratic face as he looked down at his daughter. Jamie smiled back; her father's rather faddish tendencies amused, even pleased her, for they were evidence of the softer man she knew lived beneath his sometimes rigid exterior. "You made the money, you should spend it however you want," she'd told him often, whenever his personal accountant not so subtly handed him the totals on his latest experiment.

"But it's your inheritance, too, don't forget," he'd said ruefully the last time, when the collection of custom golf clubs and the country-club membership had been donated to the local YMCA.

"Jamie, my love, you are the light of my life," he said now, rather startlingly vehement.

"Uh-oh." Her mouth twisted ruefully. "This must be a dilly. Tell me, is Arnold moving in?"

"Arnold?"

"Mr. Universe. He of the amazon wife."

"Oh. No, it's not that. As a matter of fact, this is not one of my...er, new projects."

She looked from him to the still half-full truck and then back doubtfully.

"Forgive me, Daddy dear," she said in an indulgently amused tone, "but it does have all the earmarks of another McCall special, you must admit."

"Yes, I suppose it does," he said after a moment. "You look hot and dusty, so why don't you go take a shower, then meet me in the library and I'll...explain."

She hesitated as emotion tightened his voice and the skin around his eyes. Then, with a sigh, she went into the house.

It happened occasionally, that oddly taut note in his voice as he looked at her. She knew what it meant; some unexpectedly rueful words from her Uncle Hank had told her when she was twelve.

"Lord, Jamie, you do have your mother's coloring, that honey-streaked hair and those golden eyes," he had said. "If it wasn't for that sassy nose of yours, and your mouth—" Hank had paused, grinning, to let Jamie guess if he meant what came out of that mouth, or merely the fuller, wider shape of it "—you'd be the living image of her." And Jamie had suddenly understood the reason her father never spoke about her mother, why the only photograph of her was in Jamie's room. He was living with a daily reminder of the woman he'd so loved and lost.

After a quick shower, Jamie hastily towel dried her hair, then let it fall over her shoulders in the damp version of the flyaway gold-brown mass it would become when dry, no matter what she did. Even when she pulled it tightly back, it soon escaped, wispy strands changing the severe line into a feminine softness. She dressed hurriedly and went downstairs.

Accepting the glass of soda her father had poured for her, she curled up in the big leather chair she had appropriated from him at age three, and cocked her head toward the clanking noises coming from the west wing of the house.

"Whatever is going on, I gather it's in the solarium?"

"Yes. And that's what I need to talk to you about."

James McCall sipped at his own Scotch and soda as he sat in the chair opposite his daughter, the matching chair he'd bought when he found a bright-eyed, sunny-faced toddler in the original every time he came home to this room.

"I know that's one of your favorite rooms," he finally began, uncharacteristically hesitant, "and I'm sorry to have to use it, but it seems to be the best—"

"Daddy, this house is ten times the size the two of us need. I think I can stand losing one room for a while." She raised an eyebrow at him. "I can still go in to take care of the plants, can't I?"

"Of course. You won't be losing it, not really. They're only moving the lounges and table to one side. It's just going to be used for something else, too, part of the time."

It wasn't like him to beat around the bush once he'd begun to talk, and Jamie's curiosity was mounting.

"Dad..."

"All right." He was suddenly brisk. "Do you remember what I told you about what happened last year?"

Jamie shuddered as she nodded; she couldn't help it. Every word her father had told her about his ill-fated trip to Central America was engraved in her mind. She'd come so close to losing him....

"Then you remember about the man who got us out?"

"Trey Logan? Uncle Hank's old army buddy? Yes."

Her father's face was solemn. "I've never felt right about what happened. I've had nightmares about what he must have gone through in that hellhole."

"But he told you to go on without him, Daddy. You wouldn't have gotten out if you hadn't."

"And *he* didn't get out. We left him there, alone, in that damned jungle."

Jamie uncoiled from her chair with an unconsciously regal grace and went to sit beside her father on the padded arm of his recliner.

"It wasn't your fault, Daddy—"

"I should have known. Hank tried to warn me they were on the brink of revolution, but I wouldn't listen. I had to go down there anyway...."

And he had wound up in the middle of one of the bloodiest coups ever known, in a place known for them. Jamie would never forget those days of terror, of wondering, of praying that her father would get out alive. Even now it raged on, a rebellious, out-of-control sect of the army against the government and its own forces, with the civilians, as usual, caught in the middle.

"He risked his life to get us out," her father said. "And we flew out and left him there."

"He told you to," she repeated, knowing that this was a deep, festering guilt her father had carried for a long time. "If he hadn't kept them diverted, they would have gotten all of you. And I know you started trying to find him, to get him out, as soon as you got back. You've kept after that Mr. Cárdenas, you've never given up, you've—"

She stopped, looking at her father closely.

"You've found him, haven't you?" she guessed.

He nodded.

"Then he did get away." Jamie let out a sigh of relief. Perhaps now her father could forgive himself for grasping the chance for his own survival at the cost of the man who had given him that chance.

James saw her reaction and read her relief. With a reluctant look, he corrected her gently. "He didn't get away. At least, not then. The army caught him two weeks afterward. They wouldn't have, except he'd been bitten by one of those damned poisonous centipedes they've got down there." He grimaced. "They threw him in a cell and watched to see whether he'd die or not."

Jamie paled. The rich warmth of this room, of this house, of this life, seemed to fade away in the face of the stark horror of an existence she couldn't begin to comprehend.

"But he lived," she said, in a futile hope that this was the end of the story. Instinctively she knew it wasn't.

"Yes. Although he might have been better off if he hadn't. They decided that since he was an American, he had to be CIA."

"But he works for Uncle Hank," she protested. "Hank's the one who sent him in to get you out of there."

"Yes. But they couldn't believe that a civilian company would go to so much risk just to save one businessman."

"Daddy..."

"They tried to make him confess that his true mission was to infiltrate their group, spy on them for the president's government. And they weren't gentle about it."

"Oh, God."

"He was in that jungle for months. I don't know how long they had him, and I still don't know how he escaped. I only know that Cárdenas sent Hank word he was in the capital. Hank sent a plane down to Jardín to bring him home."

He reached up and took her hand, looking at her intently. "He was in terrible shape, baby. He'd been in the hospital for days before they found out who he was. He'd been starved, beaten and shot. He's going to need a lot of rest, therapy and a place to heal."

Understanding dawned. "You're bringing him here?"

"Yes." He gestured toward the solarium, which still echoed with those clanking sounds. "That's what the gym equipment is for. A therapist will be here in a couple of days. I tried to get Carly Singer, but she's off on a job out of state."

"Too bad," Jamie said with a smile at the memory of the inordinately sassy redhead. "Carly could really whip him into shape."

"I know it will disrupt our routine, but—"

"Don't be silly, Daddy. We owe him your life. He's welcome to the whole damned house if he wants it."

There was an odd look in his eyes, a look that seemed to her one of forgiveness, although she didn't know for what. Unless, she mused suddenly, her earlier thoughts returning, it was for looking so much like her mother.

Jamie wondered if she would see him today, although she tried to deny to herself that she had decided to stay home for just that reason. Curiosity, she told herself. Just natural curiosity. Especially after last night.

The house had seemed oddly quiet when she arrived home late that Saturday, and she found herself being instinctively quiet as she made her way through the silent rooms.

"Jamie!"

She had stopped, then backtracked two steps to the doorway of the library. "Daddy? Why are you sitting in the dark? Are you all right?"

She crossed the darkened room quickly, knowing he would be in his usual chair. She knelt before it, straining to see him as her eyes adjusted to the dimness.

"How was your day, baby?"

She had sensed he was stalling, but answered anyway. "Fine. Good, actually. Chuckie did really well today, and he passed his checkup with flying colors."

She heard a low chuckle.

"I'm glad, but what I really meant was how was your date with Edward?"

She shrugged, then realized he probably couldn't see her. "The same as any date with Edward. An elegant dinner, the 'in' play and him being arrogant to the parking valets."

"I thought you liked Edward."

"He's the most tolerable of that crowd. But I can only take so much of his telling me how beautiful I am."

"But you are." His protest was immediate, and Jamie smiled.

"*You're* supposed to think so. You're my doting father."

She heard him sigh. "You really don't realize how lovely you are, my girl. But that's part of your charm."

"If I'm so charming, then perhaps I could charm out of that adoring father what it is that's bothering him?"

She heard a rustle of movement, and then light circled the leather chair. "Trey arrived today."

She had reflexively looked around at the darkened house.

"He's asleep. The long flight was . . . tough on him."

She had studied her father's face for a moment; it looked grim, shadowed with, she realized, guilt. "Daddy, you can't keep feeling that way. Even if he blames you—"

"That's just it. He doesn't. He went through hell down there, and he doesn't blame me. He just thanked me for helping Miguel to get him out."

"Then why do you still feel guilty? If he—"

"Because I've seen him now."

Jamie hadn't spoken for a moment. Her father rarely interrupted her; that he had done so twice gave her a clue as to the turmoil of his feelings.

"I'm sorry, Daddy," she had said finally, simply, unsure of what else she could say.

She had thought about that conversation for some time afterward, building an image in her mind of a beaten, broken man whose condition had put that look on her father's face. *I hope he gets better quickly,* she thought as she dressed on Sunday morning, *because I think that's the only thing that's going to stop Daddy from carrying around this load of guilt.*

In deference to her father's distaste for the worn, comfortable jeans she preferred, she slipped on a long, slender caftan of pale gold silk shot with metallic gold threads. She liked it because it made her eyes stand out vividly; she never realized that the expensive silk sliding over her slender body and long legs might bring on images of taut muscle under golden hide, images of the sinuous grace of a sleek palomino full of spirit and grace.

She hastened down the stairs, glancing briefly down the hall that led to the west wing, which held the solarium and the bedroom her father had selected for their guest. It was rather isolated, and she had wondered about the choice until she realized that it was to avoid the long staircase that might prove too difficult for him to manage.

Her vision of the man she had yet to meet became more vivid. He had been a ranger, been part of the fabled raid on

Grenada, her father had told her, before he'd left the army to go to work for Hank.

In her mind's eye she could picture the old veteran who didn't know what to do with himself without a war to fight; she wondered if he regretted having left the army before the Persian Gulf War. If it hadn't been for Hank, she supposed, the mysterious Trey Logan could have just as easily become a mercenary.

Her stomach growled as the delectable odor from the dining room reached her nose. One of Jean's incomparable breakfasts, she thought, picking out the smell of fresh orange juice from amid all the other tempting aromas.

She abandoned her idea of toast and coffee and made a right turn into the elegant room. She and her father usually passed over this room in favor of the smaller, brighter, eating nook in the kitchen that overlooked the pool, so this must be in honor of their guest.

"Ah, there you are, my dear." James rose. "I was just talking about you."

Her answer to her father's greeting died unspoken on her lips, and she stopped dead three steps into the room. On the first step she had seen her father in his usual chair. On the second she had spotted the crutches she had half expected beside the chair to his left. The final, faltering step came when she saw the man in that chair.

At first her mind wouldn't accept it. He was supposed to be old, Hank's age at least, if not her father's. He was supposed to be her stereotypical image of the old army warhorse. He was not, her mind insisted, supposed to be young and tall and lean, with thick dark hair and smoky gray eyes that seemed to look right through her without revealing anything of the soul behind them.

And then her focus narrowed, and she saw the lines grooved by pain and weariness in a face that should have been young, a face still pale beneath a deep surface tan. She saw the unnatural gauntness that spoke of too little bulk on a tall, broad frame. She saw the still-red mark of a healing cut across one high cheekbone, and the mark of another, deeper slash running from one dark brow up into thick, dark hair. And in the eyes, she saw the shadow that clouded the piercing gray, tarnishing what should have been bright, gleaming silver.

"—my daughter, Jamie."

Realizing with a start that she had just been introduced, Jamie managed a smile. It faded as she looked at the man, for the shadow in his eyes seemed to lift for a moment, revealing a distaste so strong it was almost tangible. It flashed only briefly before the cloud descended like a shutter in the silvery depths, but she knew she had seen it.

"So I presumed. Pardon me for not getting up." Was there the slightest edge in that low, deep voice, an edge that matched the look that had flashed in his eyes? "You're just what I pictured, Ms. McCall."

Yes, that edge was there. She hesitated, then spoke sweetly. Very sweetly.

"Why, thank you, Mr. Logan. A tribute to Daddy's powers of description, I'm sure, although he does tend to see me through a father's rose-colored glasses."

For an even briefer second, surprise flickered in the eyes she could feel fastened on her as she took her place to her father's right. James reached out and patted her hand, and she looked up to smile at him.

At her first look at his much-loved face, she forgot the odd feeling that cold look had given her. If it were not for this man across from her, she might never have seen that face again, and for that if for no other reason, she owed him more than she could ever repay.

She turned her gaze to him, to find him watching her steadily, his expression unreadable. Glowing with a renewed joy at having her father safe at home, she held his look.

"Thank you for my father," she said simply.

That surprise she had seen flickered again, flashing from behind the shuttered gray eyes and quickly disappearing. When he spoke, his voice was flat, uncompromising.

"It was my job."

"It wasn't your job to sacrifice yourself for him."

He shrugged. "He was the objective."

A delicate brow arched upward over one tawny gold eye. "And you were . . . ?"

He shrugged again.

"Expendable?" she guessed instinctively.

The surprise flared brightly in the gray eyes then, before he looked away. She had clearly hit a nerve. She doubted that he often avoided anyone's gaze; there was too much arrogance, too much coldness in this man.

Yet when she looked at him, when she saw the semicircles of thick, dark lashes as he stared down at his plate, he looked oddly vulnerable, softer somehow, and she felt a twinge inside, a pang of some feeling she didn't recognize.

The arrival of Jean Hooper, the loyal and efficient housekeeper who had been with them since Jamie was a baby, was a welcome break in the oddly strained atmosphere that had filled the room. She set down steaming platters of eggs, muffins, sausage, toast and bacon, and poured fresh coffee for all of them before she returned to the kitchen.

It was an uncomfortable meal, with Jamie unusually quiet as she pondered both the unexpected appearance and puzzling reactions of Trey Logan, her father hastening to fill the gap with uncharacteristic chatter, and their guest sitting in unrelieved silence.

And, Jamie noticed, not eating. He had accepted the plate Jean set before him without comment, but had barely made a dent in the generous portions of food. The only thing he seemed to eat easily was the toast, plain, forgoing both butter and the marmalade that sat in a small silver dish on the linen tablecloth.

It came to her in a rush when he reached for the glass of orange juice beside his plate and set it hastily back on the table; she had seen the brief tremor that had shaken his fingers and the cruel marks that banded his wrists below the sleeves of his shirt.

Her gaze flew to his face, seeing once more the haggard thinness. Her own stomach knotted as she realized that the bland toast was all his deprived stomach could handle. And that those marks were the signs of flesh rubbed raw by ropes . . . or chains. All the horror she had felt when her father had first told her what had happened to this man after he had gotten "the objective" safely on the helicopter came rushing back to her.

In that moment she made a silent vow. She didn't know what had brought on Trey's instant dislike, didn't care how cold or distant he might be. He had the right, she thought, after what he'd gone through for her father. He had the right to any amount of patience from her. And she would give it, no matter what.

Great. Just great. Trey Logan slumped on the weight bench, his elbows on his knees and his head cradled wearily in his hands, his thoughts whirling as he listened to the footsteps of the therapist fade away down the hall.

After three days he was still as weak as a newborn pup, his leg was throbbing and still had a tendency to buckle under the least strain, and he couldn't keep down anything stronger than toast and weak coffee. Status quo, he thought bitterly. He was in the same shape he'd been in ever since he'd awakened in that hospital in La Selva. Nothing new. Everything that could be wrong was wrong.

At least, that was what he'd thought. *You forgot Murphy's other law,* he thought wryly as he slowly straightened up. *Whenever everything's gone wrong, it hasn't.*

He reached for the towel beside him to wipe the sweat from his face. No sooner did he close his eyes than that image leapt to life again: a slender, graceful figure in a sweeping fall of pale silk lit by golden sparks that were echoed in incredible amber eyes.

Damn, he thought, snapping his eyes open quickly. His mouth twisted ruefully. "Murphy," he muttered under his breath, "was an optimist."

Determinedly he rose, ignoring the crutches he'd been ordered to use, and headed for the leg press. His gait was slow and off-balance, his face tight as he made his left leg take more weight than it wanted to. He welcomed the pain—it erased that vivid image from his mind.

Although Mark Torres, the therapist, had told him he'd done enough for one day, he began again, his back braced against the seat as he pushed the pedal to lift a total weight he would have scoffed at before. It sent searing, ripping pain from his thigh down to his ankle, and upward into the small of his back.

"Jellyfish," he muttered at himself. *Move it,* he ordered silently. *You've got a debt to pay, to that bastard in La Selva, and you aren't going to be able to do it in this kind of shape.*

He clenched his jaw and pushed again. The pain again, worse. He pushed again. And again. He pushed until the room was spinning around him, and the tearing pain seemed to have swollen to fill his entire body.

He had to stop then. He tried to sit up, but couldn't seem to remember what direction up was. Over the ringing in his ears he felt an odd, floating sensation, followed by an abrupt thud he vaguely thought would have been painful if he'd been able to feel anything more than the aching throb that began in the damaged muscles of his leg and radiated outward in waves of pulsing pain.

Although his eyes were closed, he knew he hadn't passed out, because he could still feel that screaming pain from the knotted muscles of his thigh. But it was distant, oddly removed, and he knew that his mind had instinctively retreated to that internal shelter it had built during the worst days of his captivity, when the pain of what they were doing to him had been too much for his conscious mind to bear. The days when he had filled his conscious mind with his hatred of his tormentor to the exclusion of all else, and had sworn retribution.

Yet it wasn't quite the same. This time the pain was having a very strange effect on him. He could swear he smelled fresh flowers. Gardenias, he thought rather vaguely. Like the ones his mother had grown—

That deeply ingrained safety valve snapped, cutting off the thought before it could form. He was a little amazed that the old protective device was working; nothing else seemed to be. Even though the ringing in his ears had faded, they still weren't functioning. All he could hear was a soft, soothing murmuring he couldn't recognize. And that scent, that lovely, sweet scent, lingered. He didn't want to test his eyes, but he couldn't seem to stop himself. He opened them slowly.

He was right. They weren't working any better than anything else. All they did was make him think that the radiant image was leaning over him, a look of gentle concern on her lovely face. He shut them again, shaking his head as if to free himself of the persistent vision.

Then something wonderfully cool was drawn across his forehead and cheek, and involuntarily he turned his face toward it. His movement stopped abruptly, his muscles freezing as the murmur he'd thought a side effect of the pain his mind was trying so desperately to block out coalesced into softly spoken words. His eyes flew open again.

She *was* there. It hadn't been a malfunction of a pain-wearied brain. Gone was the sweep of glistening golden silk from this morning, but there was no mistaking the mass of silky hair and those incredible tawny gold eyes, full of a softness that made it harder for him to breathe than the pain had.

"Better?"

With that one quiet word, the fog clouding his brain cleared, and his surroundings snapped into sharp focus. Only then did he realize he'd fallen from the seat and was on the floor. And Jamie McCall was kneeling beside him, the cool, damp cloth she'd used to wipe his sweating face still in her slender hand.

With a convulsive movement he tried to sit up; his aching leg told him swiftly what it thought of that idea. He fell back, disgusted once again at his own weakness.

As if she'd read his look, Jamie spoke softly. "You can't do it all in one day."

That husky voice did crazy things to his nerves, and his voice was sharp as he tried to combat its effect. "What do you know about it?"

"I know you're pushing. Doing more than you should, more than the therapist wants you to."

"Oh? And just how did you determine that?"

He bit it out as he struggled to prop himself on his elbows. And failed again. She'd probably never had a sore day in her pampered life, he thought acidly.

"I heard him leave twenty minutes ago. But you kept right on going."

"Nosy, aren't you?"

He saw something flare briefly in the golden eyes, but when she spoke, her voice was carefully even.

"I was merely waiting until you were done. I had some things to do in here, and I didn't want to interrupt you."

"Lifting weights?" he snapped as he looked at her slender figure.

He'd meant to be sarcastic, but instead found himself noticing that, although slim, her arms looked taut and fit below the short sleeves of the cheerful yellow T-shirt she wore. As did every other part of her.

Especially, he thought ruefully, the long legs clad in snug, faded jeans. Jeans that surprised him. He would have expected the very best in status-conscious designer labels, not worn, durable Levi's that somehow looked loved as they, in turn, hugged trim curves lovingly. He made himself look away.

She answered him calmly, as if she hadn't noticed his tone, although he knew by the glint that appeared in her eyes again that she had. "Gardening, actually."

He stared at her, startled, then glanced past her to the verdant profusion of plants and flowers that filled the glass-walled portion of the room. They were clearly the product of a loving hand, with a very green thumb. "The gardener's day off?"

He could see her effort to control her natural reaction to his cutting tone. When she smiled, it was as steady as if they were carrying on a normal conversation. And it made his heart begin to hammer faster than when he had been in the middle of his pitiful workout.

"The indoor gardener lives here," she said sweetly.

Damn, he thought. *Why doesn't she get mad and leave? You've been an absolute jerk. She should have been out of here the first time you snapped at her. Women like her don't stand for being talked to like that.*

He sucked in a deep breath and tried to sit up once more. He made it halfway before his muscles protested and he began to fall back. Then something stopped him, a slender but steady support that braced him, helped him make it the rest of the way.

She was too close. With her arm around his shoulders, that sweet, exotic scent of gardenia surrounding him, he couldn't breathe, couldn't slow down his racing heart.

"Don't!" he snapped, furious with himself. This was crazy, it was stupid, and if he wasn't so damned weak he wouldn't be reacting like this.

"Trey!"

His name in that soft, husky voice was the last straw. He had to get away from her. And since he was clearly unable to move, she had to.

"Just leave me alone, damn it," he grated out.

"With pleasure." She had finally been stung to anger, and got to her feet.

In his gratitude that she was leaving, he made the fatal mistake of looking up to watch her go. The sight of those legs and that trim, tight bottom in the faded jeans played havoc with his pulse all over again.

When the door swung shut behind her, a low groan broke from him as he leaned back against the weight bench. Damn, damn, damn! Why the hell did she have to look like that? And why did she have to be so blasted nice to him, even when he was being an absolute bastard?

Well, he thought as he reached for the damp cloth she'd dropped, he'd taken care of it now. She wouldn't come near him again, not after the way he'd treated her today. He could concentrate on forcing his body back into shape, on planning how he would pay back the man who had so battered it. He wiped his brow, then froze.

It was impossible, he thought. That sweet fragrance couldn't really be clinging to the cloth she had merely held in her hands. He dropped it, anyway, and let his head loll back on his shoulders wearily. Suddenly his physical convalescence, a process he'd known would be long and painful, seemed minuscule compared to what else he'd let himself in for by coming here. It was a long time before he tried to move again.

Chapter 2

He was in pain, Jamie told herself again. She couldn't expect a man to worry about things like courtesy and friendliness when he was hurting.

She didn't believe it.

Sighing, she wriggled into the swimsuit she'd dug out of a drawer. She couldn't avoid the knowledge that she alone was the recipient of his distaste. Over the last week he had exhibited quiet respect for her father, wry tolerance for Mark Torres and impeccable courtesy to Jean; with Jamie he maintained a facade of cool politeness punctuated by remarks that could easily have an innocent interpretation. She did her best to ignore the double meaning, to pretend he'd only meant the words literally, but she knew he hadn't. And worse, she could see in those cold gray eyes that he knew she knew it, and he didn't care. What the icy eyes didn't tell her was why.

It made her vow to maintain her patience very difficult to keep. If she only knew why, she thought wearily as she picked up her towel and went downstairs. But how could she when his antagonism had been obvious before they'd even spoken a word to each other? And more obvious since? For once she was thankful her father had had to go to Denver on business yesterday; keeping up a pleasant front was wearing on her.

She couldn't resist a glance down the hall to the room Trey was using, but it didn't tell her much. The door stood open, but it always did. She'd wondered about that; since he hated anyone to see him struggle with his battered body, she would have thought he would keep the door shut for privacy.

If for no other reason, she thought rather sourly, *than to keep me out of his way.* She sighed, wishing once more she could understand. Although many of his comments were veiled references to the stereotypical "poor little rich girl," she knew it wasn't envy; she had come to recognize that in people who coveted the easy life they assumed her father's money bought her. Besides, she knew instinctively that envy was a foreign emotion to the cool-eyed man to whom she owed her father's life. And *that* was a fact she needed to remember.

She padded softly through the quiet house, pulling the French doors silently closed behind her as she stepped out of the living room into the early morning chill. Mist rose from the heated water of the pool in wispy tendrils, and she paused to savor the peaceful quiet, loving these moments before the noise and clatter of the world began.

From the other side of the glass wall of the solarium, Trey Logan watched the young woman poised on the elegantly tiled edge of the custom pool. He watched as she launched her slender body into a smooth, graceful arc and cut the water cleanly and silently. Eyes that were usually clouded and shuttered were glittering silver as he watched her swim with steady, rhythmic strokes through the crystalline water.

He watched her swim, but the image of her as she had stood on the edge before her dive overlaid all else in Trey's mind. He'd been right, he thought dully. Every lovely inch of her was trim and taut and toned. And deliciously curved, even in a bathing suit that was obviously used for the purpose of swimming, not gathering admiring glances.

Yet, on her, that one-piece suit would gather as many glances as the skimpiest of bikinis, he thought wryly. Just the way the glistening white fabric set off the golden tones of her body and the highlights of her hair was enough, but with the way the French cut added impossible inches to already impossibly long legs, and the way even the plainly simple lines could not disguise the ripe curves of her breasts, the effect was breathtaking. When her natural grace and those stunning amber eyes were added, it was heart-stopping.

He meant to turn away, even began to shift the hated crutches to move, but he couldn't seem to do it. He watched as she executed a neat flip turn at the end of the pool and started back.

Once he had gotten over his surprise at seeing her at the pool at this hour, he had supposed she would, at most, indulge in a leisurely dip. But she was swimming steadily, with purpose and intent, lap after lap, each one marked by a carbon copy of that first swimmer's turn.

Discipline, he thought suddenly. This was clearly a regular routine for her, and it spoke of a self-discipline he never would have anticipated in a woman who lived the kind of life she must live.

He'd lost track of the number of laps she'd done when she headed for the steps at the side of the pool. He knew he had to turn away then, but she moved more swiftly than he had expected and he was pinned by the sight of her rising from the water, as surely as if he'd been nailed to the floor. Thin streams of water trailed along slender curves. Droplets beaded up on the golden skin, and he envied every one of them.

Inevitably his gaze dropped to the rising thrust of her breasts, and to nipples tautened by the sudden exposure to chilly air. Helplessly following their example, his own body tightened in response with a suddenness and unexpectedness that left him stunned.

He swore softly, harshly, as he at last forced himself to turn away. He had known he was in trouble from the first moment he'd looked up to see that tawny angel coming into the room that morning. He'd known it and had been furious about it. He had a promise to keep, the promise he'd made to Rodolfo Lucero before the man had battered him until his lips were too swollen to speak. The last thing he needed was some juvenile reaction to the coddled daughter of a wealthy man to distract him, especially when that man was partly responsible for pulling him out of hell.

He had tried to convince himself, rather callously, that he should be glad he felt anything, that he had responded at all. He'd had his doubts about whether his battered body could still function sexually, doubts that had been erased in the first moment he'd seen her.

He'd done everything he could think of to drive her away, to make her avoid him whenever possible. He'd been rude, abrasive and downright cruel. He couldn't understand why she hadn't told him to go to hell. Or whatever society girls said in place of that indelicate declaration.

At least, he hadn't understood until yesterday, when, after taking her father to the airport for the flight to Denver, she had returned and walked in while he was fumbling with the unfamiliar and unwelcome crutches. He was already incensed after an infuriatingly short workout, and when she had politely asked if he needed any help, he had erupted.

"I don't need your help, and I'd appreciate it if you'd leave me the hell alone!"

She had drawn back, startled at his abrupt bark, but then had merely looked at him consideringly. "Jean will have lunch ready soon,'' she said mildly. "She made that soup again, since you've been able to eat it.''

He stared at her. "What is it with you?'' he snapped. "Are you trying to kill me with kindness?''

He could have sworn he saw the corners of her mouth twitch, as if she was suppressing a smile. "Would it work?''

He'd been startled out of his determination to irritate her until she left. "Why? Why don't you just give up?''

"Stubborn?'' she suggested placidly.

He shook his head in disbelief, staring at her. Her expression was soft and warm, conversely sending a chill down his spine.

"I owe you my father's life,'' she said softly.

He stiffened. "You owe me nothing,'' he snapped, "so quit trying to be so damned nice.''

The warmth vanished. "Sorry,'' she said carefully, "but I would be nice to worse people than you, if they'd saved my father.''

She had risen then and walked from the solarium with a regal grace that seemed all the more affecting because she was so obviously unaware of it. And he had at last understood her seemingly endless patience in the face of his purposeful testiness. She thought she owed it to him.

He pushed the memory of that exchange out of his mind as he sat down near the weight rack, already weary, wondering if he would once again have the energy only to collapse after his workout. A workout that he had, after a bawling out from Mark, grudgingly shortened in return for an agreement from the therapist that he could use the pool for as long as he could stand it.

"You keep pushing like this,'' Mark had warned seriously, "and I can guarantee not only will you not be running by the end of the month, you won't even be walking. You can't do it all in one day.''

Trey had snarled something unintelligible at the words that had eerily echoed Jamie McCall's. The young therapist had blithely ignored him.

His fury at his own weakness overrode his exhaustion at the end of the exercises today, and he determinedly turned away from the beckoning door of his bedroom and began to make his way in the opposite direction. He'd been living in this house for a week and had seen only the solarium, the dining room and the room he was sleeping in. Or lying awake in, waiting for the pain to ease or the nightmare to fade and the walls to stop closing in.

He wrestled with the crutches, his only concession to his post-workout weariness, as he struggled his way down the hall. Damned house was huge, he muttered to himself as sweat broke out on his forehead once more.

He made it as far as a pair of heavy, oak double doors before his head started to spin with the effort. He pushed his way through them, hoping only for a chair to be close by, and only vaguely aware of the dark, masculine comfort of the room with its leather chairs and book-lined walls, and the bright colors of a Navajo blanket on the back of the wide sofa. He collapsed on the nearest chair, a soft, comfortable recliner, and waited with impatience for the whirling to stop. He methodically, unconsciously, rubbed at the tight skin of his healing wrists as he let his head loll back.

He'd never been a particularly patient man, except when it was the strategic thing to do. And he was especially impatient when the fit, strong body he'd always relied on failed him. And now it was telling him too clearly that he was going to have to postpone his plans. He wanted Lucero, wanted him badly. Plotting his revenge against the brutal man had been the only way he'd hung on to his sanity during his long, painful captivity.

He *would* get the man, he promised himself. He would make him pay for every blow, every stroke of the lash, every night spent shivering in a cell no bigger than a doghouse, every day spent chained like that dog in the burning sun. It might take him longer than he'd hoped, but the end result was inevitable. Rodolfo Lucero would pay. If it was the last thing Trey Logan did on this earth, he would pay.

The whirling in his head gradually slowed, then stopped. Trey didn't realize he had dozed off until Jean's voice roused him suddenly.

"Are you all right, Mr. Logan?"

His eyes snapped open. The older woman was leaning over him, her pale blue eyes full of concern.

"Fine," he said quickly. "Just resting."

She nodded in relief, one hand going up to smooth the graying dark hair that she seemed to always wear in a neat coil at the back of her neck. Unlike the coil that seemed unable to restrain the honey brown mass of spun silk that—

Stop it, he snapped inwardly.

"I won't disturb you, then," she said. "I can do this room later."

Only then did he see the duster she held in one hand and the carrying tray of other cleaning gear that sat on the floor beside her.

"Don't let me stop you." His mouth twisted wryly. "I'll be out of here as soon as I can move."

"Don't let me drive you away. I'll be done soon." She smiled. "I know this is everyone's favorite room."

I can see why, he thought, really seeing the room for the first time. The shelves of books warmed the room, books with the look of being read and loved, not placed there just for appearances. Across from him was a door that led to what appeared to be a bathroom, and next to that a large window. It let in a flood of sunlight, bringing the polished rosewood of the massive desk to a deep, rich red sheen.

Idly he watched Jean's quick, competent movements as she worked her way around the room. Then curiosity sparked when, just as she approached one corner of the room, her movements suddenly changed. Brisk efficiency had given way to tender care, and Trey twisted in the chair to see why.

He couldn't quite explain why that corner of the room was different, but it was. There was another expanse of glass, this time curving around a window seat that looked inviting with its abundance of cushions and pillows in rich, jewel colors. There was a second desk, smaller, and of oak, glowing warm and honey brown, almost the exact shade—

Jamie. He knew with sudden certainty that this enticing corner of the room was hers. It suited her, from the colors and the tempting comfort of the seat, to the glowing golden hue of the wood, to the unexpected sweep of a green stem crowned by the rich, orange grace of a single tiger lily. *Unexpected.* That word again.

Something glinted in the sunlight streaming through the window, and his gaze flicked to the source, which was held with care in Jean Hooper's hands as she polished it lovingly.

A trophy, he realized. A silver cup that shone with the unmistakable glow of sterling. His gaze went past the woman to the case that now stood open, the case that she had clearly taken the cup from. It was full, every shelf laden with similar pieces of silver and an occasional golden shape. A horse? Really curious now, he struggled to his feet.

He spurned the detested crutches and used the back of the chair that matched the one he'd been sitting in for support as he made his way to the case.

Horses, he confirmed silently when he stood beside them. Lots of them. He leaned forward to read one of the engraved inscriptions below a golden horse. First Place, Three-Day Event. What the hell was that?

"Lovely, aren't they?"

He nodded at Jean's soft words as he looked at the next piece, an exquisitely etched silver tray. First Place, Santa Barbara Fiesta Days Horse Show, Open Jumping Division.

"They were so marvelous together." Jean paused in her polishing, a reminiscent tone coming into her voice.

"They?"

"Jamie and Whiskey. Oh, he was a wonderful horse. And he'd do anything for her." She gestured to the overflowing trophy case. "But I guess you can see that Mr. McCall had this case built for her. She didn't want to make a fuss, just wanted to pack them all away somewhere."

"She...won these?" *Figures,* he thought. *Rich girl's hobby.*

"Every one." She set the silver cup back down carefully. "And she would have gone all the way."

"All the way?"

"The Olympics. She and Whiskey—her horse—made the team, at the trials. She was so excited...." She trailed off, shaking her head sadly.

Trey blinked. The Olympics? She was *that* good? Then the rest of the woman's words registered, along with her tone. "Would have?" he asked despite himself.

Jean hesitated, her kind face troubled. "It's difficult to talk about, even now. There was a horrible accident. A runaway horse got loose on the course just as she was taking a last jump. One of those horrid, spiky, fence things. They all crashed together."

He paled as a sudden vision of a ton of heavy, thrashing horseflesh and hooves flashed through his mind, made grimly horrifying by the knowledge that somewhere amid that lethal mass had been a slim, delicate young woman.

"Yes," Jean said at his look, "it was terrible. Both horses were badly hurt, and had to be put down."

"Jamie?" he asked, his voice oddly gruff.

Jean's eyes clouded. "We were afraid we would lose her. And then, for a while, they weren't sure she'd ever walk again. It was a long, terrible time."

God. And he'd thought she knew nothing about pain or suffering.

"But she's ... all right now?"

Jean paused, looking at him in surprise. He couldn't blame her, not after the way he'd been acting. But he'd long ago guessed that the woman looked upon Jamie as a beloved daughter, and he figured she wouldn't be able to resist talking about her favorite subject. He was right.

"Yes," she went on finally. "We were lucky, her spine hadn't been permanently injured. She started to get return, to regain some feeling, fairly soon, but it was a long time before we were sure she would recover completely. She spent so long in one of those horrible brace things, poor girl. And in therapy, afterward."

Therapy. No wonder she knew so much about it.

"The doctors wanted her to give up riding altogether, but she wouldn't. Even when they told her if she had another fall like that, she might not be so lucky. And Carly, her therapist—not nearly as respectful as your Mark," Jean added, her mouth twisting slightly. "Must be that red hair. Anyway, she backed Jamie up, said if she wanted to ride badly enough, she would. It gave the child something to hope for, when she could barely move."

Logan, he grated silently, *you are a bastard.* "It must have been ... hard on her."

"Yes," Jean agreed somberly. "But what hurt her the most was her horse. She barely spared a thought for herself, but when they finally had to tell her Whiskey had been put down, she was devastated. She nearly gave up then, and we began to think she would never get well. But she came through."

Came through. Such paltry words, Trey thought as he slumped tiredly in the leather recliner after Jean had gone. He'd seen enough people go through that kind of bodily hell to know how inadequate those words were.

No wonder his preconceptions wouldn't stick. She might indeed be a wealthy man's daughter, might truly have every material thing available, but none of that got a person through that kind of experience. Only guts, determination and pure backbone did, and you couldn't buy that.

Which is why, he supposed ironically, he was sitting here exhausted after the slightest of efforts. He was running short on all three of those necessary qualities. He let out a disgusted sigh, but couldn't stop his eyelids from drifting closed, or his hand from moving to massage the aching muscles of his thigh.

As he was drifting amid confused images of menacing jungle, falling horses and huge amber eyes, the throb in his leg suddenly eased slightly. He didn't remember moving, he thought groggily. He *hadn't* moved. He'd *been* moved. His eyes struggled to open. It took him a moment to realize when they had opened, for the amber eyes were still there.

"I thought it might help."

Her soft words brought him fully awake, and when he tried to sit up he realized what she'd meant: she had pulled up the footrest of the recliner, elevating his leg, and was kneeling beside it.

"I... It does. Thank you."

She sat back on her heels, staring at him with the look of someone who'd put her hand in a beehive and had come out unstung.

"You're welcome," she said after a moment.

His gaze went over her, and he wondered that he hadn't guessed before what she did when she left so early in the mornings. The worn Levi's made sense now, and he should have realized that the boots he'd thought an affectation hadn't gotten that battered look by being worn to the local shopping mall. And those taut, trim muscles hadn't come from sitting around having her nails done.

But why? He couldn't help the question that rose to the forefront of his mind. After all she'd gone through, he wouldn't blame her if she never went near a horse again.

"I saw your trophies," he began, not knowing quite how to ask, after he'd worked so hard at alienating her. That he had succeeded was obvious by the suspicion that showed in her expression as she tried to fathom the reason for this sudden softening. "It's ... quite a collection."

"I suppose." Her voice was carefully neutral.

"The Olympics..." he began again, then floundered. Damn, had he become so entrenched in this sour attitude that he couldn't even carry on a civil conversation with her? "You should be proud," he ended lamely.

"I was. For Whiskey." Her voice was level, but he saw the flicker of pain in the golden depths. "He deserved it."

"But you—"

"I was nothing without him." She looked past Trey to the glittering shelves of the trophy case. "He did everything I ever asked of him, and if I made a mistake he saved me with sheer strength and courage. He had more heart than anyone I've ever known."

Trey swallowed, his throat suddenly tight at the emotion in her voice. It stunned him, the effect the love and admiration that rang in her words had on him. He wondered suddenly if she'd ever felt like that about a person, and what it would feel like to be that person. Then her gaze swung around to fasten on him with a coolness he'd not seen from her before, even when he'd been at his rudest.

"What?" The amber eyes were flashing at him, as if daring him to speak. "No pithy observation about silly little rich girls obsessed with horses?"

He winced inwardly. "No."

She studied him, brow furrowed in puzzlement. "Why?"

He glanced at the trophies. "I may be an idiot, but even I recognize sacrosanct territory when I see it."

One delicate brow arched as she followed his gaze. "Because of some trophies?"

"Because of what it took to win them." *And to survive what happened afterward*, he thought, but didn't say it. "You still ride?"

"Yes," she said, still eyeing him warily, "but I don't compete anymore."

He ran a finger over the tucked leather on the arm of the chair. He knew she didn't trust him not to attack this precious part of her life, and he couldn't blame her.

"It must have been hard to give it up," he said at last.

"It was," she said briefly.

There was no bitterness in her tone, no self-pity at the end of what must have been a dream as well as a way of life. Guts, he thought again.

"I'm sorry." He didn't know what else to say.

Jamie's brow furrowed again. She didn't understand this. Where was the cold, mocking man of the last week? Where was the man who found her presence so distasteful that a barely civil nod was all he could manage? Who was this man whose voice held genuine feeling instead of cutting scorn?

She gazed up at him from where she crouched beside the chair. He looked, she thought, much better than he had that first day. He didn't look as pale beneath the tan, and that unhealthy grayish tinge was gone. The dark circles around his eyes had lessened, but the lines graven into his lean face by pain had, if anything, deepened, even though the cuts were healing.

He'd regained some weight, too, she thought. It was hard to tell in the loose sweats he usually wore, but the black T-shirt he had on now stretched across a chest that spoke of a broadness that would be intimidating when its full bulk was regained, and the short sleeves were already taut around leanly muscled arms. The angry red marks at his wrists were fading, but she still couldn't look at them without her stomach knotting.

She felt a sudden desire to see him recovered and healthy, at full vitality, and the image that appeared in her mind at that thought took her breath away.

She suddenly realized she had been staring, taking a silent inventory of his body as if he were a horse she was assessing for conformation. Embarrassed, she drew her gaze quickly to his face, wondering if he had noticed. The question fled her mind the moment their eyes met. Where were those wintry eyes that had always held nothing but chilly disdain when they looked at her? These eyes were glittering silver, warm in a way she hadn't known they could be. She tried, but she couldn't seem to look away.

"I'm sorry about your horse, too," he said softly, in a tone that matched the new warmth of his gaze.

"I..."

Her voice trailed off. Something about the way he was looking at her tightened her throat and made it hard for her to speak. Then what he'd said penetrated the fog that seemed to have surrounded her since she had begun that unintentional physical inventory. Her eyes widened.

"You know, don't you?" Fire sparked in her. "That's what this Mr. Nice Guy business is all of a sudden, isn't it? Somebody told you, and now you—" she rose suddenly and backed up a step "—you feel sorry for me!"

"Jamie—"

"No!"

She cried it out, ignoring the tiny part of her that seemed out of her control and had kindled with a different kind of heat than anger when he had, for the first time, used her name. She hurried on, her words tumbling out heatedly.

"I don't need pity, not from anyone, but especially not from you! Feel sorry for yourself it you want, but not me!"

She whirled and ran from the room. Even in anger she showed that same regal grace that, to Trey, seemed still more beautiful now that he knew about the battle she had fought to be on her feet at all.

He struggled to climb out of the comfortable chair. He wanted to go after her, to tell her that what he'd felt wasn't pity, not even sympathy, but admiration for what she'd done, and empathy over the loss of a loved companion. He

wanted to soothe the lines of anger from her face, he wanted
to hold her, to tell her he—

Uh-oh.

The warning echoed in his head as strongly as it had in the
dawn mist as his parachute had carried him down to the island of Grenada. He had known he was heading into trouble then, and he knew it now. The story Jean had told him
had lowered his guard, had made it impossible for him to
maintain that crucial distance from the slender, tawny gold
beauty. He had to regain that distance, and fast. He sank
back in the chair.

Maybe it would be easier now. Maybe, now that he'd
made her good and mad—ironically the first time he wasn't
trying to—she would cooperate by staying away. And staying mad.

"Great," he muttered. "Just great."

She seemed to have a knack for not doing—or being—
what he expected. Including being modest, he added to
himself dryly. He would never have known, if her father
hadn't been so proud that he had made her display her win-
nings.

And *he* would have been better off, he thought glumly. It
was difficult enough to keep snapping at her in the face of
the physical attraction he couldn't deny he felt, had felt even
when he'd thought the worst of her; to maintain that rotten
attitude when everything he learned was proving him wrong
about her, was coming close to impossible.

But it was that very attraction that he had to fight. There
was no room for that in his life, no room for anything until
he'd paid that ugly debt, and he sure as hell wouldn't insult
the man who'd brought him here to heal by getting in-
volved with his daughter.

Not, he reminded himself wryly, that there was much
chance of that. Jamie McCall was out of his league, and he
knew it. And, despite her kindness, so did she.

He sighed wearily. He could only trust that he'd managed to burn through that damned politeness of hers and make her solidly angry. Enough to stay away from him. He wasn't sure he had the strength to keep up his guard. But he didn't dare let it down, not when he could so easily wind up drowning in a pair of amber eyes.

"Oh, that man!"

Jamie slammed down the brush she had been dragging through her hair with little respect for the silken strands. The impact made the mirror over her dresser shudder, and she lifted her head to look at her quivering reflection. *That's just how I feel*, she thought grimly. *He makes me so mad, I could break something. Anything.*

When she realized she was actually looking around for something to throw, she stopped dead.

"You," she said to her reflection, "are a basket case."

She stood there for a long moment. She wished she could talk to Kylie, she thought. *She* could make sense of this. She'd been so many places, seen so many people, even though she was only six years older than Jamie. She always seemed to understand why people were the way they were, almost as well as she understood horses.

But Kylie Rainwood—Kylie West, she corrected with a smile—was gone, on the honeymoon that very nearly hadn't happened, what with the recent fire that had destroyed her barn and nearly killed the man she loved, Tyler West. No, Kylie more than deserved some peace in her life right now; even if Kylie was here, she couldn't go whining to her, Jamie thought.

"You're on your own, girl," she muttered.

With a sudden burst of determination, she tugged off her worn boots and dusty clothes and headed for her bathroom. She turned the water up to a torrent and stepped beneath it.

It was when she closed her eyes to lather her hair that the moment came back to her, that moment before she had moved to lift the footrest. She had felt incapable of movement as she had stared at the dark semicircles of his lowered lashes, and the long, strong fingers that were massaging what were clearly aching muscles.

Abruptly short of breath, she had been torn between feeling compassion for his pain and wanting to ease it herself, wanting to use her own hands to soothe and stroke. And then she had been without breath altogether as her traitorous mind wondered what it would be like to be soothed and stroked by those strong, supple hands in return.

Her eyes snapped open in shock, rewarding her with a blast of warm water that made her rub at them furiously. It wasn't until she was out of the shower and wrapped in the thick bath sheet that she allowed herself to ponder her incredible reaction again.

She approached it much like someone who had disturbed a snake and wasn't quite sure if it was poisonous or not. Common sense told her to forget it and take off running, but her own innate curiosity and boldness made her go back for a second look.

Teenage imaginings about a few rock stars and a celebrity or two aside, Jamie had never gone in much for fantasizing. At a time when most girls were gathering in giggling clusters to indulge in adolescent and frequently risqué discussion of the opposite sex, she'd been wrapped up in horses, loving their strength and gentleness, determined to make her dream of a berth on the Olympic team a reality, and caring little for the unpredictabilities of the male of the human species.

The protective cocoon of her father's wealth had strengthened that isolation, but all his care and cosseting couldn't help when she had had cold reality thrust upon her by a jagged fence and a flailing horse's hooves. She had completed her college studies from a hospital bed, with honors as a result of the voracious reading that had been the only thing keeping her sane through her long convalescence. She had missed the girl talk that fostered this kind of feminine wondering, and wasn't sure how to deal with it now. Especially since this was the first time her thoughts had ever taken this kind of intimate turn.

It didn't make any sense at all, she decided as she toweled her hair. If she was going to be having these kinds of thoughts, why on earth about Trey Logan? The man had made it clear since the day he'd arrived that he thought her an ornamental nuisance.

Until today.

"He felt sorry for you," she told her image in the steamy mirror. "Somebody told him about the accident, and he felt sorry for you. Maybe even guilty about being a jerk, but that's all."

The fact that she had felt that strange, unfamiliar stirring before she had known that, before, even, he had looked at her with that unexpected gentleness, made it only more confusing.

She wrapped the towel around her hair and went back into her bedroom. As she pulled out clean clothes, she found herself smothering a wistful longing that she hadn't felt in a long time, a longing for the mother she'd never known, for the feminine advice and closeness she'd never had.

"Good grief, McCall," she chastised herself, "you really are letting this shake you up."

And it's making you forget your promise, she added silently. And that unusual longing for her mother had reminded her sharply. She was used to a life without her mother; she couldn't imagine one without her father, as well. But she would have found out what it was like, if not for Trey Logan. She renewed her vow with fresh resolve and shoved from her mind the peculiar feelings he seemed to rouse in her.

Chapter 3

Jamie's steps faltered as she pulled open the French doors to the pool; she hadn't known Trey was there. She hadn't even realized he'd begun swimming, but remembering how Carly had recommended it as an effective yet gentle exercise, she wasn't surprised.

She was late for her own swim, but then her entire day had been turned around ever since that early-morning phone call. She lingered in the doorway hesitantly. She hadn't seen him since that day in the library, and had been somewhat shamefacedly grateful about it.

"Stop it," she ordered herself severely as she gathered her determination and stepped outside. "You can't hide in your own house."

She made her way toward the steps at the shallow end of the pool, moving slowly over the delicately hand-painted blue-and-white tiles as she watched Trey swim. He was approaching the far end, his stroke slow but steady. She wondered that he was doing as well as he was, as weak as he had seemed.

Even as she thought it, she saw him falter. She waited, expecting him to stop when he reached the far edge. Instead, after two shorter, almost awkward strokes, she saw his head come up for a gasping breath, saw him pull himself together and make a somewhat ragged turn. Then he struck out at a speed that astonished her. He kept it up the length of the pool, pushing, driving, apparently heedless that his exhaustion was evident in every forced stroke.

He came to a halt nearly at her feet, throwing one arm up over the tiled edge, his head lolling back as he gasped for breath. Just the sound of it made Jamie's chest ache. She stared at him, amazed yet again at the sheer determination of the man.

After several moments of that rasping breathing, he opened his eyes. He raised an arm that was none too steady to brush his water-slick hair back from his forehead. In the act of trying to lift his head, he froze, and she saw him swallow heavily, choking off the next gulping breath. Slowly he straightened, then turned his head toward her.

She could almost feel his gaze move up her legs, and suddenly the conservative bathing suit her friends teased her about seemed skimpy at best. She felt an odd weakness in her knees, and before they could give way as she feared, she dropped in a semicontrolled fall to sit on the tiled decking.

He didn't speak for a long moment. She could see him trying to control his body's relentless demand for air, just as she could see the strain he was feeling because she was there to observe it. She sensed that Trey Logan was not a man who took kindly to anyone witnessing his weaknesses, even when it was obviously not his fault.

Finally he sucked in one long, deep gulp of air, and seemed able to slow to mere deep breathing. He met her gaze then, and she read in his eyes the memory of how they had parted a few days before. Then that shutter dropped, and his expression was unreadable as he spoke.

"You're late today."

She couldn't hide her surprise. He knew when she usually swam? Her gaze flickered to the glass wall of the solarium, then back to him. She found no answer to her question in the impassive planes of his face.

"I had to go to the stables early," she began tentatively, willing to ignore that painful scene in the library if he was.

He raised a brow but didn't speak, and she realized he was still hoarding his breath. She hesitated, then went on, unable to restrain the gleam of excitement that lit her face.

"We had a mare foal this morning. She was having trouble, and Suzie—her owner—got scared because the vet wasn't going to get there for a while."

"So she . . . called you?" He got it out with only a single breath between words.

Jamie shrugged. "I worked with our vet for a year when I started college. Suzie thought I could help." A smile flitted across her face. "I don't know if she meant help the horse, or her."

Her smile faded as she saw a shiver ripple through him, as if someone had run a feather down his spine. But when he spoke, his voice sounded normal enough, if still a bit winded. "What happened?"

"A colt. A beauty, too." Her eyes were alight with remembered joy.

"Before or after the vet came?"

She shrugged again. "Before. The mare just needed a little help."

"Help? You call midwifing a thousand pounds of expectant mother a *little* help?"

Jamie's brow creased as she looked at him. He looked like a man who had come face-to-face with a contradiction he hadn't expected. "It wasn't as bad as I thought it might be, and it worked out all right," she said. "I still wish the vet had been there, though."

"But you did it, anyway."

"I had to," she said simply. "The horse needed help."

He just stared at her for a long moment. "I only have one question," he said at last, looking at her seriously.

"What?"

"Is a colt a boy or a girl?"

Her eyes widened and she looked at him suspiciously. Her suspicion faded into disbelief when she saw the tiny quirk at one corner of his mouth. She wanted to laugh, but she wasn't certain enough he'd meant to be funny. She took refuge in a slow, drawled retort. "Watch it. You're easily drownable at the moment."

More than a quirk this time, but still not a smile. Then it was gone as he said, "Then I guess I'd better get out of here. If I can," he added under his breath, so low she knew she wasn't meant to hear it.

He braced his hands on the tile coping to hoist himself up to sit on the edge. Jamie had to look away when she saw his arms tremble under the strain, but relaxed a little when she heard the swoosh of water that told her he'd made it. She lifted her gaze and had to smother a gasp.

At the soft, stifled sound, Trey turned to look at her. She knew the horror showing in her face as she stared at his bare back was what made him freeze, unmoving.

"I'm sorry," he said stiffly. "I thought you knew."

"I..." She trailed off, looking away. Still, the sight of that sleek skin marred by the barely faded crisscross of vicious lash marks lingered vividly, terribly, in her mind. She had barely noticed the other, older mark low on his back, so starkly did the others stand out.

His jaw was tight as he swung his legs up out of the water so he could lean over to reach for his shirt. Before he could pick it up, slender fingers touched his wrist. His head snapped around to face her.

"No," she said, her voice sounding strangely hollow. "I didn't mean ... I mean, I knew about your leg ..."

She trailed off as her gaze involuntarily strayed to the wicked, puckered new scar that marked his left thigh just below the wet nylon of the maroon running shorts he'd worn to swim in. Even had she not known, even to her naive eyes, it was clearly a gunshot wound.

The front was bad enough, but the glimpse she'd gotten of the more brutal exit wound when he'd leaned over was enough to make her stomach tighten and her mind fill with awe that he was able to move at all. She had to swallow heavily before she could go on.

"It's just that that—" she gestured toward his leg "—seems..." She faltered, her gaze flicking to his back again before she lowered her eyes. "It seems less... personal."

"I took it all very personally." His voice was cold. He wore that look again, the look of distaste she'd seen that first day.

"But your back..." she said, her voice quavering. "It's so... intentional."

He laughed, a harsh, humorless sound. "Believe me, Ms. McCall, they were both intentional."

"I know, but..." She floundered. She couldn't deal with this. She'd never seen anything like this—how could she find words for it? "It *seems* different," she said lamely.

His eyes were icier than she'd ever seen them as her words faded away. "I don't see any difference," he said brittlely. "I was chained to the same post both times."

Jamie gasped. "What...? The shot... It wasn't when you got away?"

He didn't answer. He didn't have to; his eyes told her all she needed to know of the contempt he felt for her naiveté.

"B-but why?" she stammered. "If they wanted to kill you—"

"Oh, they did. And if the general had been better at anatomy, he would have."

"Anatomy?"

"He wanted the femoral artery. He missed. Didn't get nearly as much blood as he wanted to see."

He said it bluntly, purposefully, and her color faded from pale to ashen.

"He wanted you to... bleed to death?" Her soft, husky voice echoed with horror at the vision of him, helplessly chained, his life draining away. "He wanted to watch?"

"No." His voice was the wind for the chill that had overtaken her. "He wanted *me* to watch."

He didn't even spare her a look as he got to his feet. Nor did he try to hide the unevenness of his gait as he walked away without a word.

Jamie sat there on the tile, trembling uncontrollably. She felt as if she'd been ripped out of a safe, warm womb and thrust into a cold, evil world. And she felt a fool. She'd seen, heard and read of barbarism and brutality in all parts of the world, but it had never been so real to her.

And now it was this world, this place, this house and the luxurious pool she sat beside, that seemed unreal. Reality was a pair of icy gray eyes and a set of angry welts slashing across the taut muscles of Trey Logan's back.

She couldn't stop the shaking. She wrapped her arms around herself, trying futilely to quell the rippling shudders. At last, in a convulsive, barely controlled movement, she flung herself to the edge of the pool and then over, relying on instinct to demand that her body swim rather than drown. She only hoped that it would work.

Trey watched uneasily from one of the cushioned wicker lounges in the solarium. He'd meant to put more distance between them; he hadn't meant to bludgeon her into shock.

She'd been so excited, so innocently happy about the birth of a tiny horse, and he had ripped her out of that protected cocoon and shoved the ugly side of life in her face. He remembered a time when the protection of that kind of innocence had been his goal in life, a time when he had believed in the principles that had permeated his life and his work unto death. He didn't understand what had compelled him to destroy that innocence now.

He tried to stifle the unfamiliar sense of guilt that stirred within him. He'd always easily dismissed it as a useless emotion; he did what he had to do and didn't look back. And he'd had to do this. That moment of harmony between them when she had told him of her morning had been too disarming, too close to a kind of easy companionship he'd never known with a woman.

He had to keep her away. He couldn't handle this, this ridiculous reaction to her, not when he was barely strong enough to walk the twenty feet from the pool to this room that had become his world. Maybe this would work, he thought grimly. He'd been utterly brutal this time, and he knew instinctively he'd shaken her to the core. Maybe now he would be free of the distraction she presented, free to concentrate on the goal he meant to achieve if it took the rest of his life. But still he watched her.

She was swimming now, swiftly, almost frenzied. He recognized the fierce concentration of someone trying to make the next stroke the only thing the mind had room for; he'd been there himself all too often in the last few days. She reached the end of the pool and made another of the neat flip turns, then started back at that same frantic pace.

I hope you're proud of yourself, Logan, he said harshly to himself. He turned away from the glass wall, unable to watch anymore.

Trey became a shadowy presence in her life after that day. Jamie didn't know if he was avoiding her, as, she admitted to her chagrin, she was him, but it seemed to be a mutual effort. She'd always kidded her father that they could get lost for weeks in this house; she was finding it was true.

It went on for days, until the moment when, as she found herself dodging into a spare bedroom at the sound of his labored progress down the hall, she caught a glimpse of herself in the mirror over the dresser. Slightly hunched over as she strained to hear through the door she'd pulled closed after her, she looked for all the world like a sneak thief skulking around to avoid discovery.

Slowly, her cheeks flaming, she straightened up. *Lord,* she breathed to that reflection in the mirror, *what a coward you've become. You, who always thought that if you could face the possibility of never walking again, you could face anything. And then at your first taste of an ugly reality you've never seen before, you run like a scared rabbit, blaming the man who made you see it. The man who was the victim of that reality.*

Sucking in a deep breath, she pulled open the door. The hallway was empty. She heard the clank of metal on metal and knew he was in the solarium. Pushing himself again. She scampered around the corner and up the stairs to her room.

Yes, a coward, she repeated coldly. *You creep around your own house just to avoid seeing him, to avoid having to think about it.*

"Right," she muttered to herself. As if she hadn't been thinking about him all the time, anyway. An image rose in her mind, of water glistening on the bronzed skin that was smooth and sleek between the appalling marks, and something knotted hard and tight deep inside her. The thought of him, so strong and proud, chained to a post and beaten, was—

What? Too horrible for your tender sensibilities? She snapped the words off silently, harshly. *He's the one who went through it, and he's not running. He's the one who has to live with the memories, with the pain.*

And he doesn't want your pity any more than you wanted his. The thought popped into her head fully formed and without doubt. She didn't know how she knew it, but she did. She dropped down on her bed and lay there, thinking, long after the shadows had lengthened, then faded to black.

She awoke with the startled little jump of a person unaware that she had dozed off. It had been a week of restless nights, full of too-vivid images, and she wasn't surprised she had dropped off.

She glanced at the clock on the nightstand; it was almost midnight. *No wonder my stomach is growling,* she thought. *Missed dinner again.* A little echo of that earlier self-disgust rippled through her. She'd been avoiding that, as well, fixing her own meals long after Jean had left the kitchen, and Trey the dining room. In fact, she admitted rather grimly, she'd been avoiding most of her favorite rooms lately.

She didn't flip on any lights in the darkened house as she made her way downstairs, so when she saw the sliver of light under the library doors, she was startled. She pulled one of them open quietly.

He was in the chair again, with the footrest up to ease the strain on the muscles of his leg. A book lay open in his lap, the reading lamp next to the chair throwing a circle of golden light downward, leaving his face in shadow above it. Yet she knew he was looking at her, knew he'd looked up the moment she had opened the door.

"I..." She swallowed. "I saw the light.... I just..." *Oh, damn,* she thought, her courage wavering. She backed up a step. "I'm sorry I interrupted your reading."

"It's all right." She could just make out the twist of his mouth as he went on, sounding a little rueful. "I wasn't getting much out of this, anyway."

She hesitated in the doorway. He just looked at her, waiting. *Coward,* she repeated inwardly. It got her into the room. She glanced at the book in his hands as she sat in the other chair, and despite herself her glance flew to his face in surprise.

He shrugged. "The horse world apparently has a jargon all its own."

"Yes," she said, still stunned by his choice, "it does. And that book supposes you know it all already."

He chuckled wryly. "If I knew a paddock from a fetlock, it might make some sense to me."

Jamie barely kept herself from shaking her head in numbed shock. He hadn't just been idly thumbing through the book—he'd been reading it. With interest.

"At least you know they're different things," she finally got out.

She drew in a breath and tried to fight down her edginess. She expected him to turn on her at any minute, expected to see that cold, condemning gaze again, and it made her nervous. She told herself to relax; she couldn't really see his eyes, anyway. She managed a smile, but couldn't resist the question. "What . . . made you pick that?"

He shrugged. "There was nothing in here I knew less about."

Jamie considered that for a moment, surprised. Most people in a library, she thought, would look for something they were interested in. But he had looked for the opposite, and she found that intriguing.

Admit it, McCall, she thought with rueful self-derision, *everything about this guy intrigues you.* For a brief moment, when she had asked that question, she had even wondered if his choice of books had something to do with her. *Nothing wrong with your ego,* she laughed inwardly as he spoke again.

"Is that for real?"

The book on eventing lay open to a rather startling picture of a horse and rider soaring over an obstacle that any logical mind would say was insurmountable.

She nodded. "Part of the cross-country."

"You've done that?"

She nodded again, then realized he probably couldn't see her, either. "Yes." She couldn't help smiling at the memory. "That's the fun part."

"Fun?" She saw him shift his gaze to the photograph again. "It looks suicidal."

"It looks worse than it is."

"They always say that about head wounds, too."

There was no mistaking the dry amusement in his voice, and she barely smothered a laugh. That cold, hard knot deep inside her seemed to loosen a bit.

"Really, it's not. The arena jumping is harder, with faults and jump-offs. You have to be so in control all the way. And the dressage is the toughest."

"I saw that in here. It was beyond me, whatever it is."

"Ideally, it's the invisible control of the horse. Getting him to do a specified maneuver with no visible signals."

He let out a slow, chuckling breath. "Oh, is that all? Getting an animal that weighs twenty times what you do to do something without you telling him. Easy."

A giggle escaped her this time. She thought she heard him take a quick, sharp breath, although she didn't understand why. Then he reached out and flipped on the lamp on the table beside him, filling the room with light and wiping out that golden circle that had haloed his chair.

He was wearing sweatpants again—because they were easier to get on with his leg, she imagined—and a long-sleeved pullover shirt, the cuffs carefully covering the grim marks on his wrists. It didn't matter; she could still see them in her mind's eye as clearly as she saw the puckered scar on his leg and the marks on his back. She pushed the images away, determined to hang on to her newfound calm. She concentrated on the unexpected lightness in his voice. She'd never heard him like this before. Except for that moment by the pool, before. She pushed that memory away, too.

"No, it's not easy," she finally answered, "but when it's exactly right, it's beautiful, like a dance. Unfortunately, I never got it exactly right."

"At least it's got to be safer than this." He gestured at the open book again.

"But not nearly as much fun. The cross-country is flat out, no holds barred and no form or style required. Just you and your horse, the clock and the course."

"You really miss it, don't you?"

She didn't dissemble. "Yes."

"I'm sorry."

"So am I." She shrugged. "But there's no use pining away over it. It was a long time ago."

"In years, maybe. But that kind of thing never really goes away."

Jamie stared at him. His expression told her he hadn't meant to say it; he looked uncomfortable at having let the words slip out. Quickly he looked back at the book, flipping through the pages as if he needed the release of doing something.

"What is it that never went away for you?" she asked softly.

His hands froze, and she saw his fingers tighten around the edges of the book. She knew what to expect when at last he lifted his head to look at her. And it was there—that shuttered, implacable mask.

Her first instinct was to turn and escape; only the hours she'd spent staring into the darkness, thinking, stopped her. She wasn't going to run anymore. Not from him, or from the reality he lived with that was so foreign to her. *It's time,* she repeated to herself, as she had countless times upstairs, *to grow up.*

To face that blank, cold gaze seemed somehow to take more nerve than it ever had to face Carly's grueling therapy sessions that had finally gotten her back on her feet. But she made herself do it, drawing on every ounce of stubbornness and determination that had pulled her through that painful time of her life. And after a long, silent moment, she saw something in the gray eyes shift, change—not quite a softening, yet still a change.

She was facing him down, Trey thought in amazement. Trained soldiers, men with automatic weapons in their hands, had broken before now, and this slim, pampered little rich girl was facing him down in a way that sent little shivers vibrating along his nerves.

Was this the same woman who had crumpled at the sight of him mere days ago? The same woman who had registered horror, shock and, worst of all, pity when she had seen the ruin of his back?

"I did to you the thing I hated most when it was done to me. I'm sorry."

Trey stared at her, stunned. It was as if she'd read his mind, as if she knew the exact track his thoughts had taken.

"I reacted emotionally to what happened to you," she went on softly, "and I felt everything I always hated to see when people looked at me after I was hurt. I didn't understand it then. I do now. I'm sorry," she repeated.

He couldn't seem to speak. He couldn't even move, let alone find a sharp-edged retort. He just stared at her. After a moment she let out a small sigh and got to her feet.

"Good night."

He didn't answer. She was at the door, pulling it open, when he finally spoke.

"Jamie?"

She stopped, looking back over her shoulder, an odd look of surprise and shy pleasure in her face. Why, he couldn't imagine. All he'd done was call her name.

"I..." He paused, letting out a long breath. "Good night."

After a moment, she nodded. She pulled the door quietly closed behind her.

Trey stared at that closed door for a long time, his mind whirling. Every time he thought he had her figured out, she threw him a curve. He had thought that he'd finally found the answer, that her reaction to the scars that marked him would put the distance between them that he so needed.

That she had approached him at all after that surprised him; that she had been so open, so relaxed with him, had amazed him.

What had followed had put him at more of a loss than he could ever remember being. That she had seemed to read his thoughts had been startling enough; her eloquent, poignant apology had taken him completely aback, it was so unexpected.

Unexpected. That word again.

"For somebody who's spent practically half his life being trained to expect the unexpected, you've sure as hell been surprised a lot lately," he muttered ruefully to himself. To be precise, ever since he'd sat in that elegant dining room and looked up to see a golden vision of sparkling cloth over slender, curved flesh, and amber eyes that matched the honey-colored streaks in a mass of silken hair.

He had expected a spoiled child with an expensive finishing-school polish; instead, he found a woman bright with the light of joy and love for her father. He had expected a wealthy socialite who did nothing more strenuous than sign credit-card receipts; he'd found a woman who wasn't far removed from the girl who had taken a ton of horseflesh careening over an insane succession of obstacles for the sheer love of it. He had expected a pampered little rich girl who had never had a real problem in her life; he'd found a woman who had faced the destruction of a dream, and nearly of her life, who had overcome tragedy and pain with courage and dignity, and at an age when the idea of tragedy usually meant not getting the classes you wanted. He had expected an imperious debutante who looked down her elegant nose at the world, beyond reproach; he'd found a woman who had the grace and courage to apologize for something most people would never realize they'd done.

What he'd found was a woman with loyalty, spirit, nerve and fire, tempered with a gentleness and patience that astounded him. What he'd found was the kind of woman he didn't think existed, especially not in this luxurious world. That she came wrapped up in such an intriguingly attractive package only made it more difficult to believe.

He pondered it all for a long time, until he realized that he hadn't thought of Lucero, of revenge, for hours. The realization bothered him. It bothered him a lot.

He struggled to his feet, moving to put the book back on the shelf beside the trophy case, purposely ignoring the crutches that lay on the floor beside the chair. He grimaced in disgust when his aching leg nearly buckled under him and he had to grab at the bookcase to stay upright. A thick, heavy book fell sideways, pushed by his grasping fingers. When he was steady again, he reached to straighten it, but froze in the act, staring at the space behind it, and what occupied it.

It was a photo album, tucked away out of sight behind the row of books that filled the shelf. It held at least three inches of the plastic pages, and for a moment he felt as if he'd disturbed the contents of some carefully hidden and precious shrine. He shook off the odd feeling, then moved once more to return the book to its place.

At least, that was what he meant to do. Instead he found himself lifting the thick album and lopsidedly hobbling back to the chair. He felt guilty, as if he was prying into something intensely personal and private, but he couldn't seem to help it.

Nor could he help the instant tightening of his throat at the first page of the album. It held a single snapshot of a child, a beaming face surrounded by a halo of gold-tipped hair and full of excitement. She was astride a short, chunky pinto pony, riding alone at an age when most children were struggling with the complexities of walking. And already the joy, the exuberance, was there. With the reluctance of one who knew the tragic turn the story was to take, he began to turn the pages.

It was like watching her grow up. The toddler became a sunny-faced child, then a gangly, coltish girl with the promise of the future beauty she would become. He felt the twinge of guilt again but smothered it; he was too caught up in the life unfolding before him.

He found the exultant look of pride at the first blue ribbon, at the first silver cup. He found the photo of a sleek, rangy chestnut horse labeled simply "Whiskey." He followed their progress now as if it were a film rather than a series of still pictures. He saw the young horse and rider training relentlessly, saw the weariness, the determination, and at last the flashes of glory as rider and horse became a unified being rather than two separate entities.

He saw the height of the jumps increase along with their breadth. He saw the pair leaping impossible fences, skidding recklessly down impossible slopes and, finally, clearing with room to spare the very same impossible jump he had seen in the book, a towering rail fence jutting viciously out of a deep, yawning hole in the rocky ground.

He flipped to the next page. The pictures had stopped.

"Oh, God," he murmured, knowing.

The blank pages stared up at him, a grim reminder. A shudder rippled through him before he could stop it. He wanted to shove the album out of sight; he wanted to forget he'd ever seen it. *That's what you get,* he told himself angrily, *for sticking your nose in where it doesn't belong.*

With a swift, sharp movement he jerked his hands to the leather cover of the album, ready to slam it shut. Something slipped from between the pages of the blank section, and he reached for it instinctively. It was an envelope from a local photo shop, and it was thick with the familiar shape of more photographs.

Never in his life had he so strongly ordered himself not to do something, and never in his life had it been so useless. He lifted the flap.

Even beneath the austere formality of the velvet hunt cap, her hair escaped in wispy tendrils that softened the severe lines. She looked elegant in the formal hunt coat, and atop the big, powerful horse she looked impossibly slender and delicate.

He knew without having to see the famous linked-rings symbol that these were the Olympic trials. And he knew that she had been doing well. Not from the pictures of the chestnut soaring so easily over the solid obstacles; he didn't have the knowledge to judge those. To him they all looked incredible, they all looked as if the pair had taken wing, scorning the earth below. But he knew it from the look on her face, from the high color in her cheeks, the jubilation evident in the last of the photos.

The newspaper clippings that fluttered down from behind that last picture were folded carefully, and every nerve in his body screamed at his hands to leave them that way. He watched his rebellious fingers unfold the yellowed newsprint as if they belonged to someone else.

He breathed a silent prayer of thanks, something that felt strange even as the words formed in his mind, so long had it been since he'd felt that thankful about anything; there was no gruesome photo accompanying the stark, emotionless account of the accident at the Olympic trials. The story had been, he realized as he stared at the clippings, big local news for a while.

Tragedy always was, he thought bitterly, remembering the headlines in an Oregon paper thirteen years ago, and the grim pictures of twisted wreckage, an angry man and a devastated boy. It was always big news until something new, or more tragic, took its place.

But she hadn't had the option he had had then. She had been tied to a hospital bed, unable to avoid the reporters, the chaos. *Unable to run, you mean,* he told himself coldly. *Like you did. Not that she would have. No, Logan, she had more backbone, even broken, than you had.*

He put the clippings back and slammed the book shut. He sat with it on his lap for a long time before he finally began the struggle to stand up and replace it on the shelf. Braced against the bookcase, he stood staring at the trophy case. Then his gaze shifted to the golden oak desk and the ever-present tiger lily. Like her, he thought—graceful, fragile looking, yet with a depth of color and strength that gave it the fierce name.

He stood there until his leg began to throb in protest. Until at last he thought he was tired enough. His eyes demanded to close no matter what hell awaited in sleep, and he turned out both lights, then reached for the hated crutches.

He wondered if it would be the old perdition tonight, or a new edition, full of images of a golden-eyed woman facing adversity with a far greater courage than he had ever had.

Chapter 4

"I see she was right."

There was a splash as a startled Trey nearly slipped off the edge of the pool. He pulled himself the rest of the way out, then twisted around to stare at the tall, lanky man who was lounging in one of the chairs beside a table that held a bright blue umbrella.

"You never did make any more noise than a snake," Trey muttered as he walked—hobbled, he thought sourly—over to pick up the towel he'd left on the chair across the table from the unexpectedly occupied one.

"I'll take that as a compliment," the older man said, his lips twisting wryly as he ran a hand over the stiff brush of his close-cropped gray hair. "Especially coming from you."

A pair of cool blue eyes looked Trey up and down, pausing for a barely perceptible moment on the still-angry scar on his thigh. They swept over the marks that circled his wrists and the ones that slashed across his back without hesitating, and Trey felt his mouth twist in a look that matched the older man's. *Trust him,* he thought as he ran the towel over his chest, *to go right to the crucial damage, wasting no time on the surface dents.*

"Checking out your property?"

The older man shrugged.

"Sorry," Trey said tightly. "I won't be moving very quickly for a while yet."

"There's always a desk waiting."

Trey jerked around to look sharply at the man unconcernedly watching him. The quick movement cost him—the leg he'd pushed to the limit once more today gave way under him. Only being within reach of the heavy patio table kept him from going down, enabled him to direct his fall awkwardly into the empty chair.

For a long moment he could barely breathe. He hunched over the throbbing, torn muscles, unable even to care that the man who was his boss was there, kneeling beside him. When he could, he gulped in a quick breath, then another, willing his head to stop spinning.

"I think my niece, for once, understated the facts," Hank McCall said dryly when he was sure Trey would hear him. "You're supposed to be healing, not trying to permanently cripple yourself."

"Your...niece?" Trey hoped the unsteadiness in his voice would be put down to his breathless state.

Hank's brows shot up. "Jamie. You remember. Pretty girl, lives here?"

"Sarcasm," Trey panted out, "doesn't become you. I meant—" He cut himself off, only now aware of what he'd been about to do, to reveal. *Whoa,* he muttered inwardly, *just because your head's spinning, don't let your guard down.*

"You mean, why were we talking about you?"

Damn, Trey thought. Sometimes it was scary, the way he could read people. It must run in the family.

When he didn't answer, Hank went on as if he had agreed. "She asked if you were always so tough on yourself."

Trey's head shot up. On himself? He'd been tougher on her than he'd been on anyone in his life. Hank was looking at him oddly, and a flush suffused him when he suddenly realized that Hank had been talking oranges while he had been thinking apples. Hank had meant physically, while his first thought had been emotional.

Emotional? He stared down at the ugly mark that dented the muscle of his thigh. He thought he'd walled away emotion long ago. He'd sworn off emotion as torture on that day long ago when his father had laid the responsibility for the ruin of his life at his son's door.

God, what was wrong with him? He hadn't thought about that in years. He had buried those memories, put them into a securely locked, hidden part of his mind, never to let them out again. With a tremendous effort, he drew himself up and pulled back the armor that had slipped for a moment.

"I'm glad you found something to talk about," he said stiffly.

A speculative gleam came into Hank's eyes as he studied him for a moment. "We always find something to talk about. She's a very bright girl."

I know, Trey thought wearily.

"Of course, the family always said she took after me," he said with a laugh. "Especially James, who never has quite forgiven me for doing the unspeakable for a McCall and joining the lowly army. Bit of an elitist, is my brother. Unlike his daughter."

"Mmph," Trey muttered, hoping Hank would change the subject.

"I remember arguing with her once over some fine point of philosophy," Hank went on, destroying Trey's hope. "She pinned me on every possible fallacy, every shaky support." He paused, chuckling. "Then she hit me with the fact that she felt the same way I did. She just wanted to know how I'd defend my position.''

"Figures," Trey muttered. *Ornery little imp. She—*

"Even at twenty, she was a formidable opponent."

Trey's gaze shot up to the other man. Twenty. When she'd been hurt.

"You know about her accident," Hank said slowly.

Trey sighed. He'd never been able to hide much from this man; Hank seemed to be able to look right through his fabled poker face.

"Yes," he said shortly, then hastily changed the subject before Hank McCall got a hint of the turmoil his niece caused in his employee. "You weren't serious, were you?"

"Serious?"

"About a desk," Trey said warily. He didn't want to have to fight Hank when he was at last well enough to go after Lucero.

Hank laughed, diverted for the moment. "A fate worse than death, huh?"

"Close."

At the flat tone of his voice, Hank had the grace to try to atone. "I'm sorry, Trey. You've been too close to death too recently to joke about it."

"Forget it."

"I can't. I owe you my brother's life."

Damn, Trey thought. He forced his body to cooperate and got to his feet. "You don't owe me anything," he said carefully, tightly. "I did a job. If I'd done it better, I wouldn't be here, like this, now."

"Trey—"

"I did what you pay me to do. No more."

"What you did was far beyond anything that can be paid for. And despite what you seem to think, as I've told you before, you are not expendable."

Trey winced. He'd heard those words too recently, from the lips of that vision in gold.

Hank went on, unperturbed. "We owe you for what you went through, if nothing else."

Trey gritted his teeth. "You don't owe me anything," he repeated. "Your brother doesn't owe me anything." His jaw tightened. "And your... niece doesn't owe me anything. And if that's why I'm here, because you think you're under some kind of obligation to me, then I'll get the hell out right now."

He'd never been more furious at the frailty of his body than he was in that moment. He was trapped by his own weakness, still a prisoner of a maniacal revolutionary general's savagery. He wanted out of here, out of this soft, luxurious existence. He wanted to either force his battered body to function or curl up and wait until it was over. Like a wounded wolf needed a lair, he needed someplace quiet, safe... someplace that didn't play havoc with old memories, someplace that didn't stir up emotions he'd thought long dead. Someplace that didn't have an amber-eyed enchantress with the power to throw his mind and body into chaos, the power to make him lose track of what was most important: the payback of Rodolfo Lucero.

Hank looked at him with an interest that seemed oddly intent. "You're here," he finally said, "because my brother feels he owes you, despite his lack of use for us army-types in general, and he won't get off my back about it. So consider it part of your job to accept gracefully."

As a rebuke it was mild enough, but it told Trey he'd pushed a little too far. The years since Hank McCall had retired from the army to run the development division of the McCall Corporation had done nothing to lessen his aura of command, and Trey responded to it instinctively. Hank had been one of the few men he thoroughly respected, in the army or out, and he still felt that way.

"Yes, sir," he said after a moment. "Was there something else you wanted?"

Hank barely suppressed a twitch at the corners of his mouth. "Don't go all punctilious on me now, Captain."

"I'm not a captain anymore," he responded automatically.

"And I'm not a colonel. So let's drop the military protocol, all right?"

"Yes, *si—*" He caught himself, and let out a rueful chuckle. "Sorry," he said with a grimace. "I think it's cabin fever."

Hank looked around at the pool, the house and the cloudless blue sky. "Some cabin."

Trey shrugged, but looked a little abashed.

"Or is something else bothering you?"

There was that oddly intent look again. "No," Trey said, a little too quickly. "I'm just tired of... being tired."

That odd expression his boss had worn stayed with Trey long after Hank had left, having given him stern instructions to take it easy. Something was brewing behind those blue eyes; he'd learned to sense the workings of the man who had, for a brief time, been his commanding officer.

"Take it easy," he muttered. "If I take it any easier, I'll turn into a vegetable. Or maybe oatmeal." He let out a sigh as he sat down and raised the footrest on the chair in the library once again. He never would have guessed such a little thing would make such a difference until Jamie had done it for him.

Jamie. Hovering in the wings as usual, waiting for the slightest of chances to take over the center stage of his mind. He was running out of ways to fight her off.

He made himself turn his attention back to the book he'd selected. He was startled when, at the sound of the front door, he looked up to see the hands of the antique schoolroom clock on the far wall showing nearly seven. He heard the sound of boots on the tiled entry and knew Jamie was home. He wondered why she hadn't come in through the garage, as she usually did, then shook his head at the realization that he had become so familiar with her routine that the slightest variation had him wondering.

He found out when she came into the room, dropped a tangle of leather and metal that he managed to recognize as a bridle on the back of the sofa next to the Navajo blanket, nodded briefly to him and walked over to dial the phone.

"Can you tell me if flight 574 is on time?"

She waited, leaning against the front of the rosewood desk. She looked hot and dusty, but somehow still exquisite, even straight from the stable. She was wearing those faded, worn jeans that seemed molded to her slender hips and long legs, and were no less sexy for the dust that marked them. The soft green-knit tank top she wore hugged the full curve of her breasts and bared the firm, golden flesh of her arms and throat. He tore his gaze away the moment he realized he was wondering if her skin felt half as silken as it looked.

As she waited, she reached up and tugged at the elastic band that held the mass of her hair at the back of her neck. The movement caught his eye, and he glanced up again. When the band came free she shook her head, sending the silken cloud flying around her head. It was an offhand, unstudied motion, a long-familiar routine, done as casually as if she were alone in the privacy of her bedroom.

There was no sensuous intent in the shaking out of that mane of gold-streaked hair, no sexual taunt in the movement of her breasts beneath the cotton top. There was absolutely no reason for his body to surge violently in response, for the blood to begin to pulse heavily in his veins. He looked away again.

"Thank you," she said after another moment, then hung up, glancing with a grimace at the clock he'd just looked at.

"Running late?" He was almost proud of the steadiness of his voice.

"Yes, a little." She looked at him, and he sighed inwardly at the way the wariness in her eyes gave him a pang.

Although they had spent the last two days in relative peace after her heartfelt apology, she still didn't quite trust him not to turn on her.

He couldn't blame her, in fact told himself that if he had any sense he *would* turn on her, but somehow he was too tired to make the effort. And it was an effort to think of how to be rude or cold to her. It was becoming more of an effort every day.

"Daddy took an earlier flight, so I'm cutting it pretty close," she added after a moment. "Excuse me. At the least I need a shower, and I've only got twenty minutes."

He would have bet there wasn't a woman alive who could have done it, but with three minutes to spare he heard her coming back down the stairs. He barely flinched anymore when she defied his expectations. He looked up when she stuck her head around the library door.

"I'm expecting a call, but the machine is on, so it shouldn't bother you."

He nodded, his gaze sliding over her. She had worked wonders in that short twenty minutes; she looked quietly elegant in a pair of trim khaki tan pants and a soft cotton sweater in the same shade, with a peach-colored scarf shot with golden threads draped softly over her shoulder. High-heeled pumps and a belt in that same peach, and small gold earrings completed the outfit, and he thought she looked like what she was—a woman who belonged in this house, in this neighborhood, in this exclusive beach community.

But when she had gone, the image that lingered in his mind was that dusty, jean-clad figure, which, but for the more womanly curves, had reminded him sharply of the girl he had seen in the photographs, in the album whose contents had haunted him ever since he'd looked at it.

She'd only been gone fifteen minutes when the phone rang. He heard the answering machine click on and turned his attention back to the book, but when he heard the recording that answered the call, he realized it was turned up enough that he would hear the call, as well. He considered turning it down, but thought in disgust that by the time he managed to drag himself up and over to it, it would be over, anyway.

He tried not to listen, but the unexpected sounds of a high, childish voice startled him. It was someone named Chuckie, and he was so excited about something happening next Saturday that he was barely understandable. This was the call she'd been waiting for? His forehead creased in puzzlement.

Where was the string of admirers that had to be dangling after her? Come to think of it, she'd only been out once in the two weeks he'd been here, and that had been to a charity event she'd attended in her father's place, Jean had told him. And she'd gone alone. And unwillingly.

"I hate these things," he'd heard her grumble from the hallway before she walked through the kitchen as she headed for the garage.

He'd been sitting at the breakfast bar, trying to eat the rather bland meal of macaroni and cheese Jean had fixed, wishing his stomach would get back to normal so he could quit putting the kindly woman to so much extra work. *I hope Hank is paying her extra for me,* he had thought glumly as he waited to see if the last bite would stay down.

He'd looked up at the sound of her voice, and the sight of her as she came into the room had taken his breath away. Her gown had been a demure yet sexy sweep of some glistening white knit, the high cowl neckline falling in soft drapes over her breasts and sliding caressingly over her slender body, its pristine white setting off her golden skin.

"You know you'll be fine once you get there," Jean had said, as she followed her into the kitchen and reached up in a motherly gesture to straighten the clip that held a sweep of the sun-touched honey brown hair back over her left ear. It was a stunning piece, he noticed, a spray of gold alive with the sparkle of diamonds.

This was the woman he'd pictured—cool, regal, unapproachable and, above all, untouchable. She even walked royally in a pair of strappy, high-heeled gold sandals. He laughed scornfully at himself for the spasm of regret that seized him. Then she turned, and he nearly choked on the sip of water he'd just taken.

The back of the dress was a deep V that dipped almost to her waist. Although the opening was narrower than the slender space between her shoulder blades, and bared only a slim band of golden skin, the suggestion was instantaneous and potent, and the contrast between the decorous front of the dress and the tantalizing sexiness of the back left him stunned.

Yet wasn't it her? he thought. Wasn't that the very essence of her? She was both. She was more than both. She was more kinds of woman wrapped up in one than he had ever seen, ever thought possible. Aware he'd been gaping at her, he turned his gaze to his plate, staring at the cooling pasta as if it was utterly fascinating.

"There you go, dear, and don't forget your purse." Jean picked up the small gold bag and handed it to her.

"I'd like to forget the whole thing."

"Now, now, you don't mean that. Besides, honey, you look so lovely. Doesn't she, Mr. Logan?"

His head had shot up at that. He felt Jamie looking at him, and when he shifted his gaze to her face, he saw, to his amazement, vulnerable insecurity reflected there. How could someone who looked like her not know, not be sure? Yet she wasn't; he couldn't mistake that look.

He realized with a little shock that this, too, was part of the woman she was. This shy uncertainty was as much a part of her as the regal carriage and the sexy daring. He had a fleeting sensation that he was on the trail to untangling the intriguing mystery that was Jamie McCall; then it was gone.

But that vulnerability was still there, and he knew he'd been handed the weapon that would drive her from him forever, the tool that could restore sanity to his life by removing the disruption of her presence. With a few well-chosen, maiming words he could drive a wedge between them that would never be removed. He opened his mouth to say them.

"She looks...beautiful. Very beautiful."

The smile she gave him kindled the tiny flame that had begun deep and low inside him at the first sight of her in that gown, a flame growing from the embers that remained from the fire that had leapt to life the morning he'd seen her for the first time.

"Thank you."

Her husky whisper had whipped that tiny flame into a blaze, and by the time she had gone, he had been more than grateful for the concealment of the bar he was sitting at.

Just the memory of that vision in white and gold had the power to stir that fire now, and he shifted in the chair uncomfortably. He was almost grateful when the phone rang again and this time the voice of a young man, his words peppered with trendy slang, cheerfully reminded her of their date next Friday. This, he told himself firmly, was the call she'd been waiting for. And he was going back to *King Lear;* he'd purposely picked something he had to concentrate on to appreciate.

They were back sooner than he'd expected, the cheerful sounds of father and daughter echoing in the entry. James set down his bags before he stepped into the library and started toward him. Trey closed the book and reached for the arm of the chair to lever himself up, but James stopped him.

"Relax," James said heartily. "I hear you've been pushing it too hard, anyway."

Trey's gaze flicked to Jamie; she met his gaze steadily.

"No," James said, catching his look, "I spoke to Hank today. He suggested a tranquilizer in your morning orange juice." Jamie smothered a giggle; Trey scowled. "However, since he also suggested I have a ticket out of the country ready for when you found out, I decided to forgo the idea.''

Jamie's giggle became a laugh, and Trey couldn't stop his own wry smile.

It turned into an evening unlike any Trey had ever had. James sat in the other chair, talking expansively about the results of his successful trip. While Trey knew little about the financial details of the company's operations, he knew enough about the various branches to get the gist and ask a fairly reasonable question or two. Jamie, having changed once more into a set of comfortable sweatpants and shirt in a soft shade of yellow, sat quietly working on the bridle she had left on the sofa earlier.

She spoke rarely, but Trey was constantly aware of her presence. For once it made him feel not uneasy, but comfortable, in a way he didn't understand.

''—what you did at the warehouse in San Diego.''

Trey tuned back in to James's words. ''It was easy, just being in the right place and waiting until they messed up.''

''Easy?'' James shook his head. ''One man against five, armed with semiautomatic weapons? What do you call difficult?''

''Explaining to the police afterward,'' he said wryly.

James laughed, and Trey heard the silvery notes of Jamie's laughter, as well. It warmed him, adding to that feeling of contentment he'd never before experienced and didn't quite know how to deal with.

''Well, I must say that I'm not sorry we're no longer in the explosives business,'' James said.

''I'm not real broken up about it myself,'' Trey said dryly.

''If they'd gotten away with stealing those—''

''They didn't. They were amateurs. More dangerous to themselves than anybody else.''

''You still took quite a chance.''

Trey grinned suddenly. "Nope. Number five on Roger's Rangers standing orders: 'Don't never take a chance you don't have to.' It was good in 1759, and it still is."

While Jamie stared, as if startled by the sight of that flashing grin, her father laughed, with an oddly bitter undertone.

"Good Lord, you sound like Hank."

"I could do worse."

"I suppose," James said, his tone belying his words. "Although I never understood why he felt the need to join the army. I mean, our family has ... other things to do."

Had he hesitated on that word, Trey wondered, at the last minute substituting *other* for *better*? Was this a trace of that elitism Hank had mentioned? He glanced at Jamie. She was intent on the bridle, although it seemed to him she was concentrating a little harder than necessary.

"He's a good man," he said at last, neutrally. "And a better commander."

James was silent for a moment as he studied the young man sitting across from him. "Once a ranger, always a ranger, he used to say." Trey tensed, but James seemed unaware as he went on. "He never told me why you left. The army, I mean."

"I wasn't cashiered," Trey said stiffly, "if that's what you mean."

James looked startled. "Of course not. I just—"

"I'd rather not talk about it, sir, if you don't mind."

Jamie's hands had stopped on the bridle, and the cessation of motion drew Trey's gaze to her. Her head came up and she met his look. As clearly as if she'd spoken, he knew she was thinking of the day she'd asked him what it was he'd had to give up, what was the thing that never went away for him. The moment of silent communication was intense and, for Trey, uncomfortable. She was getting too close, tangling him up inside when he should be focused on one thing only. It would be too easy to let thoughts of her push thoughts of retribution out of his mind. He couldn't let it happen. After a moment she lowered her gaze, turning it back to the bridle she'd been stitching.

"—class today?"

Trey only heard the last words, and Jamie's head came up as if her father's question had startled her out of equally deep thought. "I'm sorry, Daddy, what?"

A vision of the elegant woman in the incredible white gown flashed through Trey's mind. It should have been at odds with the loving "Daddy" she used, but oddly, it wasn't. It was all part of her, he thought again.

"I asked how your class went today."

"Fine. They're all getting nervous, though."

"Class?" Trey asked.

"My riding class," she explained.

"You . . . teach?"

She looked at him quizzically. "What did you think I was doing?"

"I . . . Just riding, I guess."

What he'd thought, he realized in chagrin, was that she had been spending her days pursuing what was left of a life that had been taken from her. What he'd thought was that her father's money enabled her to do it without worrying about working.

"I've tried to get her to put that business degree to some use and come to work for us, but—"

"Daddy, please, not now." She said it with a touch of weariness that told Trey this was an old, worn topic. "I like teaching my classes."

"Well, at least your charity classes for the Orange County riding center are—"

"They aren't charity classes." she said, a little tightly.

"Well, you certainly don't get paid much for them."

"I don't do it for the money. I do it because I love it. And because . . . I could have been one of them."

James's voice softened slightly. "I know that, honey. But you could be making fifty times the money if only—"

"Daddy," Jamie cut him off smoothly. "I'm sure Trey doesn't want to hear all that." Before her father could protest, she went on to finish answering his original question. "Some of the kids aren't ready for the show Saturday, but it would break their hearts not to compete. They don't expect to win, so hopefully their feelings won't be hurt. It'll be good experience for them."

"What about Chuckie?" her father said. Trey sat up, recognizing the name.

"My pride and joy?" she said with a laugh. "He's doing great. If he doesn't take at least one of the three classes he's in, I'll want to know why."

"Is Chuckie a smaller human with a voice about an octave above a dog whistle?"

Jamie stared at Trey, then burst out laughing. James joined her, and between chuckles managed to say, "Exactly."

As she caught her breath, Jamie glanced at the answering machine as if realizing what had brought on the question. "He did call, then?"

Trey nodded. Then stopped, when it penetrated that the child had indeed been the call she'd been expecting. "Uh...so did somebody else...."

He let his words trail off; she was already at the machine. The high little voice played back again, the message making more sense now that he knew what it was about. He couldn't seem to stop watching her as she listened to the second message. He felt an odd sense of satisfaction when, after hearing that the young man was calling only to confirm their plans, she shut off the machine without even listening to the rest of the message.

He had thought she would go upstairs when James did, but she only continued working on the bridle in her lap, lifting her head to return her father's good-night kiss. Trey returned determinedly to the book in his hands.

When at last he closed it, she looked up. "It's worth the work, once you get the rhythm, isn't it?" Startled at how closely she echoed his own thoughts about the play, he nodded. She smiled. "I never understood all the fuss about Shakespeare, until I had the time to read it properly."

He knew instinctively she meant when she'd been hurt, but he didn't say so. He didn't want to risk this comfortable peace they'd attained.

He wondered about that feeling after she had finally gone upstairs, wondered at the odd sensation of contentment he'd felt tonight. It was so unlike anything he'd known before that he wasn't even sure what to call it.

It wasn't just that he'd never seen such an easy relationship as she and her father seemed to have; it was more. It was as if, despite her father's feelings about "army-types," it had somehow expanded to include him. He had the feeling it should make him uneasy, but he couldn't quite find the energy for that.

Maybe, just maybe, he'd be able to sleep tonight, he thought. With a grimace he reached for the crutches he'd thought to be long rid of by now.

It was barely dawn when Jamie awoke, but the alertness of her mind told her she wouldn't be able to go back to sleep as clearly as her gritty eyes told her she hadn't had enough. With a sigh she sat up, yawning as she stretched, wondering if she should just go for her swim now.

No, she thought groggily, she'd wait at least until it was light out. In the meantime, she'd go down and check the plants she'd been neglecting. Trey must be still asleep, as late as they'd been up, so the solarium would be empty.

She reached for her robe and slipped it on, the rich, turquoise satin contrasting with the deep wine of the silk nightgown she wore. The robe was piped in the same burgundy shade, although it had been a gift from her father and the gown a present from two of her girlfriends, to cheer her up after she'd been told she had to face another two weeks in the hospital when she'd thought she was going home.

She yawned as she went down the stairs, knotting the belt of the robe, then pushing a hand through her tousled hair. She went through the arched entryway to the solarium and was several steps into the room when she heard the sound. A low, smothered sound that, even though she couldn't make it out, seemed to tighten that knot that had taken up residence somewhere deep inside the day Trey had arrived.

She stopped, holding her breath, listening, her eyes searching the room. Because of the glass sky wall, there was more light here than in any other room, but it was still gray and shadowed. She was about to go on, thinking it was her imagination, when it came again.

Her gaze went to the low brick wall of the planter area, and the deeply shadowed area below it. There was an exercise mat on the floor, pushed up against the bricks. And on it huddled an even darker shape.

She crept closer, certain she was imagining things. It couldn't be. Why would he—

The sound came again. A low, muffled groan. And the huddled shape grew up into a tighter curve. The knot within her clenched, and a little chill swept over her as she knelt down beside the mat. Had he fallen? Or hurt himself in some late-night flurry of overwork? He'd have been on one of the lounges if he was only sleeping, wouldn't he? God, how long had he been here like this?

It didn't seem possible that his long, lean body could take up so little space. Yet it did as he lay facing—almost jammed against—that low brick barrier, curled in on himself like a wounded animal protecting its vulnerable parts. She bent over him.

He was asleep. His lashes lay in dark semicircles on his lean cheeks, and he looked younger, vulnerable. That knot

tightened another notch, but the chill became an odd
warmth. She meant to back away quietly, to leave him to
rest, when that sound escaped again. He drew up even
tighter, coming up against the bricks, his head moving rest-
lessly.

She couldn't leave him like that. He needed the sleep, but
she couldn't leave him in the grips of a nightmare.

"Trey," she whispered. Nothing. With a sigh, she reached
out and gently touched his shoulder. And nearly cried out
herself when his shout echoed through the room.

"No!"

Chapter 5

He erupted into motion as the startled cry broke from him, his hands going up instantly, as if to fight off some horrible threat. In that brief second, when she ducked reflexively out of the way of his attack, she saw something in his eyes that stunned her.

Fear. Even in the shadows, it was there, unexpectedly, unbelievably. She'd seen those eyes icy cold and full of contempt. She'd seen them shuttered and blank. She'd seen them puzzled, she'd seen them angry. And even more rarely, she'd seen them glittering with that warmth, with that silver sparkle that took her breath away. But never, ever, had she seen them like this. She wouldn't have thought it possible. Instinctively, she reached out and grabbed his hands.

"It's all right, Trey. It was just a dream."

He stared at her blankly, his fingers tightening painfully around hers, the remnants of the nightmare swirling in his widened eyes. He took one long, shuddering breath, then dropped back onto the mat. He closed his eyes as he took a second breath, then a third, fighting for calm.

"It's okay, everything's all right, it's over now."

She was speaking slowly, softly, almost crooning, as she would to a frightened horse. It was instinctive, automatic, and it seemed to work. His gasping breathing slowed. Hoping to keep him from thinking about it, she spoke quickly, saying the first thing that came to mind.

"What are you doing in here?"

The dark lashes lifted, and his gaze flickered over her face for a moment before he turned his head to stare at the brick wall bare inches from his face. He pulled his hands away from hers and she saw them curl into taut fists. For a moment she didn't think he was going to answer, then she heard the low, rasping words.

"I couldn't . . . sleep in there. Closed in."

Her brow furrowed for a moment. The bedroom he'd been given wasn't small; in fact, it was larger than most of the bedrooms in the house, with its own bath and sitting area. She studied him as his gaze shifted upward.

When she saw him staring out through the top of the sky wall at the gradually lightening sky, when she saw his muscles begin to relax and the tension begin to drain away, it all made sense to her. The door to his room, which was always open, his coming in here to sleep, yet being curled up so tightly as if he only had a few square feet to sleep in. . . .

That knot deep within her was almost unbearably tight now as she fought off images of him chained in some tiny cell, at any moment expecting the beating, the abuse, to begin again. Although her chains had been different, she knew the feeling. But her "captors" had been trying to help her; he had had to deal with the knowledge that his pain was all intentional, that it was for the sick enjoyment of a twisted mind.

She sat back, drawing her legs up and wrapping her arms around them, resting her chin on her knees as she looked out at the sky with him. After a moment she spoke, in a softly reminiscent tone that was soothing in the dim light.

"I remember when I came home from the hospital, I couldn't sleep at all. I was always afraid I would wake up and be back in that room—trapped, helpless, waiting for them to come give me some damned pill, or make me try to move, or jab me with another needle."

He didn't say anything, didn't even look at her, but she sensed he was listening.

"And I had to be in one of those hospital beds here, and a brace, so it was even worse. It felt just the same, and sometimes I woke up screaming that I wanted to go home, never realizing that I was already there. Finally Daddy got desperate." She smiled softly, even though she knew Trey probably wouldn't see. "I know he's too protective, that he'd wrap me in cotton wool forever if he could. He was that way before I got hurt, and it was even worse afterward. But this time he was right. He moved me in here, where the first thing I'd see when I woke up was the sky."

She felt him tense again, felt his gaze on her then. But she didn't look at him, just kept watching the pink streaks of dawn that were beginning to stripe the sky, and kept talking. Softly, calmingly.

"It worked. Oh, I still had the nightmares, for a long time, but the moment I woke up and saw the sky, I knew I was home, and safe."

He was intent on her now, watching, listening to every word; she could feel it as clearly as she could see the dawn breaking.

"I knew I'd be all right, eventually. Carly—my therapist—kept telling me that. That someday it would stop hurting, or I'd get used to it enough to live with it. And when I woke up in the night sometimes, and watched the stars, watched the moon rise and fall, I even knew that someday I wouldn't be afraid anymore."

Long, silent minutes drew out. She didn't dare look at him, wondering if she'd once more made a fool of herself.

She stared outside as the lovely pink dawn sky faded away and the brilliant blue of a California morning took over.

"You're an incredible woman, Jamie McCall."

The words were soft, low and husky, and they sent a shiver racing through her. She remembered the night in the kitchen, when she had expected some cutting comment about rich women and society balls, and instead had gotten a quiet, heartfelt compliment. It had robbed her of the power to even breathe, as his words had now.

"Thank you," he added quietly, and in the two little words was an acknowledgment of everything she'd said and meant to do. Of the baring of a painful part of her past, a past she had made it clear she didn't share easily. Of the understanding of the source of his nightmare. And of his reaction to her awakening him. And, most of all, of the complete absence of any pity in her gentle, caring words.

"You're welcome," she said, and in the soft words was an acknowledgment of everything he'd meant and hadn't said.

"I know... how it must have felt," he said after a moment, the words coming in broken spurts. "When I woke up in the hospital in Jardín... and Miguel, the La Selva agent who'd helped us, was there, and told me... I was safe... I didn't believe it. Thought it was a dream."

"Dreams can be the worst—and the best," she agreed softly. "Especially when you dream nothing will ever change. If Carly hadn't sworn I'd ride again someday, I think I would have gone crazy."

"Sometimes... I think I *am* going crazy." His voice was low with tension. "I... keep hoping it will all go away. And most of it has. I can forget what happened... except at night, it's all there.... I could live with it... except for..." The pause in the broken, hesitant phrases was strained, painful. When at last he finished, his voice was barely a whisper. "Except for feeling so damned helpless...."

Jamie bit her lip against the tears that were welling behind her eyelids, knowing he wouldn't welcome them. Just the tortured sound of his words, as if they were being pulled from deep within him, against his will, told her how very careful she had to be.

"You're not helpless anymore."

"Only when I'm asleep," he said bitterly.

"I told Daddy once that the only good part about the bad dreams was that they made waking up and finding out it was only a dream even better."

She heard him make a sound, a tiny rush of air that could have been a sigh. He didn't speak, but she could almost feel him letting go of the last remnants of his nightmare, and for a long time they sat in a peaceful silence.

Trey didn't know if there was a connection between his recovery and the lessening of tension between them; he only knew that after that golden morning, when he at last admitted that he couldn't keep up the pretense of antipathy any longer, he'd felt so much better it stunned him. Even his battered body responded to the change, letting him push a little further, a little harder, and making the aching payment a little less harsh the next day. Or maybe it was just that he noticed it less.

James's first day home seemed to have begun a routine. Trey grew to look forward to the evenings spent in easy companionship in the library. It bothered him a little, as if he were slipping into a trap of softness that it would be difficult to escape from, but he enjoyed the conversations too much to do anything about it. He was even able to ignore the occasional dig James seemed compelled to make; Hank had clearly been right about his brother's touch of elitism.

Trey told himself it was just the novelty of it all, and that when he was well he'd be able to walk away without a backward glance. That when he was well, he wouldn't waste a moment in regrets, but would get on with the task at hand, finding Lucero and making him rue the day he'd ever come across Trey Logan.

And that day would come sooner than he'd at first expected, he thought. He'd managed to make it all the way to the library without the hated crutches, although it had been slow and painful and had resulted in his collapsing, rather than sitting, in the big leather chair.

It was Thursday just after dinner when James had returned, looking glum, from answering the phone.

"Daddy?"

"I'm afraid it's back to Denver for your old man, baby."

"But you just got back!"

"I know, but there's a problem with the zoning for the new warehouse. I have to personally appear before the zoning commission." He glanced at his watch.

"I gather because you're looking at your watch and not a calendar, you're leaving soon?" Jamie said with a grimace.

"Right, my clever little girl." He sighed. "The earliest flight is out of LAX, in three hours. Do you feel up to driving me in? I'd hate to leave the car there when I don't know how long I'll be."

"Sure. But for LAX in three hours, we're already an hour late," she said dryly.

James chuckled. "You do hate traffic, don't you?"

"I swear, I'm going to move to an island with no cars."

"I can call a cab—"

"No, Daddy, I was only being silly. But really, you'd better hurry and pack."

"You're right, as usual." He glanced at Trey, who had been pointedly studying his half-empty cup of coffee; a half was still about all his stomach could handle. "Perhaps Trey is up to going along—at least you'd have company on the drive back."

Trey's head came up abruptly. He stared at James, then his gaze flicked to Jamie.

"Of course, if he feels up to it," she was saying.

No, his mind said, recoiling at the thought of being in such close quarters with her without the barricade of his feigned animosity toward her.

"Yes." It was out before he could stop it. "I'd like to...get out."

"I'm sure you would," James said brusquely as he stood up to go pack. "Hank said you had a touch of cabin fever."

As Trey sat in the passenger seat of the luxurious Mercedes on the way back from the busy airport, he realized how true those words had been. He sat with the window open, letting the wind blow through his hair, looking up at the sky that seemed beautiful and open and free to him despite the haze of L.A. smog.

Jamie left him to enjoy it, driving with a quiet competence that belied her alleged distaste for the traffic that plagued the freeways they traveled. He relaxed, realizing that she was content to be quiet, not feeling the need of most women he'd known to fill every minute with talk. As a result the silence was easy, not strained, not feeling like an awkward lapse in conversation.

"Can you make it?" Jamie asked when they had pulled into the garage.

To his own surprise, her words didn't send his temper—touchy when it came to his condition—flaring.

"If I can get out," he said evenly enough as he opened the car door. Then she was there, offering a hand for support, bracing herself to provide leverage for his weight. *Don't,* his mind said as he looked at that outstretched hand. A moment later he'd taken it and was on his feet with ease.

"Thanks."

Jamie nodded, staring up at him. He hadn't released her hand, and his fingers closed around hers. Something odd was happening—a strange, glowing heat was radiating out from that warm grasp. She moved, as if meaning to step back, but somehow she wound up closer to him. The heat that seemed to go through him in waves collided with the heat that was kindling beneath his fingers, combining and growing with a speed that left him breathless.

Trey saw her lips part as if she, too, felt the shortage of air; he saw the color that was rising in her face, saw the widening of the amber eyes as she looked up at him. His jaw tightened against the swelling response of his body to that look, battling it down once more.

Then she swayed against him, and even her slight weight was enough to back him up against the car. The muscles of his injured leg protested, and he automatically shifted to ease them. The movement brought her even closer, until he could feel the slender length of her against him from shoulder to knee. He nearly gasped aloud as the soft curves of her breasts pressed against his chest.

She lifted her arms as if to push away, but then her hands spread wide over his chest in an almost stroking motion. Fire leapt along nerves long cold and abandoned, and he barely stopped himself from lowering his head and taking those soft, parted lips fiercely.

"Jamie," he said tightly, warningly.

"Yes?" Her voice was soft and vibrant, and she barely remembered to make it a question.

Trey heard the answer it had almost become, the answer to a question he hadn't dared ask. His body screamed at him to make it what she'd meant, the answer to that unspoken query. For once his mind won. "My leg hurts."

"Oh!"

Startled, she backed away as if she'd only now realized she'd been plastered against him like a wet shirt. Color flooded her face, and she avoided his eyes.

"I'll be in in a minute," he said, rather gruffly. Without a word she whirled and disappeared into the house.

He sagged back against the car gratefully, willing his body to stop, to retreat. *You are out of your mind, Logan,* he said to himself. *She's James McCall's daughter, for God's sake. He might think he owes you his life, but it's for damned sure that the payment doesn't include fondling his only daughter.* That was hardly in the company benefit plan.

And an affair with a lowly, beat-up company security man was hardly what class-conscious James McCall would have in mind for that daughter. Or, for that matter, what Hank McCall would have in mind for his niece, no matter what he thought of his former ranger comrade and current employee.

So keep your damned hands to yourself, Logan, and quit acting like a teenager whose hormones just kicked in. She's too young, anyway. Maybe not chronologically, but at that moment, he felt as if his battered, weary spirit was at least a hundred years older. He took considerably longer than the minute he'd promised before he finally limped inside.

Jamie was on the phone in the library when he came in after his swim the next afternoon. He turned around to leave, but Jamie saw him and shook her head at him, signaling him to wait. She quickly finished her conversation and hung up.

"It's all right," she said as she shuffled through a stack of papers. "I'm just trying to finish up the last of the details for the horse show tomorrow."

"Are you in charge of it?"

"No, just in charge of my fifteen kids, horses and too many anxious parents," she said with a rueful look.

She had determined to put the episode in the garage out of her mind, and he obviously wasn't about to argue with her decision. He dropped down into his usual chair; it seemed to be getting easier for him. And, she realized suddenly, for the first time he was without props.

"Did you burn the crutches?"

He grinned. "Not yet. But it's not a bad idea. Except that they're aluminum."

She shrugged. "Toast 'em anyway. Just for the satisfaction of it."

He laughed. "I'm afraid I'm not quite rid of them yet. Someday I might want to walk farther than fifty feet."

Jamie stared at him. She'd seen him smile, that wry smile that tugged at her heart; she'd seen him grin, that brilliant, flashing grin that sent her pulse racing; she'd even heard him chuckle, low and deep in his chest in a way that set up an answering echo somewhere deep inside her. But never had she heard him laugh like that, and she didn't know what to call the feeling it gave her.

"How about tomorrow?" she asked hastily, before she forgot what she'd meant to say in the wonder of the sound of that laugh. "If you're feeling all right, that is."

"I'm fine. I rested all day. How about tomorrow what?"

"Walking. I know you're not into this, but I thought maybe you might want to come to the show tomorrow."

"The horse show?" He looked startled.

"You'd pretty much be on your own—I'll be running like a fool all day—but it would be a chance to get out." She hadn't forgotten the look on his face on the way home from the airport. "We pack up lounge chairs to sit on, so you can rest if you get tired. And Jean packs us a mean lunch, too."

He hesitated, but she could see that he was tempted by the thought of getting out, of being away from this house that she knew all too well could, no matter how lovely, become a prison of its own.

"I'd like to go. If you're sure I—and those damned crutches—won't be in the way."

"You won't. They'll probably put you to work if you don't watch out."

"Work? You mean doing something constructive instead of sitting around vegetating? Perish the thought."

She stared at him, then burst out laughing. He let it wash over him, loving the lighthearted sound of it and feeling absurdly pleased that his silliness had caused it. She was still smiling widely when the phone rang, and she rolled her eyes as she began to reassure a nervous would-be ribbon winner.

While Trey sat with the newspaper in his hands, Jamie made call after call, switching from brisk efficiency to soft cajoling, from placating parents to encouraging children. She verified transportation, feed—both human and horse—and times, reminded each caller of everything that would be needed, and assigned each one to call someone else in the morning to make sure nothing was forgotten. When at last she checked off the last name on her list, Trey lowered the unread front page and looked at her.

"You can be my APL anytime, lady."

She set down her pen. "APL?"

"Assistant patrol leader. The one who makes sure the patrol leader doesn't screw anything up in planning a mission."

"What's a patrol leader, besides what it sounds like?"

"Senior ranking member of the group."

"Is that what you were? In the rangers?"

He nodded. "Your uncle was my C.O." He smiled. "And he's still ordering me around."

"But now you can say no."

His brows shot up, then he smiled wryly. "I suppose so. Somehow it never occurred to me. He's not an easy man to say no to."

"I never had a problem," she said sweetly.

He laughed again, and again that shiver went up her spine. "I'll bet you didn't," he said. "He said you were just like him. Stubborn, bossy, a smart aleck—"

She threw the pen at him. "He did not say that!"

"Well, maybe not in those words," he said, laughing as he fended off the wad of paper that followed the pen.

"Besides, I wouldn't mind being just like him," she said.

"I wouldn't, either."

He said it softly, and she didn't think he'd meant her to hear, but she did. After a moment she spoke again.

"He said you won three medals in Grenada."

He tensed. "Everybody who went there got medals."

"He said that too. Thousands of them. That anybody who had anything to do with the operation got at least one pinned on him."

"Everybody who showed up at a meeting about it got one," he grated. "Anybody who could say he even knew about operation Urgent Fury got one."

"He also said yours were different."

The shutters in his eyes were up again when he looked at her. "Different?"

"He said you earned yours. That they dumped you on top of the main Cuban stronghold. And that the enemy knew you were coming."

"Oh, they knew, all right. We parachuted right into an ambush." The edge in his voice was bitter. "Some of the guys were WIA before they even made it to the ground."

She'd listened to her uncle enough to know WIA meant wounded in action. And enough to know how he had felt about the whole thing. "Hank said if the . . . well, if the bureaucrats would have stayed out of it, it could have been a very efficient operation."

As she gave him the edited edition of her uncle's comments, she could almost feel his anger draining away, and the shuttered look faded.

"It's okay. I heard the original version," he said with a grin.

She studied him for a moment. Then, as her certainty grew, she said softly, "That's why you left, isn't it?"

He stared at her, suddenly rigid again. She knew without his saying it that he didn't intend to answer her question. He opened his mouth and she waited for some scathing rebuff. He seemed as surprised as she was at the words that came out.

"Good men died that didn't have to. Friends of mine." Once he'd begun, the words kept coming, as if against his will. "In the end we outnumbered them ten to one. No one should have had to die. And if the…bureaucrats had stayed out of it, no one would have. And yes, that's why I left."

It came out in choppy bursts, with an awkward sound that told her he rarely, if ever, spoke about this. She remembered when he had told her father he didn't want to discuss it at all. Yet he had told her.

"I'm sorry, Trey." *For prying. For your friends who died. For what happened to you. For the end of the life you loved.* She couldn't say the words, but when she met his gaze again, she had the feeling that he'd heard them, anyway.

"So am I," he said after a moment, and the tense moment passed. As if to insure he wouldn't be lured into any further confessions, he picked up the newspaper once more.

Jamie went back to her lists, checking items off one by one. Trey lowered the newspaper again and watched her. She set down one pile of papers and lifted another list that had been sitting on top of the answering machine.

The answering machine.

"Er," he began, clearing his throat, "don't you have a…date tonight, or something?"

She looked blank, then her eyes widened in shock. "Edward."

Lucky Edward, Trey thought.

"Oh, no."

Maybe not lucky Edward, he amended as she groaned. "You…don't sound happy about it."

"Edward," she said succinctly, "is a pain."

He raised one brow at her, trying to ignore the rush of relief that filled him at her offhand dismissal of the unfortunate Edward. "You're going out with a pain?"

She sighed. "I didn't know he was a pain when I agreed to this concert. He bought tickets, so now I'm stuck."

"Can't you tell him…you're sick or something?" He watched her as she stood up.

"I could."

But she wouldn't. He'd known that even when he'd said it. Jamie McCall wouldn't play that kind of game.

She gathered up her papers and came out from behind the desk. Trey watched her cross the room, and when she got to the door, she stopped and turned back toward him.

"Are you sure you're up to going tomorrow?"

"No. But I'd like to, anyway."

"We have to leave at six in the morning."

He nodded, and she turned to go.

"Jamie?"

She looked back.

"Thanks."

The smile that spread across her face did absurd things to his composure. "You know, Mr. Logan, when you're not working so hard at throwing up walls, you're quite a guy."

She was gone before he could do more than gape at her. What was it with these McCalls? Did every one of them have this eerie gift to read his mind and his motives? Did they do it to everyone, or just him? And how did she manage to get him talking when he didn't want to? And why didn't it hurt when he did?

It was a long time before he went back to the paper he hadn't read a word of yet. And when he did, he had a hard time concentrating. She was as distracting in her absence as she had been in person. Only the memory of her casual dismissal of the importance of this date with the hapless Edward kept his imagination in check; he almost felt sorry for the guy. Almost.

"No, Edward. It's late."

"Not that late, babe." The young blond man's voice was as thick and syrupy as the casual endearment. "Just one little drink."

"You've had one little drink too many already." Jamie wrinkled her nose at the smell of alcohol as he leaned toward her. "I think we'd better call a cab. You can pick up your car in the morning."

"Or I could just stay." Edward Chapman's slightly glazed brown eyes leered at her. "C'mon, Jamie, you've put me off for too long. It's time we got serious."

"I am serious." She turned away and crossed the entry hall to the phone. A startled little yelp escaped her when Edward grabbed her wrist and yanked the phone away.

"Oh, no. I don't need a cab. A Chapman can hol' his liquor." He slammed the phone down in the cradle.

"I didn't say you couldn't," Jamie said warily, her nose wrinkling again. "I just don't think you—or anybody—can hold that much and drive responsibly."

"'Sponsi—Respons'bly," he stammered with a snort. "That's all you ever think about."

"Edward—"

He grabbed her wrists suddenly, tightly enough to hurt.

"Stop it!" she snapped, trying to twist away.

"Stop, huh? Your favorite word, isn't it? Think nobody's good enough for you 'cause your father's James McCall!"

"Go home, Edward." Her voice was weary now; she'd heard it all so many times before.

"Oh, no, babe, not this time. You're not pushin' me off again. I've waited long enough."

He pulled her roughly against him, aiming his mouth for hers but missing sloppily. For one brief second her arms went around him, searching. Then she twisted in his grasp, pushing at his chest. He pulled her closer, shoving his hips against her crudely.

"Edward!" She stomped her high heel fiercely down on his foot, and he stumbled backward. She backed up several steps out of his reach.

"I'm sorry I missed Act I."

They both whirled at the cool, dry words that came from the open one of the double library doors. Edward's jaw dropped, and Jamie flushed in embarrassment. In her retreat she had come up against the closed door, and now stood bare inches away from where Trey was looking at Edward impassively.

He was leaning casually against the doorjamb, his legs crossed at the ankle. The light from the room behind him threw his face into shadow, hiding the lines of weariness and the hollowness of his eyes. He looked tall and strong and intimidating, and Edward gaped at him.

Only Jamie knew the significance of that casual posture, that he was carrying his weight on his uninjured leg. Only she knew that the appearance of capable strength was a facade, but she suddenly knew as well that that was exactly how Trey had meant to appear.

"Wh—who the hell is that?" Edward sputtered.

"Just an . . . interested observer," Trey said mildly before Jamie had a chance to speak. "Don't let me interrupt you."

"He was just leaving," Jamie ground out, glaring at Edward.

"So that's it," Edward spat out. "You shove me out the door and hop in the sack with him!"

Jamie's cheeks flamed. "You're drunk, Edward, so I'll forget you said that. Now go. And don't bother calling again."

"Oh, I'll go. Three's a crowd. Unless you like it that way," he said nastily. "Is that it, Miss Innocent? Are you into groups, under that phony sweet little face of yours?" He took a step toward her, and Trey straightened suddenly. Edward stopped dead.

Jamie's color heightened, but her voice was steady. "Now, Edward."

Jamie shuddered as the door slammed after him, but she knew Trey was still there, watching, and she fought to control it. She turned back to the phone, picked it up and dialed.

"A cab?"

She didn't look at him. "He's too drunk to drive."

An edge crept into his voice. "Why didn't you just let him stay, if you care so much?"

"I care," she said tightly after she'd given the address and hung up, "about the innocent people he might take with him."

The hard gray eyes softened with apology for a moment, but Jamie wasn't looking. "What makes you think he'll wait for a cab?"

"These."

Trey stared at the ring of keys dangling from her slender finger. She saw his gaze go unfocused for a moment, as if the scene he'd just witnessed was playing back in his head, including that moment when she had yielded to Edward's embrace. Realization cleared his furrowed brow, and she knew he'd guessed she'd been after Edward's keys. A look oddly like relief flickered over his face, but was gone so quickly she couldn't be sure.

"You'd better lock the door, then. He'll be back."

She sighed and nodded wearily. She crossed to the heavy, carved front door and turned the lock, then the dead bolt. She turned, leaning back against the door as she looked at Trey. His face was impassive, his look once again shuttered. Embarrassment flooded her as she realized what he'd seen, what he was probably thinking, after all she'd said about Edward being a pain. She'd had enough humiliation for one evening.

"I didn't need your help, you know," she snapped.

One dark eyebrow rose at her uncharacteristic attack. "I didn't say you did."

"Edward is . . . harmless, really."

"Just a pain."

She flushed. "Yes."

"But a pain of the proper social standing, no doubt." She stared at him. His mouth twisted wryly, as if he hadn't meant to let that out. "Somebody just needs to harness that tongue of his for him, that's all."

"At least he has the excuse of being drunk," she said quietly.

Trey barely suppressed a wince, and she knew she'd struck home. A sudden, loud pounding at the door beneath her back made her jump.

"A cab's on the way," she called in response to Edward's muffled shouts. "Just wait. Good night, Edward."

The pounding went on, rattling the heavy door. She stepped away from it, squaring her shoulders as she crossed the tiled entry and flipped off the light, plunging the area into darkness except for the shaft of light that shot out from the library. Jamie kept walking toward that light, and the shadow thrown by the man standing there. At the last second before she stepped into the light, she stopped.

"I apologize for disturbing you." She knew her voice sounded small and tight, but she was feeling suddenly exhausted and couldn't seem to care.

"Jamie..."

Something in his voice stopped her, and she stared up at the dark shape of him.

"I...didn't mean that." When she didn't respond, he sighed and went on. "I know you're not...a snob. Guys like him just rub me the wrong way. I wanted to punch him."

There was a pause, then a light feminine chuckle. "I almost wish you had. I never realized what a horrible mouth he had."

Trey let out a breath, as if he'd been holding it, as if he'd expected her to toss his apology back in his face. "If I hadn't been reasonably certain I'd fall on my face, I would have," he said ruefully.

She immediately stepped into the light, peering up at him. "Are you all right?"

He nodded. "Nothing damaged but my already battered pride."

"It's just as well you didn't hit him. His father's the original headline attorney."

"I'm surprised you didn't slap him yourself, Ms. Firebrand."

She blushed. "I would have, if he hadn't been drunk."

And if she hadn't been so busy trying to beat down the images that had leapt to life in her mind when Edward had made that crack about her hopping into the sack with Trey. Images that were too easily fanned to flames again. Especially when he had been so ready to defend her, when she had gotten a glimpse of the power of the man, the power he was regaining every day. She shuddered to think of what the sight of a healthy, healed Trey Logan would do to her.

"Morning's going to come early," she said hastily. "That is, if you still want to go."

"Yes."

"We'd better go to bed." We? God, that sounded as if she meant—

"Good night, Jamie."

"Yes." She whirled and raced up the stairs.

Trey leaned back against the doorjamb, trying to slow his racing heart. *Way to go,* he sneered at himself. *First you go into overdrive at the mere suggestion of her hopping in the sack with you. Then she mentions going to bed, so your imagination immediately goes into a core meltdown while she turns the color of a stoplight. The operative word here is* stoplight, *Logan. And it's one you'd damned well better obey.*

With a muttered curse, he went back to turn the light out before he made the futile effort to sleep.

Chapter 6

"Jamie! Over here!"

"Jamie, Zinger threw a shoe—"

"Jamie, Heather forgot her hat—"

"Hurry, Jamie!"

As she parked beside the big barn, Jamie threw Trey a rueful look. He smiled back.

"Go ahead. I'll manage."

She slid out of the driver's seat and in seconds was engulfed in a swarm of children. Trey reached for the doomed crutches, knowing he was going to need them before the day was over.

He'd been surprised when she first wheeled her vehicle out of the garage. He'd expected some sleek little sports car, or maybe a convertible version of her father's Mercedes. Then he wondered when he was going to learn that he couldn't push her into some preconceived slot—she wouldn't fit.

The big Range Rover was obviously perfect for what she did. And barely big enough for everything she had in it. He'd felt utterly useless this morning, standing there watching as she'd tossed saddles, boxes and things he didn't recognize into the back of the multipurpose vehicle.

At least, he had felt that way at first. After a few minutes of watching the easy grace of her movements, and the flex and stretch of her trim, taut body, a feeling of a totally different kind began to build in him. He beat it down, thinking it should be getting easier to do with all the practice he'd had.

He maneuvered out of the passenger seat, managing to land mostly on his healthy leg, and looked around with interest. Banners flew everywhere, and the entire population seemed to consist of children, horses and hovering parents. Except, he thought curiously, for the small group that appeared to be a video crew. He glanced around and, after a moment, spotted a van with the logo of the local television network affiliates. His brows rose; he hadn't realized this was such a big deal.

When he walked around the front of the Rover and toward the group that surrounded Jamie, he left the crutches leaning against the rounded pipe grille guard, thinking that if anyone needed them worse than he did, they were welcome to them. He'd only taken a few steps past the sizable front bumper when it hit him. He stared at the excited, milling groups of children.

They were of diverse ages, all dressed in varying styles of equestrian wear, and all eagerly shouting questions at Jamie. And every one of them, he saw with a little ripple of shock, had some sort of visible handicap.

There were leg braces in evidence, missing limbs, and the unfocused look of eyes that had lost the ability to see. He knew there were other disabilities that he didn't have the knowledge to recognize.

I could have been one of them.

Jamie's words echoed in his mind. He looked back over his shoulder at the banner that hung below what appeared to be some sort of judging booth above a large, white-fenced arena. The Orange County Therapeutic Riding Center, it said, was sponsoring this show, and in smaller letters it rather gleefully added, Able-bodied Riders Welcome!

"Jamieeeeeee!"

His head whipped around; he recognized that high-pitched young voice. A slender, sandy-haired little boy clad in a bright red Western shirt was headed for her at a run, shrieking her name joyfully. She laughed and turned to catch him up in her arms, nearly losing the battered straw Stetson, adorned with a bright feather band, that sat on her head.

"I was afraid you'd decided not to come," she teased, and he made a face at her. "I'm glad you're here, Mr. Lowell. I'm going to need your help."

"You bet, Jamie!"

Trey watched until he realized he was trying to see what this boy's hidden disability was; then he looked away hastily, ashamed of his own actions. He felt like a self-involved fool for spending so much time groaning about his own problems. At least his would heal. And in the midst of all this was Jamie, the woman he'd thought had no conception of reality.

"Have you seen Greg?" she was asking the boy.

"He's holdin' Scout for me."

"Okay, let's get moving, kids!"

The scene erupted into action, with, inevitably it seemed, Jamie at the center.

He began to get the feel of it as the morning went by, the excitement, the commotion, yet the underlying organization that kept everything going. He watched the classes with no idea of what they were being judged on, but found himself rooting for the kids he'd seen with Jamie. He began to see what a wonderful thing she was doing here. Because after a while, he forgot the differences in these kids; they were just kids, and every last one of them was having a great time. Her father had condescendingly called them "charity classes," but Trey was willing to bet she got more out of them than she gave.

He was vaguely aware of the other member of her entourage—a young, lanky teenager who kept looking at him rather suspiciously. The boy was blond, tan and good-looking, if a little sullen. The other kids called him Greg, and Trey gathered he worked here at the stables. Why Greg was watching so carefully, he didn't know.

It was nearly noon before Jamie had a free minute and came over to where Trey was standing near the fence, watching the group of riders circle the arena. It was the first class she hadn't had a rider in, and she leaned against the fence rail gratefully.

"How's it going?" He knew the results of the classes, but didn't know what she'd expected.

"Not bad. Nobody's gotten hurt, or upset, or fallen off."

He chuckled. He should have known those would be her priorities, not winning. "And a couple of ribbons to boot."

She grinned. "Yep. That's the gravy." She looked him up and down. "How are you doing?"

He shrugged. "Fine."

"They kind of make you forget, don't they?"

He stiffened; then, as he heard another shriek of delight from the class winner, relaxed. "Yeah," he muttered.

"I've got a minute before the next class," she said. "Would you like to see the new arrival?"

When he nodded, she led him over to a small enclosure behind the big barn she'd parked next to. A placid-looking brown mare, dozing despite the chaos going on around her, stood quietly in one corner. And peeking curiously out from behind her was a tiny equine face, with a white stripe running crookedly, rather endearingly, down its center.

"Isn't he adorable?" she crooned, leaning to rest her arms on the pipe railing. The tiny horse's ears flicked forward, and he trotted out from behind the protective bulk of his mother, looking as if he'd recognized her voice.

Probably did, Trey thought, as he watched the little colt come to her without hesitation. *He's not even afraid of me as long as she's here.* He couldn't stop his smile at the ridiculous length of the spindly legs.

"All elbows," he said. "Or whatever they are on a horse."

She flashed a grin at him; it took his breath away. "Hocks," she said. "And you're right, it does look like that, doesn't it? But he's going to be a beauty someday."

"Thanks to you."

"I just helped."

"You should be proud." She shook her head, but the color that rose to her cheeks told him she was pleased. "Is there anybody you don't—"

"Jamie!" Greg came skidding to a halt beside her. "Chuckie needs help with Scout. He's acting up again."

"All right."

She gave Trey an apologetic look and left at a trot. Trey watched her go, his jaw tightening as his body responded to the sight of her long legs and trim bottom in those snug jeans. Only when she was out of sight did he realize that Greg had stayed.

"You her boyfriend or somethin'?"

He jerked around to look at the boy, startled. "What?"

The teenager shrugged, but his almost belligerent tone belied the casual attitude he assumed. "She's been actin' kind of different lately. Figured it must be you."

It didn't take long for Trey to figure out the reason for the boy's attitude; he'd stuck to Jamie like glue all day, and it was obvious he had a heavy crush on her. His manner was understandable if he thought Trey was— He swallowed tightly at the thought of what the boy had assumed, and at the swift, wayward wish that rose in him, the wish that it could be true.

"What makes you think that?" he said carefully.

Greg snorted derisively. "You think I'm dumb or something? I've seen the way she looks at you, the way she watches you."

Trey gaped at him. She watched him? And just how did she look at him?

"Besides, she's never brought anybody here before." Greg looked at the crutches Trey had had to resort to after the first hour on his feet. "Unless you're just another one of her strays."

Stung, Trey stiffened. "Strays?"

"Yeah. Like me."

Before he could demand an explanation, a chorus of shouts drew their attention.

"All right, Jamie!"

"Ride 'em, cowgirl!"

The cries turned both of them around toward the source, and Trey's heart seemed to lodge in his throat, his hands tightening convulsively around the grips of the crutches.

It looked like something out of a rodeo, the black-and-white-spotted horse dancing wickedly sideways, his rider clinging like a burr to the saddle. Except the rider aboard the protesting pinto was Jamie, and she looked impossibly fragile atop the half ton of horse, which rose suddenly straight up in the air on its hind legs.

Trey let out a choked sound as he stared. God, what if she was thrown—she could get hurt again! She shouldn't be doing that—what if—

A vision of her, pale and drawn, chained to a hospital bed as surely as he had been chained to a post in that jungle compound came to him, and the chill that enveloped him made him shiver as he started toward her, not sure what he was going to do, but feeling he had to do something.

"Don't." Greg grabbed his arm. "You'll just spook the horse. She's all right." Trey looked at him incredulously. "She is. That's nothing compared to what I've seen her ride. She'll talk him down."

The horse had come back on all fours, still dancing sideways. Jamie leaned forward, and he could hear bits of her soft, calming phrases.

"...my pretty one...full of yourself, aren't you, my boy...know how good you are, don't you now...that's the way..."

The dancing slowed, then stopped. Then she nudged him, still whispering. The horse's ears were turned back attentively, and he walked forward as politely as a gentleman out for a stroll.

Trey let out a long breath, feeling the ebb of adrenaline in the relaxing of taut muscles. He watched as she slid off the now-docile horse and turned the reins over to the slender youngster who had stood cheering along with the others. Greg had gone to rejoin the group, and she spoke to him for a moment before she came back to where Trey stood. The boy watched her go, and with an odd little shock Trey recognized that avid look. Trey couldn't meet her eyes, and kept his gaze lowered as they made their way back to the arena.

"Sorry," she said a little breathlessly. "Scout always has to get in his token protest before a show."

"He does that a lot?" He leaned the crutches against the fence, shifting to use the top rail for support.

"Only on show days. And afterward he's angelic."

He glanced up at the boy now astride the flashy horse that was entering the ring. "Don't his parents worry?"

"They're just so glad he's able to ride, they don't care. Besides, other than that little quirk, he's a perfectly safe horse."

He wanted to ask her what was wrong with the ebullient Chuckie, who looked like any ten-year-old, but he couldn't seem to find the words. And then she was so intent on the class in progress that he didn't want to disturb her.

On each round, she called encouragement to the boy, and occasionally a quick piece of instruction. Trey was watching her so closely that when the class was over, he had no idea what had happened. That is, until Jamie let out a shout of delight and threw her arms around him.

"He did it!" she cried, her amber eyes gleaming no less than the sun that lit the sky. She hugged him fiercely, her slender body pressing against him. He stared down at her, his breath caught in his throat.

She went suddenly still as she looked up at him, her lips still parted from her joyous cry. Her mouth felt suddenly dry, and unconsciously she touched her lips with the tip of her tongue. Trey groaned as his heart began to hammer in his chest. He tried to stop, but the temptation was too much, and he lowered his head.

He told himself he could just taste her, just the slightest brushing of his mouth over hers, but the resolution was lost in the first touch of her lips. She was so warm and soft in his arms, and her mouth was so sweet. . . .

Her arms tightened around him, and he felt her hands flexing against his back. His mouth coaxed, cajoled, and when he let his tongue flicker over the delicate line of her lips, she gave a little sigh that fired his blood and parted them for him.

Heedless of the surroundings, he slid his hands upward to cup her head and tilt it back to deepen the kiss. A low, husky sound rose from deep in his chest as his fingers threaded through her hair; it felt exactly as he'd known it would—like thick, heavy silk against his hands.

He probed tentatively past the soft barrier of her lips, his tongue finding and tracing the even ridge of her teeth. She made that sound again and swayed against him. The pressure of her weight against his rapidly swelling body was a sweet, hot pain, and he barely managed to stop himself from sliding his hands down to her hips to press her even closer, harder against him.

Then he felt the brief, tentative brush of her tongue against his, and he groaned deep in his throat. That touch of hesitancy was somehow more erotic than any practiced smoothness, and his body rose to it with a fierceness that took his breath away.

"Jamie! Jamie, did you see? I won!"

Trey's head snapped up, nearly knocking off Jamie's battered straw cowboy hat. The hot, golden haze lifted a little. Jamie tried to stand but swayed, and Trey's hands went to her shoulders to steady her. She stared at him, looking dazed, her breath coming in quick little pants. He lowered his gaze, trying not to look at her parted lips, but found himself instead staring at the soft curve of her breasts. He closed his eyes, but not before the sight of her taut, straining nipples pressing against the soft fabric of her shirt was engraved indelibly in his mind.

"Jamie!"

With a strangled little sound she turned away, and he saw a little shiver go through her as she started toward the jubilant Chuckie. He leaned back against the fence, struggling for control. *Damn,* he thought. *Oh, damn.*

He'd almost had himself convinced that his response to her was just the result of his long isolation, the long months he'd gone without a woman. Or even reaction to what had happened to him in that damned jungle. But he'd done without before, and been close to death before. And never in his life had he experienced anything like this.

My God, he thought, *it was just a kiss. Just a simple, harmless kiss.* Harmless? He laughed harshly. About as harmless as a baseball grenade, and with the same potential for damage. His hands clamped around the top fence rail; without it, he wouldn't have been surprised if he'd fallen down. He was weaker than he'd been when Lucero had been doing his bloody worst, and even the fury that the general's image brought roaring to life wasn't enough to overcome the effects of kissing Jamie McCall.

He suddenly decided it was time to give in to the emphatic demands of his leg and seek the relief of the chairs Jamie had brought.

"Here, Mr. Logan." He turned at the high, piping voice and saw Chuckie standing beside an unfolded chaise longue. "Jamie brought this one for you, so you could stretch out your leg."

The child gestured at the waiting chair with all the flair of a maître d' at an expensive restaurant. Trey stifled a smile and thanked him gravely. The boy turned away as he dropped down gratefully, trying not to wince as the damaged muscles let him know he'd waited too long.

"Hurts, huh?"

His head snapped around to see Chuckie back again, a look of empathy on his young face. Not sympathy—empathy. This child knew about pain, he thought, and the realization was oddly distressing.

"Yeah," he agreed softly, "it does."

The boy nodded, a world of torturous experience in the soft brown eyes. He held out an icy can of soda, which Trey took gratefully. It was hot out. He was hot. And, to his surprise, hungry. He supposed it was being outdoors, but whatever the cause, it was the first time in weeks he'd really had an appetite.

As if he'd read his mind, Chuckie was back again, a sandwich in each hand.

"Ham or peanut butter?" he asked solemnly.

"Did somebody appoint you to take care of me?" Trey asked suspiciously.

"Yep. Jamie." The boy grinned happily. "I never took care of anybody before."

Leave it to her, he thought wryly, *to pick somebody I can't tell to go away.* "Ham."

"Good." Chuckie handed over the sandwich. "I'll have the peanut butter."

Trey had had a feeling that was coming, and he grinned inwardly as the boy pulled a chair up close and sat down.

"Jamie said you got hurt helping her dad," the boy said between bites.

Trey tensed, then realized it and made himself relax. It had become a reflex, he thought. "Yeah. Sort of."

"I'm glad you helped him. I was scared for Jamie."

He had a wisdom much too old for his age, and Trey couldn't help wondering yet again if there was some invisible problem plaguing this child. Perhaps he was just related to one of the others, he thought, pleased with the idea. The child chattered on happily, still flushed with the success of his earlier win.

"Where's your ribbon?" Trey asked after a while. He'd figured the boy would be wearing it, he was so proud.

"On Scout's halter, of course. He won it, really."

It didn't take much to recognize Jamie's teaching, and he smiled.

"Greg put it there for me. I'm not tall enough."

"Greg . . ." Trey began slowly. "He . . . works here?"

"Yeah. He's okay, but he's kind of in a bad mood today."

"Oh?" *Uh-oh, you mean.*

"Yeah. Like he used to be when he first came."

"He used to be in a bad mood?"

"All the time. He was in trouble a lot then, I guess, till Jamie got him the job here."

"Jamie got him the job?"

"Yeah." Chuckie clearly had no qualms about discussing it. "She talked Mr. Doyle into it. Said it wasn't his fault, that his dad used to hit him a lot, and that's why he was in trouble all the time."

One of her strays. The words echoed in his mind. A sense of wonder at the seemingly limitless capacity she had for caring warred with an uncomfortable speculation as to whether that was how she saw him. He was glad the boy kept up a steady stream of talk until Greg, with a glance rife with antipathy for Trey, came to get Chuckie for his next class.

To his embarrassment he dozed off then, and Jamie had to wake him up when the last class had been judged and she had gotten her satisfied pupils on their way home. He was even more embarrassed when he found everything already loaded except for the lounge he was on. He felt useless once more.

"You have . . . quite a fan club."

They were almost to the house, but it was the first thing he'd said since they'd gotten in the Rover to come back. He hadn't known what to say; the memory of that kiss was too vividly in his mind, even though she seemed to have put it out of hers.

She smiled. "They're good kids."

"Are they . . . hard to teach?"

She didn't say anything until she pulled the Rover into the garage and stopped. Then she glanced over, looking him up and down with an expression that made him slightly uncomfortable. "No. Teaching *you* would be hard." He looked startled. "They're flexible, and they want to learn. I can teach them. You're too stubborn."

He flushed; then it faded as he caught a glimpse of a smile tugging at the corners of her mouth as she slid out of the driver's seat.

"Brat," he muttered as he got out on his side. It was a lot harder this time, and he knew that he'd pushed the mutilated muscles of his leg too far.

Jamie came around the Rover and stopped dead. He was leaning against the door he'd just closed, sweat beading up on his forehead, and he was as white as her shirt had been when she'd started out this morning. His lowered lashes looked thick and black against his suddenly ashen skin.

"Trey!" She set the empty cooler down abruptly and rushed over to him. His eyes snapped open.

"I'm fine," he grated.

"If you're fine, why do you look like you're about to pass out?"

"I'm not about to pass out." At least, not if the world would stop spinning so fast, he amended to himself.

He became aware of her silence, and when the whirling at last slowed, he realized she was watching him with that same penetrating expression. He swore under his breath and grabbed for the crutches.

His petulant departure cost him; he barely made it to the library before he collapsed. He didn't make it to the chair, and only his battered pride made him drag his aching body off the floor before she came in and found him.

He was still breathing hard and kneading at his rebelling muscles when she came in twenty minutes later. She sat down without a word, but he could feel her gaze on him. He didn't look up; he didn't dare. Then a tempting aroma began to tickle his nose and he glanced up reflexively. And grimaced when his stomach growled loudly.

"I just brought it," she said, gesturing to the tray that held a steaming bowl of Jean's clam chowder and another sandwich. "I figured if I asked, you'd just say no."

"Stubborn?" he asked wryly.

"Stubborn," she agreed with a smile.

He sighed and gave up. And finished the food so quickly he was embarrassed. His appetite was finally, it appeared, on the mend.

Later, when she came down from her shower, Jamie found the library deserted. She glanced at the clock and thought perhaps he'd gone to bed after the long day. It was nearly ten. A smile curved her lips when she saw he had picked up the tray and the empty dishes. She'd never seen him eat like this in the entire month he'd been here, and it made her feel warm in a way she didn't quite understand.

She let out a small sigh. *He* made her feel warm in a hundred ways she didn't understand. All day, despite the chaos around her, she had found herself watching him. She had caught herself more times than she could count looking for him in the middle of the crowd and flushing at the little rush of pleasure that flooded her when she found him, tall and dark and still amid the flurry of activity.

He looked so much better now, even with the crutches. In fact, she barely noticed them at all. How could she notice something like that when she was too busy looking at the expanse of his chest beneath the snug knit shirt, and at the way the pale blue color of it seemed to turn his eyes to a shimmering silver-blue?

And those jeans... After seeing him always in sweatpants, she was totally unprepared for those jeans, for the way they hugged the long, muscled lines of his legs, rode low on his narrow hips and emphasized the flat, trim belly. And the way they cupped the taut swell of his buttocks made her stare with a blatant enjoyment that embarrassed her as soon as she realized it.

And that, she thought with a breathless little gasp, was before he'd kissed her. Lord, she thought, *warm* wasn't the word for what *that* made her feel. She didn't know *what* the word was for that. She only knew that she'd never felt it before.

With a sigh, she went into the kitchen to get a glass of milk, but stopped when she glanced out the window and saw the light on in the solarium.

No, not even he could be *that* stubborn. Could he? He wouldn't try to work out after today? He'd been on his feet for hours, for the first time; his leg had to be hurting terribly. She knew it was hurting; she'd seen his face when he'd landed on the leg as he got out of the Rover.

She put the glass back and headed down the hall. And breathed a sigh of relief when she saw him, not at the gym pushing weights, but sitting on the planter wall. His hair was damp, and he was back in sweatpants after his shower. Sweatpants, and nothing else.

She had to swallow against the sudden tightness in her throat at the sight of his bare torso. It had nothing to do with the fading marks on his back, and everything to do with taut muscle and sleek skin, his bare chest and the way soft, dark hair began a path just below his navel and plunged temptingly downward out of sight. Her swift steps faltered.

He was staring, not, for once, out at the night sky, but at the plants beside him, the fragrant gardenias that were her pets. He looked up as she came in. Noticing her pause when she saw where he was, he grinned wryly.

"Stubborn, but not necessarily stupid," he said.

She didn't deny it; she was too busy trying to rein in senses that seemed suddenly out of control. After a moment she was able to steady herself.

"There are times," she said as she crossed the room and sat beside him, "when stubborn is all that gets you through."

He looked away, fingering one of the white flower petals idly. After a long moment he looked up at her again. "Yeah. Even when you forget why."

She knew what he meant. She would never forget the long days when she had wanted to give up, and she saw in his eyes that he knew she understood.

One of the petals of the pure white flower fell into his hand, and he raised it to breathe in the exotic, rich scent. Something odd flickered across his face, something almost like pain.

"My mother used to grow these."

He didn't go on, and she said in low tones, "They're my favorites. I love the scent."

He looked up at her then. "I know. Every time I smell them, I think of that perfume you wear."

His gaze flickered over her with an expression she couldn't quite interpret. She had put on the caftan again, that silken fall of yellow shot with gold threads that flowed over her. When his gaze met hers again, the memory of that kiss leapt between them, and she suddenly knew that he had been thinking of how she had felt in his arms, just as she had been thinking of the burst of heat that had rocketed through her when his mouth had come down on hers. As if he'd read her thoughts, he looked hastily away. It was a moment before she could speak, grasping a neutral topic.

"Does your mother still grow them?" she asked, watching him toy with the piece of the flower.

"No." Convulsively his hand curled into a fist, crushing the delicate petal. "She's dead."

Jamie felt a familiar pang. "I'm sorry," she whispered.

He shrugged, but the tension in his body gave the lie to the casual gesture.

"How long . . . ?"

"Thirteen years. An aeon ago."

"Or just yesterday." She drew in a shaky breath. "I know how it . . . it's so hard."

His eyes narrowed suddenly. "You don't know the half of it, so don't go feeling sorry for me."

She drew back, startled. She hadn't heard that tone from him for a while. "I don't—"

"Just drop it, will you? You don't know anything about it, all right?"

Color rose in her cheeks; she'd thought they were through with this. "I know how hard it is. I know what it's like to wonder what it would have been like if she hadn't died. I know what it's like to live without—"

"Do you know what it's like living with knowing you killed her?" His head had come up sharply, every muscle gone rigid, and Jamie stared at him. "I do," he said flatly. "I live with it every damned day."

"Trey, what—"

"I killed her," he repeated, as if she'd disputed it. "If I had seen that damned car when it came over the center line, if I'd just let my old man drive—"

He shuddered, his body jerking slightly as he turned his face from her. One hand went to the mark low on his back, the older scar, and rubbed at it in a gesture that looked automatic. It was, she knew instinctively, not from Lucero's abuse, but from the accident that had taken his mother. Jamie watched him, her throat tight. This, then, was the real thing that wouldn't go away for him.

"An accident—" she began, but he whirled back on her.

"I should have seen it coming. I could have avoided it."

"They...told you that? When the other car was at fault?"

He laughed harshly. "They didn't have to. I knew. And even if I hadn't, my old man made sure of it."

She gasped. "Your father?"

"He knew. He was in the car. If he'd been driving—"

"The same thing could have happened," she burst out. "How could he blame you?"

"Easy. He did it quite thoroughly. Right before he told me to get the hell out of his life, he never wanted to lay eyes on me again."

She couldn't stop the rapid calculation in her mind. Thirteen years. He'd been seventeen. So young to be cast out, on his own. Had he joined the army because he had nowhere else to go? Her heart twisted inside her.

"Trey—"

"Just drop it," he bit out. "You don't understand—"

"I think I do," she cut in softly.

"How could you?"

"My mother died having me."

That brought him around to face her again. She held his gaze, seeing the eyes that had gone cold again shift, seeing the quandary in their depths, and then the slow, growing ruefulness.

"You'd think I would have learned, after today, wouldn't you?" he said wryly after a long silence. "I never realized I was such a self-centered bastard."

"We all are, sometimes."

"Not all of us." His voice was quiet, soft, and the pointed way he looked at her was unmistakable.

She colored. "Me as much as anyone else. Sometimes more."

"I doubt that."

"Don't. It's true. I'm just—"

"Beautiful."

She caught her breath as color flooded her face again. Something in his steady gaze made her think of that kiss again, and her pulse began to race.

"And the outside matches," he said softly, lifting one hand to her face, to run the back of his fingers over her cheek. Her lips parted; she couldn't seem to breathe when he touched her. She didn't mean to do it, but somehow she had turned her head and was pressing her lips against his fingers.

She heard his sudden intake of breath, felt him tense. Then, slowly, he moved his hand until he was cupping her face. And again, unable to stop and not sure she wanted to, she turned her head and pressed a soft kiss into his palm.

She heard him let out the breath he'd taken in a long sigh. He raised his other hand to her shoulder, fingers flexing as if to trace the delicate structure of it, then softening as if he were savoring the warmth of her beneath the gold silk. Then his arms tensed, and his grip tightened as if he fought against pulling her to him.

She supposed if she had given the slightest sign of resistance, he would have stopped. But at the first increase in pressure she melted into his arms like wax to the flame, and with a smothered groan he lowered his mouth to hers.

Oh, God, Jamie thought as he feathered his tongue over her lips. It had been like this, it really had. How could her body turn to liquid so fast? How could he reduce her to golden, flowing heat in mere seconds? She didn't know, and at that moment she didn't care. All she cared about was being closer, wanting more.

Her arms crept up to encircle his neck, her slender fingers tangling in the thick, damp hair at his nape. He pulled her closer as he thrust his tongue forward. She opened for him, welcomed him, and a bolt of searing heat shot through her at the sound that rose from him when her tongue rose to meet his with eagerness this time.

His arms tightened around her convulsively, drawing her up onto his lap, seemingly heedless of his tender leg muscles. Nothing seemed to matter next to the inferno that had leapt so suddenly, so fiercely, to life, and she wondered dazedly if he, too, couldn't feel anything except the sweet, honeyed heat. She twisted, driven by a need she'd never known before to feel his skin, that expanse of bare chest beneath her hands. She flattened her palms against him, her fingers curling involuntarily. He let out a strangled groan as her flexing fingertips brushed his nipples, and he wrenched his mouth away.

Jamie froze at his movement. Then slowly, tentatively, she moved her fingers again, stroking the flat, male nubs that were tautening beneath her touch. For an instant something near puzzlement showed in his face, but it vanished in the fire that ignited in the gray depths when her hands moved on him again.

His hands slid down her slender back, stroking over her shoulders to her waist. She twisted sinuously, and shivered with pleasure when he reached to cup her trim bottom, to bring her tighter against him. His hands moved again, then stopped as a rippling, convulsive shudder ripped through him.

"God," he murmured thickly, "you're naked under this, aren't you?"

Jamie knew that color was flooding her face, but she couldn't stop it. She couldn't do anything but feel, and flow with the heat that was sweeping over her in wave after wave. Her heart was rejoicing, and all the years when she'd wondered if something unknown had been damaged in her, when she'd wondered if she would ever feel anything but a quiet affection for a man, were gone as if they'd never been. This stubborn, solitary man with the eyes that could turn her soul to ice or flame had ripped them away with one kiss and was burning them to ash with the caressing touch of his hands.

She felt the unmistakable pressure of aroused male flesh against her thigh, and her color deepened. It seemed so strange, so unknown, and yet so right....

Trey saw her fierce blush, felt her tentative movements. God, he thought, she made him feel as if he was the only one who had ever touched her, as if he was making her feel things she'd never felt. He groaned, reeling under the strength of it. He knew he was careening out of control, and thought desperately that he had to do something.

"Jamie," he said thickly, "I can't..."

She raised her head, never relinquishing her clinging hold on him, and looked at him with eyes that seemed the exact color of sunlight through honey—hot and golden. It took her a moment to speak, and when she did the huskiness of her voice sent another ripple of flame straight to that hot, pulsing core of him that was rapidly taking control.

"Are you hurting?" She shifted on his lap, trying to lift her weight from his injured leg. He groaned again as her innocent movement brought her hard against his rigid flesh.

"Yes I'm hurting," he ground out.

"I'm sorry," she said with another blush. "Your leg—"

"It has nothing to do with my leg," he said through gritted teeth.

Her delicate brows furrowed, then cleared as color once more flooded her face. Her tongue crept out to wet her suddenly dry lips as her hands slipped from behind his neck, sliding down over his chest. Her fingers found and scraped gently over his nipples once more, and his body clenched with a violence that made him gasp, closing his eyes.

"Jamie," he warned hoarsely.

"I don't want you to hurt anymore."

His eyes shot open to look at hers at her whispered words, and when he saw the heat, the desire, and the longing that were swirling in the amber depths, whatever protest, whatever warning he'd been going to give her went up in a fiery burst of heat. And when she leaned forward to kiss him hungrily, so did he.

Chapter 7

Trey sensed her uncertainty, although he doubted his interpretation when she dragged her fingers over his chest again, then followed his lead and nibbled gently along his lower lip. Involuntarily that low sound broke from deep within him, and he felt her press her fingertips against him as if feeling the vibration of it through the heated skin of his chest. She looked at him with a touch of awe, as if she couldn't believe the effect she was having on him. He nearly groaned aloud; he couldn't believe it, either. He shivered at her touch; it grew to a shudder when her movement pressed her hip once more against his all-too-ready flesh.

"Oh, Jamie!"

It burst from him as his hips bucked beneath her, his hands pulling her hard against him. Any sign of awe vanished from her face, to be replaced with a shocked pleasure when his fingers stroked over her breasts to her nipples, finding and tugging the puckering flesh. She whimpered, her breath rushing from her as his fingertips gently squeezed and rubbed.

Trey looked at her from beneath half-lowered lids, seeing the swollen fullness of her lips, the hot, dreamy look of the topaz eyes, feeling the sweet pressure of her against him, making him want to take her here and now, sitting up, heedless of anything except the driving need to bury himself deep inside her. It would be so easy—he could just lift her over him, slide that golden silk up the smooth, satin length of her legs, free his hot, begging flesh and—

He shuddered violently, shaken to the core by a need unlike anything he'd ever felt. He was mindless with it, with want, with urgency, with the pleasure just touching her gave him. And they'd barely begun.

His gaze dropped to her breasts, the breasts he could swear were swelling and growing heavier even as he caressed them. His gaze locked on the sight of his hands cradling that precious flesh, his skin darkened by days chained in the Central American sun, and his wrists still banded by the fading marks of those chains. The contrast with the rich, elegant silk of the caftan, with the rich, elegant woman herself, brought him to a quivering halt.

"Jamie," he panted. "Jamie, we've got to stop."

She leaned back a bare fraction of an inch, looking up at him through the thick fringe of her lashes, eyes hot and wanting.

"Why?" She said it with such shy wonder that he groaned again.

Why indeed? *Because you're who you are, and I'm what I am. Because we're in your father's house. Because I work for your uncle and respect him more than any man I know. Because your father trusted me here. Because I'm a hundred years older than you in what I've seen and what I've done. Because I want you too damned much, and I'll hurt you.*

All the good, solid, logical reasons were there, poised and ready, and he couldn't say a word. She had leaned forward to press her sweet, warm mouth to his chest, taking away his breath and his power of speech.

Then her tongue slipped between her lips to lay a trail of wet fire across his skin and his mind short-circuited, jumping from answering the why to asking "Why not?" She wasn't a kid—she knew what she was doing. She couldn't not know, not the way she was kissing him, not the way she turned all soft and hot in his arms, so why not? It had been so long, and he'd been to hell and back, so why not? She'd made it clear, more than clear that she wanted him back....

Jamie sensed the change in him, sensed the moment when he gave up the battle. For one split second she felt a little shiver of apprehension at the irrevocable step she was about to take with this man she'd known for barely a month. But he was also the man who made her feel like no one ever had, the man who'd fascinated her ever since he'd shattered her preconceptions to splinters. And then he was kissing her, soft teasing little caresses, and nothing mattered except the feel of his lips against her skin and the way her breasts nestled into his hands.

She let her head loll back, offering her throat to him. The movement arched her back, and her breasts pressed harder against his hands. She wondered with a little thrill what it would feel like to have those hands, those strong, tough hands, on her bare flesh. Would he be gentle, or rough? Both thoughts made her gasp in anticipation.

As if he'd read her thoughts, he released one breast and reached for the zipper at the neck of the caftan, still trailing sweet, hot kisses down the side of her throat and cuddling her other breast in his other hand, his thumb teasing the crest to rigid, tingling awareness.

She moaned, a tiny, eager little sound that seemed to make his hands clumsy as he tugged at the caftan. At last the fastener slid open, the golden threads sparkling as the silk fell away, slipping off her slender shoulders and tumbling to her waist.

"Oh, Jamie," he groaned, staring at the lush, full curves tipped with coral pink crests that drew up even tighter under his gaze.

She blushed, deep and rosy, wondering how she could feel so shy and at the same time so incredibly wanton. She looked at Trey, whose face reflected the same kind of confusion she was feeling, as if he was being swamped by a rush of so many tangled emotions that he couldn't begin to sort them out.

Trey reached for her, pulling her hard against his chest, sucking in a long, harsh breath at the feel of her naked breasts against the skin of his chest.

How could she be so shy yet so sensual? Seem so innocent yet so incredibly erotic and arousing? He didn't know; he only knew he'd never been so full, so hard, so desperate for the sweet relief that could only come from her. He'd guessed she hadn't much experience, and told himself he had to be gentle, but when she kissed him, when wildfire slashed through him as her seeking tongue found his, gentle was the last thing he wanted to be.

He wanted her naked beneath him, he wanted to take those tight, straining nipples in his mouth, carefully raking his teeth across them until they were pebble hard against his tongue; he wanted to hear her moan with the pleasure of it, he wanted to drive his aching, throbbing flesh into her....

But more than anything, he wanted her to want it. He wanted her to want it as badly, as desperately as he did. He wanted her to cry out for it, to beseech him to take her, to plead for his body inside her. He had to know, had to be sure, that she wanted him, that she was ready for him, that she had to have him. He'd never cared so much about it before, and it might have scared him if there had been room in his thoughts for anything but this raging compulsion.

He stood up, holding her tightly against his chest as he let her slide down until her feet touched the floor. He reached for the caftan that was caught between their bodies, then paused as his fingers touched the bunched silk.

"Jamie," he said hoarsely, "this is it. It's been too damned long for me. If you stop me now, I might be able to walk away. But if you don't—"

His words, words that gave her the chance he'd felt compelled to give her for a reason he didn't understand, broke off with a strangled groan. She had given him her answer. With a quick, unsteady movement she had backed a half step away from him and given a trembling little twist of her body. The shimmering silk slid down from her waist and over her slim hips to puddle on the floor. She kicked it away, the certainty of that motion at odds with the flushed self-consciousness in her expression. Modesty battled with hunger on her delicate features, shyness with wanton need, and the combination nearly sent Trey to his knees.

Convulsively he reached for her, pulling her hard against him once more. The feel of her, slender, trembling, and naked in his arms, nearly sent him over the edge, and he tried to rein in his surging senses.

What was wrong with him? True, it had been a long time, since long before the ill-fated trip to Central America, but he'd gone longer. He hadn't expected to nearly lose control at just the sight of her, at the sight of her smooth, lovely curves, the full swells of her breasts, the slender indentation of her waist, the trim yet womanly hips and the silken mane of hair falling over her naked shoulders.

"You're so beautiful," he breathed against her hair.

He didn't deserve this, he thought. He didn't deserve this soft, delicate beauty; she deserved better than him, better than some battered, beaten soldier of fortune who would carry the scars of his kind of life forever. But for some reason he didn't comprehend, she wanted him, and he couldn't find the strength to turn away.

He lifted her in his arms, and with exquisite care he took her down to the mat that had become his bed. He kicked free of his sweats as she clung to him, small little sounds of pleasure rising from her as his hands moved over her, caressing every inch of silken skin.

He tried to control his haste as he bent over her, seeking and finding one taut nipple with his lips, the other with his hand. He suckled deeply at the one, rolled the other between his thumb and forefinger and tried to check the flame that rocketed through him at the low, husky cry of pleasure that broke from her. She arched upward to him, her head rolling back as she offered her breasts to him more fully, and he couldn't stop the tremor that swept him.

Jamie clutched at him when he shifted, afraid he would leave her, that the glorious torment of his mouth on her breast would cease. She didn't want it to ever end, wanted the hot, golden ripples to go on and on. Yet she wanted more, was striving, arching for more, even though she wasn't sure what it was she wanted.

Her hands slid down from his shoulders, nails digging into his flesh. Then, with the last tiny fragment of her sanity she remembered his back and realized that her fingers were scraping that tender, barely healed skin. For a moment she froze, as did he.

The halting of that sweet, drawing motion of his lips at her breast left her feeling oddly bereft. With a forlorn little sound she moved, her hands going to tangle in the thick, dark hair as she urged his mouth back to her nipple. She thought she should feel embarrassed by her own boldness, but somehow all she could feel was need, and all she knew was that if he didn't resume that hot, wet, luscious caress, she would die.

Quaking in his effort to control his body's response to her silent entreaty, Trey moved over her, lowering his head to her breast once more. He took each nipple in turn, trying to concentrate on how sweet she tasted, on the rich, exotic scent of her, more intoxicating than the flowers it was drawn from, and to ignore the teasing, tormenting feel of the silken skin of her belly against his swollen, aching shaft. He couldn't quite do it—his hips moved involuntarily, pressing himself between them, and a harsh, throttled sound broke from deep in his chest.

Jamie gasped, her eyes widening as she felt the hot, rigid length of him. A brief moment of doubt assailed her at the thought of that throbbing column of flesh invading her body. Almost at the same second, fire ignited, erupting deep inside her, in the very place that would accept the invasion. It melted her lower body to some heavy, pooling liquid, wanting, needing that invasion, needing that part of him inside her more than she needed her next breath.

"Please," she moaned, only realizing she had spoken her need when she heard the breathy little sound of a voice she barely recognized as hers.

"Please, what?" His voice was low and vibrant against her breasts.

Oh, no, she couldn't ask, didn't know how to ask. She quivered in his arms, felt his hips move once more.

"Trey, please," she gasped.

He smiled a primal smile at his name on her lips, at the urgency in her voice.

"What?" he repeated, his voice nearly a growl as he nuzzled her soft flesh. "What do you want, Jamie?"

She shuddered, her need overcoming her shyness. "You," she moaned.

"You want me?" He lifted his head to look at her, his eyes hot, smoky gray now. "You want me inside you?"

"Yes," she hissed, writhing beneath him now, her hips lifting instinctively, eagerly.

The voluptuous movement shattered the last fragile threads of his control, and he began to unravel with such speed he knew he couldn't stop. He parted her legs and knelt between them, the muscles of his belly rippling when he saw her glance slide down his body to rest wide-eyed on his jutting manhood. Something in her eyes nagged at him, but when his own gaze came to rest on the tangle of sandy curls at the top of her thighs, that tiny remaining bit of sanity fled before the blast of fire that exploded within him.

He came forward over her, his mouth taking hers with a swift fierceness as his body homed toward her soft heat. He probed, a violent shudder taking him when he found her slick and ready. She did want him, she really did....

The first searing clasp of her flesh around the tip of his was his undoing. He thrust forward fiercely, wanting to sheath himself completely in that coaxing, luring hot wetness. Halfway there he had to stop—she was tight, so very tight....

He shuddered again as she bucked beneath him and gave an odd little cry that he smothered with his lips. It had almost sounded like pain, his reeling mind thought. She seemed so small, she couldn't seem to take him; he should stop, he had to be hurting her, but he couldn't, he couldn't stop now....

He thrust hard once more, and then he was there, buried in her, feeling her body clench around him.

"Ah, Jamie!"

His shout was hoarse, thick and choked. He was aware of her odd stillness and wanted to ask. He wanted to go slowly, to savor every sweet moment. He wanted to pull back, then reclaim her inch by hot, slick inch. He wanted to linger over the feel of her body holding him, stroking him. He wanted all these things, but the rupture of his control was complete. His body, already too long denied satisfaction, was careering headlong toward a height he'd never reached, never known existed. He was driving deep into her, into the haven she had become to him. A little sound of wonder rose from her, and his name was on a breathy sigh. It made him tremble as he braced himself over her.

Her warmth, her tenderness, her care in the face of his screen of insults had drawn him to this moment seemingly inexorably. She had taken a weary, resistant and untrusting

NO RISK, NO OBLIGATION TO BUY ... NOW OR EVER!

CASINO JUBILEE
"Scratch'n Match" Game

Here's how to play:

1. Peel off label from front cover. Place it in space provided at right. With a coin, carefully scratch off the silver box. Then check the claim chart to see what we have for you – FREE BOOKS and a gift – ALL YOURS! ALL FREE!

2. Send back this card and you'll receive brand-new Silhouette Intimate Moments® novels. These books have a cover price of $3.50 each, but they are yours to keep absolutely free.

3. There's no catch. You're under no obligation to buy anything. We charge nothing – ZERO – for your first shipment. And you don't have to make any minimum number of purchases – not even one!

4. The fact is thousands of readers enjoy receiving books by mail from the Silhouette Reader Service™ months before they're available in stores. They like the convenience of home delivery and they love our discount prices!

5. We hope that after receiving your free books you'll want to remain a subscriber. But the choice is yours – to continue or cancel, anytime at all! So why not take us up on our invitation, with no risk of any kind. You'll be glad you did!

YOURS FREE!

This lovely Victorian pewter-finish miniature is perfect for displaying a treasured photograph – and it's yours absolutely free – when you accept our no-risk offer.

CASINO JUBILEE
"Scratch'n Match" Game

CHECK CLAIM CHART BELOW
FOR YOUR FREE GIFTS!

YES! I have placed my label from the front cover in the space provided above and scratched off the silver box. Please send me all the gifts for which I qualify. I understand that I am under no obligation to purchase any books, as explained on the back and on the opposite page.

245 CIS ANFC (U-SIL-IM-03/94)

Name _____

Address _____ Apt._____

City _____ State _____ Zip _____

▼ DETACH AND MAIL CARD TODAY!

soul and softened it, gentled it, made it wonder if it could dare to risk, to believe. And in the face of the incredible sensations sweeping him, shaking him to that very soul, he let fly the last of his doubts.

She began to move with him, slowly, uncertainly, but even the slight motion of her body beneath him was too much. He slid his arms under her shoulders, his hands curling back over them as he gripped her as if for his life. His hips jerked forward sharply, uncontrollably, then again. He tried to hold back, tried to stop the boiling tide that was rising in him, but he'd fought it for too long, denying his need for her, and he knew he was going to lose.

"Jamie ... I ... Sorry ... I can't wait!"

With a harsh, guttural cry he slammed forward. His back arched as he drove into her, his head thrown back, the cords of his neck standing out as his face contorted with a pleasure that was almost pain.

Jamie thought she had never seen anything quite so wondrous, so beautiful, as the sight of him soaring over her. Her heart, full and tight, made it hard for her to breathe. She felt wonderful, despite the twinges of her body, despite the odd longing she didn't quite comprehend, the feeling that there was something more than even this sweet pleasure. And when he collapsed atop her, his breath coming in harsh, quick pants, she raised her arms to hold him close.

"I'm sorry," he whispered against her ear. He nuzzled his face into the curve of her neck. "But, Jamie ..."

Sorry? Her brows furrowed slightly as she let her hand drift upward to tangle her fingers in his hair. Why? She felt the tickling flutter of his eyelashes against her skin and the slight motion as he gave a short shake of his head.

"You shot my control all to hell, lady."

She felt his lips brush over the sensitive skin just below her ear, and a little shiver rippled through her.

"I know, honey," he murmured. "I'll make it up to you."

The little thrill that rocketed through her at the endearment faded to puzzlement as she watched him raise himself on his elbows. "Trey...?"

"I promise," he said solemnly, even now feeling his body responding again to the heat of her, to the fierce pleasure of still being deep inside her. There was something to be said for going without, he thought wryly. He knew he'd been alone on that incredible flight, but he would make sure she joined him next time, he—

"Damn!"

It escaped him on a compressed burst of air, and all color drained from his face. His jaw clenched, and he closed his eyes against the force of the sudden, agonizing pain ripping upward through him from the lacerated muscles of his leg. He fell sideways off her, his hands grabbing for the violently cramping muscles at the back of his thigh.

"Trey!"

Jamie's cry was immediate, as was her movement as she slid out from under his other leg. She stared for one stunned moment at the scarred flesh, stared at the muscles that were knotting, clenching as if with life of their own. Sweat was breaking out in a fine sheen over his skin, and a low, choking groan escaped him despite his efforts to smother it. She reached for him, frightened by the ashen cast of his face.

"Don't!" he bit out. "Please, don't...touch me."

The pain in his voice, raw and brutal, took any sting out of the words, and she ignored them as she moved to kneel beside him.

"Please," he repeated on a gasp, "it'll pass. Just—"

He broke off as the torn muscles bunched again, drawing his leg up in a tight bend as every nerve in his body screamed. He rolled over onto his stomach, burying his face in the mat before the protest could echo from his lips.

"Just leave me alone," he ground out through teeth gritted so tightly he thought they would break. He heard her move, leave, and that small part of him that could still think of how much he hated her to see him like this relaxed. He grabbed at the rock-hard knot of muscle again, his entire being concentrated on riding this out without screaming his lungs out.

And then she was back, kneeling once more beside him.

"Damn it, Jamie, just—"

"Hush!"

It was short, sharp and most definitely an order, and even through the pain it startled him into silence. He lifted his head.

Jamie repeated her command, then quickly looked away. She couldn't bear to look at his pale face, couldn't stand the sight of unshed tears of agony blurring the eyes that had so recently been hot and smoky with passion. She tried to ignore her own pain at the knowledge that he had gone through this before, and tried not to wonder how often.

She pressed him back, facedown on the mat with a firm but gentle hand, and at last, burying his face in the crook of his arms, he gave in. He had to—it was taking every bit of his strength to bite back a scream. When she moved to touch his doubled-up leg, that strength wasn't enough, and that throttled groan escaped again.

"Let it out," she urged. "I'm going to straighten out your leg."

"Don't—"

"Quiet," she said as she grasped his ankle and began to press downward. "I swear, you're more stubborn than any horse I've ever had to deal with."

And almost as strong, she thought as she found she had to lean nearly all of her weight against his calf to get his leg extended. The abused muscles protested again, and she saw his fingers curl around the edge of the mat.

His breath left him in a rush and he spat out a short, pungent oath when she dropped the scalding towel from his bathroom on the scarred flesh. She kept his leg pressed flat with her knee braced on his ankle, and began to knead the knotted muscles through the steaming cloth.

"Can you hold it now?" she asked when the towel began to cool. "With your other foot?"

He made a small, low sound, as if he was going to protest again, but it never turned into words. Instead he did as she asked, lifting his foot to lock it on the back of the heel of his wounded leg and hold it flat. She lifted the towel and went quickly to reheat it.

He didn't make a sound when she came back, just let her knee once more take the burden of keeping the knotting muscles stretched out. He flinched when she dropped the steaming towel over the back of his thigh, lifting his head to look at her, but he still stayed silent as she again began pressing, rubbing at the knotted flesh. After a moment she saw the muscles of his back relax as he dropped his head back to lay on his forearm.

It took three more trips to run fresh hot water on the towel before the rigid, cramped muscles began to loosen and turn pliable beneath her fingers. He murmured something softly once or twice, but didn't move. Gradually his breathing slowed, then deepened. She kept on, knowing what he'd be in for tomorrow after such violent strain on impaired and still-tender muscle.

At last, her fingers tiring, she began to slow. He didn't stir. She leaned forward, studying the thick, lowered lashes for a moment.

"Trey?"

She said it softly enough so that it wouldn't awaken him if he was truly asleep. He never moved.

Jamie sat back on her heels, looking at him. Color touched her cheeks when she realized she was staring avidly at the strong, taut swell of his buttocks. She looked hastily away and then caught herself. They'd been as intimate as two people could be. Didn't she have the right to look? And to enjoy?

Her gaze moved once more to that tight, muscled curve, and this time she let herself look, barely resisting the urge to reach out and cup that tempting flesh. Only the fear of awakening him enabled her to hold back.

Slowly she let her gaze slide over him, from the broad shoulders, more solid now with regained weight, down to the trim, narrow waist and hips. The wicked marks that marred the sleek skin were fading, but she supposed he would always carry some faint reminder of his ordeal. They were, she thought suddenly, as much a badge of honor as the medals he'd won, an outward sign of the courage and determination of the inner man. An ache rose in her, tight and poignant, at the thought of his pain, but she was surprised to realize that it was accompanied by a sense of pride that he had withstood it so well. She'd never had this kind of possessive feeling before, so it was a moment before what that pride implied sent a little ripple of stunned, self-realization through her.

She loved him. This stubborn, contrary man, this man who held himself carefully behind a pair of shuttered gray eyes, had somehow done what no one ever had. He had found and stoked fires inside her that she'd never known were there, that she had doubted she had the capacity for.

And he had done it despite the fact that he had tried so hard to drive her away. She realized that now, realized that his resistance was part of the protective wall he'd so solidly built around himself. And she knew instinctively that the scars that marked his body were only the ones that showed; that shell hid scars that ran even deeper.

She sat there, wrestling with the wonder of it. She loved him. And she had well before tonight, she thought. If she hadn't, last night never would have happened at all.

She drew up her legs and encircled her knees with her arms, strangely unconcerned with the fact that she was still nude, sitting there gazing at the equally bare, sleeping body of the man who had so dizzied her senses.

She was content, for the moment, to think of nothing beyond the realization that had come to her. She loved him, she who had wondered if she would ever love anyone the way her father had loved her mother, to the point where he had never remarried after her death. It had frightened her, knowing deep down that she would never settle for anything less, for she wondered if it meant she would be left with nothing. It had seemed a very real possibility until Trey Logan had come into her life.

She shivered slightly as the night chill began to penetrate the glass-walled room. Seized with a sudden urge, she got up and ran to his room, tugging free a blanket from the double bed she knew now he rarely used. She came back to the solarium, pausing after she flipped off the light until she could see enough to go on. She dropped back down beside him, snuggling up to his heat, and pulled the blanket over them both. He moved slightly, as if to make room for her on the narrow mat. She shivered at the little thrill that went through her when he mumbled her name sleepily and lifted one arm to bring it around her and draw her close.

It was a long time before she slept.

Trey twisted, trying to ignore that nagging little ache, but it refused to go away. He'd pushed it too hard yesterday, he thought groggily. All that walking, and then—

Shock brought him bolt upright, gasping for air. He looked around, a little wild-eyed. He was alone on the exercise mat, alone in the room.

Had he dreamed it? Had he dreamed that incredible night? Lord knows, it seemed possible, with all the other crazy dreams he'd had about her. Then the presence of the blanket that covered his naked body, and the lingering discomfort in his leg told him the truth; he remembered the moment when the screaming pain had brought everything to an abrupt halt.

He flushed, groaning under his breath. He'd fallen asleep. She'd saved him from hours of pain, reduced what should have been an aching throb this morning to a mild tightness, and he'd gone and fallen asleep on her. And before he'd had the chance to atone for leaving her unsatisfied after his deprived body had made a fool of him.

He rubbed at bleary eyes, wondering what time it was. Sunlight streamed through the solarium glass, and he guessed it was late morning. It had to be—for the first time in months he felt rested. He ran a hand through his tousled hair, pausing at the shudder that rippled through him at the thought of her slender fingers doing the same thing as she pressed his head to her breast.

He tried to suppress the sudden qualm that swept him. He had known, even as he had taken her last night, that he had only postponed the guilt. All the reasons he had ignored then came rushing back now, but he smothered them with the certain knowledge that she had wanted him, too. It was powerful, potent, and it worked. He reached to throw back the blanket.

Halfway out from under the pale blue wool he froze, staring down at himself. Damn, he thought, his gaze fastening on the ridge of scar tissue that puckered his thigh. Had he done that much damage? He had torn it open somehow, after all this time? He couldn't have—she wouldn't have left him like that. Puzzlement furrowed his brow when he found the mending flesh intact. Then what—

He paled, shock stopping his breath like a blow. The brownish smear of dried blood looked dark and ominous against the skin of his leg. The only explanation leapt fully formed and indisputable into his mind.

"My God," he gasped, stunned.

It all came together now, with the rapid-fire speed of artillery. The innocence that had been so at odds with the sensuous eagerness, the awe in her voice, in her eyes. That moment when he had wondered at her extreme tightness, and most of all that moment when, as he first sheathed himself in her searing heat, she had been so very, very still....

"You idiot!" He spat it out viciously. "You damned, stupid idiot!"

A string of curses he hadn't used since he'd left the army rolled off his tongue, all furious, all aimed at himself. He yanked on his sweatpants with short, enraged movements. All the guilt he had managed to quash came rushing back, overwhelming him with its force.

Great, he thought bitterly. *You seduce her in her father's house, take her on the damned floor, like an animal or something, take advantage of her innocence and goodness, and you don't have the brains to realize what you're doing. You just assume that there's no such thing as a twenty-four-year-old virgin. You wondered if you hurt her? If you had one fraction of an ounce of sensitivity or sense, you would have known you were hurting her. And, for God's sake, you would have known why. All the signs were there, you were just too damned dumb to see them.*

Why? Why had she done it? Why had she chosen him to give that most precious gift? And why on earth hadn't she told him? He wouldn't have been so rough, he would have done it differently; God, he would have done it so differently....

The hell you would, he told himself, guilt flooding him again. *You wouldn't have done it at all if you'd known.*

He scrambled to his feet, anger and guilt digging at him, the guilt compounded by the fact that he could move at all without the crutches, a fact that he knew was entirely due to her.

I hope you're happy, Logan, he castigated himself as he left the solarium to look for her. *You made damned sure her first experience with sex was miserable, then you collapsed after you got what you needed, leaving her still wanting.*

He found her in the kitchen, sitting with a mug before her on the bar. She was in the caftan again, looking tousled and marvelously sweet, and he faltered beneath the wave of emotion that engulfed him. Then he saw she was on the phone, and he halted just short of the doorway.

"I know," she said into the receiver as she idly stirred whatever steaming liquid the mug held.

Trey backed up a step, not wanting the distraction of the phone to intrude on what he had to say to her. He would wait for her in the library, he thought. She always wound up there sooner or later. Then— His thoughts came to an abrupt halt as something she said froze him in his tracks.

"—sorry he got hurt. I'm sorry for him, too." He cocked his head back, listening, unable to stop himself. "It was just a temporary aberration on my part," she was saying with a rueful chuckle. "I know now that he's got as much class as a . . . a . . ." There was a pause, then a giggle as whoever she was talking to apparently supplied an appropriate word.

"No, it's my fault," she was saying now. "I should have known better than to let it go so far. He's not my type at all. I should have realized it a lot sooner."

Trey leaned back against the wall in the hallway, clamping his jaw against the surge of pain, pain as fierce as any his battered body had put him through. He wanted to move, to leave, to not hear the rest, more than he'd wanted anything in his life. But, unlike the times in his life he'd spent under enemy fire, the times he'd had to move or die, his nerves failed him, refusing to send the signals. So he stayed, pinned as helplessly as if by a bayonet, or chained once more to that post of torture, to hear those final, crushing words.

"Well, I may have made bigger mistakes in my life, but I don't remember any."

And the light, airy laugh he loved had become a jagged-edged knife, slashing deep and hard into the soul she had softened up for the blow.

Chapter 8

He'd been right all along.

The phrase played over and over in Trey's head as he stumbled to his room. He should have trusted the instinct that had, before he'd ever met her, warned him about spoiled little rich girls. He should never have let her lull him, let her convince him she was different.

But she *was* different! His heart rose to defend her swiftly, completely. His stomach contracted as the fierceness of it grabbed him, and then a sudden, wintry chill took him as he realized what it meant, that eager, ready defense.

"Damn."

He pulled the door shut behind him and leaned back against it for a moment, trying to reel in his spinning thoughts. *You knew she was out of your league,* he told himself harshly. *She went slumming, for whatever reason, and now she's sorry. You were a mistake. A temporary aberration, that's all, just like she said.*

And why shouldn't she feel that way? You handle her like a piece of meat, never even notice what's being given to you, and then you go off like a rocket with a short fuse. What did you expect?

His head lolled back as if his neck was too weary to hold it, coming to rest against the door with a faint thud. He'd had women say many different things to him on the proverbial morning after, but never had one been so ashamed of having been with him. Of course, he'd never been with anyone like Jamie McCall.

He squared his shoulders and lifted his head as the real truth of that struck home. Yes, he'd never been with anyone like Jamie. And he'd never been like he was with her, either—mindlessly out of control. He'd never known he could be like he was with her.

Don't be a bigger fool than you've already been, he said to that stubborn, hopeful part of him that refused to believe what he'd heard with his own ears. *You can't help that, but, by God, you can keep from making it worse. You can make damned sure she doesn't know how she got to you. And you can get your sorry butt back on track, get out of here and get started on what you should have been working on all along: making plans to make Gen. Rodolfo Lucero's life the same kind of living hell he made yours.*

For starters, he thought bitterly, he would go take a shower. He would scrub the evidence of his idiocy away. He only wished he could wash her image from his mind as easily as he could wash her blood from his body.

As he stood under the stinging spray, he dug around inside himself, searching for the walls, for the barriers he'd built so long ago, when fear and guilt had threatened to swamp him. At seventeen, all he'd been able to do was to shut down completely, to cut off all feeling, all emotion. He'd gotten very, very good at it, and his early days in the army had only perfected his technique of withdrawing behind those solid, impenetrable barricades. At least, he'd thought they were solid. But a slender, golden-eyed woman had proven him wrong, and now he couldn't seem to find those walls at all.

He dressed hastily, stoically ignoring the ache in his leg as he pulled on worn jeans and a faded gray T-shirt. Somehow getting fully dressed instead of just pulling on the more comfortable sweats made him feel stronger, closer to leaving—and reminded him less of last night.

Forget last night, he ordered silently. *Just worry about getting out of here.* He sat on the edge of the bed and was pulling on his socks and black high-top running shoes when it hit him: Where the hell was he going to go? Hank had told him he'd closed up the apartment in L.A. after the third call from the landlord, when Trey had been missing for two months. And he had no cash on hand, although Hank had also told him his salary was waiting for him when he needed it.

He got up and went for the phone on the nightstand and quickly dialed the office. After enduring the surprised greetings, he finally got to the payroll office and the matter at hand, only to be regretfully but resolutely told it would take two days to process the check, did he want a bank transfer instead?

"Hell, I don't even know if I still have a bank account," he muttered. He thought briefly of asking Hank for a loan, but the bitter irony was too much. Hank would surely want to know why he was in such a hurry to leave, and Trey wasn't about to tell him.

"Cut the check," he said into the phone. "I'll get there to pick it up somehow. I'm going to be out of here by then, anyway." No matter what he had to do, he assured himself.

He hung up the phone and turned around to see Jamie in the doorway, staring at him. He stared back; he hadn't even heard the door open.

"I... The door was closed. You never close it. I was worried." She bit her lip as he just stood there, not speaking. At last she went on. "You're ... leaving?"

"Sure," he said easily, suddenly finding those walls. He'd be damned if he'd let her think he was going because of her. "It's about time." *It's one night too late,* he amended silently, but buried that last remnant of tearing regret before she could see it in his eyes.

"But I..." She broke off, coloring as she swallowed tightly. "Your leg," she began again.

"It's fine." His voice was cool and even, he thought in satisfaction.

"How can you say that when—"

"Look," he said sharply, his calm wavering, "I'm not one of your wounded strays, all right?"

Stunned, she gaped at him. God, he thought, she almost looked hurt. If he didn't know better, he'd think she gave a damn.

"Trey," she began, and his name on her lips in that bewildered little voice sent such a burst of pain through him that it took every ounce of his will not to visibly wince. But the words she had spoken in the kitchen, disparaging what had happened between them to someone he didn't even know, were burned into his mind. They gave him the strength to look at her coolly, unemotionally.

Her eyes were full of confusion. Of course, he thought, she didn't know he'd overheard her little summation of him, and what he was—or wasn't—to her.

"What—what's wrong?" she stammered. "Last night—"

"Oh, yeah." He gave her a cavalier grin. "I wondered if the old body was going to function or not. Now I know."

She paled, staring at him in wide-eyed shock. "Wh-what?"

"So, thanks, I guess," he said coolly, still grinning. "I needed that."

He couldn't look at her anymore, couldn't stand that wounded look, the ashen paleness of her face. Why the hell did she look like that? He was putting it on the same level she had; she should be glad.

His mind, safe now behind those walls, was quick with the answer—her ego was bruised. She couldn't believe that making love to her hadn't been the most incredible experience of his life. Hadn't been what it truly had been, his stubborn heart tried to say. He quashed it coldly as he met her dazed eyes again.

"Hey," he said flippantly, "don't get tense about it. We're consenting adults. I needed to know if I could still do it, and you were handy. Grow up. Don't take it so seriously."

With a strangled little cry she whirled, running from the room. It was a long moment after she'd gone before he realized he was shaking. He slumped against the wall, gripping the edge of the nightstand to try to steady himself.

She was a hell of an actress, he thought. If he hadn't heard the careless, casual words with which she'd destroyed what had grown between them, he would have believed it. He would have thought her bafflement genuine, her pain real.

He felt exhausted. Just minutes ago he'd felt better than he had in months—rested, satisfied and at last on the mend. Now it was taking all his strength to hold on to that protective shell while he was still seesawing between raging guilt at what he'd done and anguish over what she'd said. He shuddered; then his head came up and his spine went rigidly straight as he fought it, controlled it. When at last he pushed himself away from the wall, his eyes were as flat and cold as gray marble, more shuttered than they had ever been. But they weren't nearly as cold as he was inside.

Jamie hadn't known it was possible to cry so much. She'd thought she'd wept more than was humanly possible when they'd told her about Whiskey, but it seemed minuscule in comparison to the storm of weeping that had overtaken her now.

It was so useless, she told herself, time after time trying to control the helpless sobbing. It didn't matter if it was for herself, for the pain of losing him or the pain of finding she'd never really had him. It didn't even matter if it was for the misery of finding she had been such an utter fool; the tears were useless, exhausting things, changing nothing.

Yet she couldn't seem to stop. She'd been lying in this tiny, huddled curl on her bed for hours, powerless to halt the hysteria that had gripped her. And every movement of her body reminded her—that soreness that was so new, that had been so unexpectedly pleasant this morning, now served only as a brutal reminder of how laughably stupid she'd been.

Grow up, he'd said. She'd said it to herself, that day after she'd reacted so foolishly by the pool. Well, now she knew just how much of a child she'd been, to think that a man like Trey Logan could truly care for her. She supposed that was what hurt the most, that destruction of her fanciful, romantic dream. She'd thought, last night, that he must care, he had to care, or he wouldn't have wanted her, wouldn't have looked at her with that passion turning his eyes to that breathtaking smoky gray. She'd forgotten everything she'd ever heard about pure lust, and male drives that let some of them enjoy sex totally without love.

Well, you know better now, don't you? she told herself acidly. *You were handy. That's all, just handy for a man who wondered if he could still perform after the treatment his body had received. Perfectly logical.*

Any faith she'd ever had in her own judgment was shattered; any pride she'd had in what she'd accomplished in her life was in splinters. She felt used, but that, at least, she understood. What she didn't understand was the gnawing regret that wouldn't let her rest. She should hate him for what he'd done, what he'd said; why couldn't she? Why did she keep seeing his face when he'd looked at her, hear his voice when he had crooned those soft, sweet words in her ear?

She rolled over to bury her tearstained face in her pillow, shaking once more with fierce sobs. Every insecurity she'd ever had, every doubt about her own femininity, rose to haunt her just as every trace of courage and determination seemed to desert her, leaving her shaken and lost.

She clung desperately to the last tiny thread of sanity, trying not to let it snap, fearing the abyss she would tumble into if it did. Drawing up into a tight, fetal curl, she wrapped her arms around herself as if that would keep her from flying apart. She lost track of time, but it didn't matter. She knew this hell would go on forever.

Trey slammed the foot press down, the clanking of the weights echoing through the solarium. He'd nearly doubled the weight, daring his leg to protest, to buckle. He almost wanted it to; he needed something to blame his fury on.

He hated this room, he hated being here, hated looking at it. He couldn't go anywhere near the spot where the exercise mat had been; he'd rolled it up and crammed it out of sight yesterday morning, his first action after having been blown to bits by a few laughing words. He'd made himself sleep—or try to—in the bedroom, with the door he'd never been able to bear having even halfway shut closed tight. The nightmares, the old, breathless feeling of being trapped seemed suddenly a pleasant alternative.

But the dreams didn't come. The old anxiety had been replaced, supplanted by erotic visions of a naked honey-maned sylph who beckoned, teased and lured, only to confront him with a pair of innocent, wounded eyes. They seemed almost accusing as they looked at him, and he awoke in a sweat, wondering how she could make him feel so horribly guilty when it had been she who had driven the wedge between them.

All he had done, he told himself repeatedly, was to salvage a little of his battered pride, to wield the ax himself, before she did. He'd made it easier for her, really—she hadn't had to tell him she'd made the biggest mistake of her life by making love with him. So why did he feel like this? Why did the image of her stunned, tormented expression linger, when he knew it wasn't real?

He growled in frustration, then got up and removed the metal rod that was inserted below the marked weight he'd been working with on the leg press. He was still able to think too damned much, so obviously he needed to work harder.

He almost wished for the return of that debilitating pain; at least it had stopped his mind from straying down paths that brought a different, harsher pain. But it, too, was gone. In fact, he hadn't felt that ripping, tearing spasm in his leg since she'd tended him so sweetly that night, since she had kneaded away that knotting agony with her gentle, healing fingers.

"Damn it!"

He spat it out as he jammed the rod in at fully double the weight he'd been up to before. Why the hell had she done that, if she felt that way? Why had she bothered? Or had it not been until morning that the reaction had set in, the realization of what she had done?

He dropped back in the seat and began again, setting up a driving rhythm with the clanging weights that was furious in its speed and intensity. His fierce determination stemmed from one source only: he had to get out of this house. Not to mention being gone before James arrived home Friday night. He wasn't up to facing her father, not when he was so confused. His paycheck would be ready tomorrow, and so, he thought with icy determination, would he. He would be away from her, from those haunting eyes.

He hadn't seen her at all since that morning, and he had no doubt it was intentional. She had left early today for the stables and had come home late, apparently abandoning her morning swim altogether. He was grimly glad about it; the less he saw of her, the better he felt. He didn't relish being reminded of what a fool he'd been. Or trying to figure out which felt worse—the guilt about that night, or about what he'd done to her the next morning.

Why did he keep thinking that? He slammed the leg press down again. Why was he always catching himself thinking of her as the injured party, of her as the one who'd been wronged? She'd been willing—was it his fault if she'd decided later that she regretted it, if she'd decided he wasn't good enough for her? She'd known who he was, what he was; it wasn't his fault if she hadn't realized she had more of her father's class awareness than she'd thought until it was too late.

Her father. Memories of those pleasant evenings in the library played in his mind. Trey had never experienced that kind of relationship, of parent to adult child. His mother had been killed long before he'd reached that point, and his father had never been a man to invite confidences, even before he had laid the blame for his wife's death at the feet of his frightened, devastated son. But Trey had imagined what it must be like, and seen it in action here in this house, between father and daughter.

Would she tell him?

The thought made his hands tighten around the edges of the seat beneath him. He knew the man felt he owed him his life, but Trey also knew his sense of indebtedness wouldn't forgive the seducing of his only daughter. Yes, he'd have to be out of here before James got back, he thought, and lifted his foot to the press again. And stopped again as his last thought replayed through his mind, again and again like an unwelcome taunting refrain.

"You lousy, sniveling coward," he spat out in intense self-loathing. *Running away. Again. You ran away when you were seventeen, because you didn't have the guts to face your old man. And you're getting ready to run again now, because you don't have the nerve to face hers. You're a real gem, Logan. And she's absolutely right—you're nowhere near good enough for her.*

He let the weights fall noisily as he jerked himself upright from the bench. He strode out of the room, yanking on the T-shirt he'd shed earlier as he headed for the front door. He'd added walks around the exclusive neighborhood that nestled in the foothills of the Pacific in these last two days, pushing himself mercilessly toward his goal of escape. And it was only there that he found some small measure of relief from the constant thoughts of her.

He went much farther than he intended, and without paying much attention to where he was. *Some recon specialist you are,* he muttered when he finally stopped and looked around. *You'll be lucky to find your way back without stopping for directions. Give me a jungle anytime—* He cut off the old, familiar joke with a shiver. It had been a long-standing quip among the men of his patrol that they would prefer finding their way through any jungle, forest or desert on earth to navigating the wilds of civilization. He'd agreed then, and had since—until he'd left pints of his blood and too much of his nerve in that compound in Central America. He didn't find it funny anymore. And the jungle of La Selva held no attraction for him—except that it hid the one man on earth he wanted to kill with his bare hands.

It was late when he finally made his way back to the house. So late that the dark green Rover sat in the driveway. Steeling himself, he headed up the long, curving ribbon of concrete to the front door. The healing Jamie had managed seemed to be holding. His leg was tired, but a mild ache had supplanted the raging, cramping pain that usually followed such exertion.

It wasn't until he walked past the big vehicle that it struck him how oddly it was parked, haphazardly, at a crazy angle. He wondered why she hadn't put it in the garage, but reminded himself rather intensely that what she did wasn't his business anymore. If it ever had been, he thought as he went inside.

The house seemed dark until he got to the end of the large entryway and could see the light cast from the kitchen. Quietly he made his way down the hall, feeling more of a coward than ever as he listened, hoping the sounds from the kitchen wouldn't stop as he went by.

He showered quickly, then pulled on the clean pair of jeans he'd left out. He was still warm from his long walk, so he left his shirt on a chair with his shoes and shaving gear, then stuffed everything else in the duffel bag he'd already gotten out. He'd be ready to go first thing in the morning. He'd hitchhike if he had to, to get to the office. Then... He wasn't sure what then, only that he'd be safely away from this place, from Jamie....

He knew he was too restless to even try to sleep, so he went, on quiet, bare feet, toward the solarium. He heard Jean murmuring in the kitchen and smelled the inviting, rich odor of baking cookies. He'd miss this, he thought with a little shock. This house might be big, and only be home to two, but it was just that—a home. It had the feel, the scent of a home: the mementos, the comfort, the well-loved rooms.

Like this one, he thought as he eased open the solarium doors. He'd grown attached to the warmth of this sky-filled sanctuary, despite the twinges of painful memory caused by the sweet-smelling gardenias.

The room was dark, but he knew it now and could find his way without the main lights. He was at the gym, vaguely wondering what James would do with it after he was gone, when the barest whisper of sound stopped him. He froze, then went back to the wall and flipped on the light.

"Jamie." It came out in the tone of an invocation.

She was huddled on one of the lounges, her hair tangled, her clothes wrinkled but minus the usual stable dust, her boots lying discarded on the floor. Her legs were drawn up under her, her arms wrapped around them as she sat there, staring out through the skylight wall into the darkness with a blankness that told him she was seeing nothing. She didn't even react to his presence. Little tremors rippled visibly through her, and she was breathing in odd little gulps, as if she had to think about doing it.

"My God," he breathed.

He had gotten a look at her face. It was tear streaked and pale, and her eyes were huge and darkened. Shadows circled them, making them look bruised in her colorless, drawn face.

He knelt beside her, instinctively reaching for her in a movement that came from his heart, not the mind that told him he didn't care. But when she jerked away, curling up even tighter and pulling back into the corner of the lounge as if even his presence hurt her, he drew back sharply.

It was the first time he'd seen her since the morning his words had sent her running from his room. She looked ghastly, thin and ashen, the silken tousle of hair dulled, and even those incredible eyes flat, their golden fire extinguished.

God, he thought as that horrible, swamping guilt rose up in him again, had he done this to her? Had what he'd done made her look like this? He couldn't help himself; he reached for her again, his hand coming down gently on hers where they were clasped tightly around her knees, her knuckles white with tension.

She shuddered violently, as if his touch was more than she could bear. As if he repulsed her. A choking little sound, half gasp, half moan, rose from her, and tears began to spill once more down cheeks that hadn't dried from the ones shed before he'd found her.

Her reaction bit deep, and he jerked back, stung. Then he berated himself silently for expecting anything different from her. Bitterness welled up in him, and it spilled over into the acid words that broke from him.

"Pardon me. I was only trying to help."

She mumbled something soft and unintelligible.

"Sorry, Ms. McCall. I'm hearing about as well as I see the truth when it stares me in the face these days. What did you say?"

Her voice matched the terrible, hollow look in her eyes. Involuntarily his hand moved toward her again. He yanked it back, cursing himself for being a fool a third time. Hell, for being a fool for the umpteenth time. She would only turn him away. Once a mistake, always a mistake. Anger surged in him, hot and savage, and it poured into his voice before he could stop it.

"What's wrong, Ms. McCall? Horse lose a shoe?"

She flinched, then recoiled, staring up at him with those horror-filled eyes. Cringing away from him, she crawled out of the lounge, tottering toward the doors unsteadily, as if drunk. Still reeling from the appalling shock on her face, he took a step after her, his mind racing. Had she hurt herself? Been thrown, or kicked? God, if she had, she should be at a hospital, she should—

He caught himself just as she went out of sight. What the hell was he doing? She didn't want his sympathy, his concern, or whatever the hell it was he was feeling. She'd made it clear she didn't want anything to do with him. She didn't want him, period.

He turned around and sank wearily down on the planter wall. She wanted nothing from him but his absence. Well, he could give her that. And he would, at first light. He'd be out of her house, out of her life.

"Out of sight, out of mind," he muttered, wishing he could have the slightest certainty that she would ever be out of his. He had the sinking feeling that she would always be there, her image rising before his eyes every time he closed them, thoughts of her invading his mind every time he let his guard down.

He didn't know how long he'd been sitting there when the sound of the door opening again made him look up quickly.

"Here now, dear, you just eat these and—"

Jean stopped abruptly, balancing the plate of cookies and the glass of milk she held while she took in the fact that he was the only one in the room.

"I'm sorry, I thought Jamie was here," she explained.

"She...was," he said, eyeing the woman carefully. If Jamie had been hurt, Jean would be doing more than baking her cookies, he thought, and relaxed a little.

"Where did she go?"

"I'm not sure. Upstairs, maybe." It seemed a safe guess; she hadn't left her room at all yesterday, once she'd gotten there.

"I suppose," Jean said as she set the plate down on the low table. "Is she coming back?" The woman's normally cheerful countenance was troubled, her voice heavy with concern.

"I doubt it," he answered wryly, figuring he'd pretty well taken care of that.

"Oh, dear. Well, perhaps I'll take these up to her. She needs to eat something."

"I...noticed."

Jean let out a sigh as she bent to pick up the plate and glass once more. "Poor girl. You'd think she'd had enough heartache in her life, without adding this."

Trey's head snapped around, away from the glass wall he'd been staring through unseeingly. She knew. God, she knew. So why was she talking to him? Why was she even in the same room with him?

Jean was looking at him oddly. She had straightened at his sudden movement, leaving the plate of cookies untouched. His heart was hammering as that familiar wave of guilt crashed home again.

"I...I'm sorry, I..." *Oh, shut up, Logan. You can't apologize for something like that.* He looked away.

"So am I," the woman said softly. "Poor child."

Her words hit a very tender spot. "She's not a child," he grated out.

"Pardon?" Jean looked startled now.

"She's twenty-four years old. Hardly a child." His voice was taut as his hands tightened against the brick wall, the edges digging into his flesh.

"Jamie?"

Trey's brow furrowed; the woman had sounded totally bewildered. "Yes," he said slowly. "Who else?"

"Oh, no, I was talking about that poor child. So young."

He was relieved at first, but then, as what she'd said got through, he looked at her blankly. "What child?"

"You didn't know? She didn't tell you?"

"No. She . . . didn't feel like talking." *Not to me, anyway.*

"Oh, my poor little girl."

He'd never seen anyone actually wring her hands before. He sucked in a breath, wondering what little item he'd missed that would make sense out of this. Poor child, poor girl . . . What the hell had happened?

"Jean," he said slowly, trying to rein in his impatience, "what are you talking about?"

"Why, the bad news, of course. I've never seen her like this, except when she was hurt and Whiskey was put down."

Trey was on his feet now, staring at the woman.

"What bad news?" he demanded hoarsely.

"Why, her little pupil, the one from the riding center."

"What pupil?"

"Chuckie. Chuckie Lowell. He died this afternoon."

Chapter 9

Trey swayed on his feet, and he groped blindly for the support of the low wall behind him.

"No," he choked out, shaking his head in protest, "not— He was fine— Just Saturday..."

"Oh, dear, I'm sorry, I didn't realize you knew the child, too."

Jean's words fell on stunned, uncomprehending ears. No, his mind protested violently. He'd seen him, just days ago, and the bright-eyed, blond youngster had been fine. There hadn't been anything wrong with him at all.

Nothing visible, you mean, he thought, remembering the day of the show again, and how he'd wondered what hidden malady had plagued the lively child. *Lively.* Not anymore—

His mind shied furiously away from the thought. He'd seen his mother buried, he'd seen friends fall beside him under fire, he'd fought off the grim reaper himself, but the thought of that clever, animated child, so very young... He lowered his head, shaking it slowly, blinking rapidly against the stinging of his eyes. "He was . . . just a . . ."

"A baby," Jean agreed softly, then her voice turned brusque. "But it's my baby I have to worry about now. She loved that little boy."

Jamie. Trey's head shot up. My God, he thought, Jamie. What had he done to her?

He couldn't stop the moan that rumbled up from somewhere so deep inside him it was physically painful. Jean, her movement toward the plate and glass arrested once more, looked at him with a sudden intentness.

You might as well have plunged a knife into Jamie's heart and twisted it, he thought dully. And suddenly it didn't matter that she had done the same to him. All that mattered was that she was in horrible, harrowing pain, and that he had made it immeasurably worse. And that thought was somehow more than he could bear. He straightened up.

"I . . ." He swallowed again. "I'll take it to her."

Jean's brows lowered.

"I . . . Please. I need to . . ."

He trailed off, unable to find the words. But Jean seemed to understand and come to a decision. She lifted the plate and the glass and held them out to him. He reached for them, not able to hide the tremor in his hands when he did.

"I'll just go up to bed, then," she said after a moment. "You tell her, if she needs anything, to call me." He nodded, a short little movement of his head. "Good night, Trey."

He nodded again, realizing only after the woman had gone that she had never used his first name before. He wondered vaguely about it for a fraction of a second before he started toward the door.

He didn't think about steeling his nerves as he left the solarium. He thought only, as he had in combat, that it had to be done and he would do it. She would, no doubt, tell him to go to hell. And rightfully so. He'd been callously, coldly cruel, lacerating a wound that was already so deep it would never heal. He knew too well how that felt. That he hadn't known what had happened was no excuse.

He was nearly to the stairs when something caught the corner of his eye; he turned to look and through the open library doors saw the strip of light shining from under the door of the bathroom that opened off the moonlit room. Of course, he thought. Where else would she run when she was hurting? He walked into the library, setting the plate and glass down on a table before crossing to the closed bathroom door and tapping lightly.

He hadn't expected an answer, and he got none. He reached for the knob without hesitation; whether he would go in if she didn't respond had never been in question. He didn't have a choice.

The bathroom was spacious and luxurious, with a screen of plants flourishing in front of the large window at the end of the counter, beyond the sink. At a tiny sound his head jerked around toward the smaller, separate room to his left. His gaze narrowed when he saw her, crouched on the floor beside the porcelain bowl.

He crossed the room in one long stride. She made another small sound, this time intelligible as a protest, as he knelt beside her. She buried her face in the towel she held in hands that were trembling violently. She'd obviously been sick, and just as obviously didn't want him there.

He ignored it. He bent to her, gathering her up in his arms, bracing himself against the flurry of blows delivered to his bare chest by her tightly clenched little fists. She was strong, and the pelting hits hurt. He ignored that, too.

"Don't...touch...me..."

"Shhh."

He stood up, lifting her slight weight easily, turning sideways to maneuver her long legs through the doorway. She hit him again, with less energy this time, a small, harsh sound breaking from her throat. He carried her gently, cradling her body as if it were fragile, delicate crystal. It was how she felt to him, wound so tightly she would shatter at the slightest pressure. Instinctively he headed for the comfort of the library, forgoing his usual chair for the roomier couch.

"Don't," she moaned again, quivering against him.

"Shhh," he repeated, sitting down with her carefully on his lap. "I know you don't want me here, I know how you feel about me, but you can't be alone, not now."

She squirmed in an effort to get away; he tightened his arms around her.

"Just relax, honey."

It slipped out, he hadn't meant to say it, and she went rigid in his arms. "Damn you."

It was low, hoarse and grating, full of a twisting, tortured pain she didn't even try to hide. His entire being cringed at the sound of it.

"Yes. You can damn me all you want. Later." And she would, he thought, as soon as she got through the shock, the grief.

"I already have," she spat out.

He winced. "I know. You've got every right."

Her gaze was fixed on him, wide with a mix of pain and anger, lit eerily by the silver light that fell across them.

"Yes," she said coldly, "I do."

He let out a long breath. He hadn't wanted to get into this, but if it would distract her from the real reason for her distress, he would stand it. Somehow.

"You were right," he said with a weary sigh. "It should never have gone so far."

A touch of puzzlement joined the turmoil in her face as she looked at him.

"I'm sorry." His mouth twisted bitterly. "Inadequate little word, isn't it? Sorry. If you hadn't…felt sorry for me, you never would have given in to that…'temporary aberration,' would you?"

She caught her breath, staring at him. "What... do you mean?"

He shrugged. It could hardly matter now. "I heard you on the phone."

"The phone?"

A spurt of annoyance shot through him at her pretense of mystification.

"Don't play games, Jamie. I know I'm not in your class. You don't have to pretend you didn't say it."

"Trey, what—?"

"Damn it, I'm saying you were right. It probably was the biggest mistake of your life. Of mine, too. I never should have touched you. I knew it then, and I did it, anyway."

"You... heard me?"

It was his turn to be puzzled. He'd admitted that, hadn't he?

"Yesterday morning? On the phone?"

Why was she looking at him like that, with that utterly stunned expression?

"I didn't mean to," he said uncomfortably. "I was looking for you, to... to apologize. Because I..." He lowered his gaze. "Because I hurt you, because I didn't realize you were a—"

"Oh, God, Trey!"

She was staring at him, tears flooding down her cheeks, her lips parted as she struggled for breath. The stunned realization in her face dumbfounded him.

"Jamie?"

"That morning," she gasped out, "I was talking about Edward!"

He drew back from her, his eyes narrowing.

"He'd gotten drunk again, got in a fight in some seedy bar somewhere. My friend Gina heard about it and called me. She thought we... were dating." She gulped in a shuddering breath. "That's what I meant when I said I'd let it go too far. I never should have kept seeing him once I realized what he was really like.''

He was gaping at her. ''You... That was your mistake?''

''Yes.'' She swiped at her tears with an unsteady hand. ''Oh, God, you thought I meant you?''

Beyond speech, he nodded numbly.

She took a gulping breath. ''That was what you meant? When you said that about being one of... my strays?''

''You said... I thought you were just... sorry for me.''

''Oh, Trey,'' she moaned. ''I never—''

A choking sob cut off her words as she remembered what she'd said that morning, and what he must have thought.

''No,'' she gasped out. ''Oh, no. It wasn't you. I couldn't—I could never think of you as a mistake!''

Warmth hit him, flooded him at her vehemence. ''Jamie—''

''Please, Trey, it wasn't you. I couldn't stand for you to think I said those things about you!'' Her voice was rising toward hysteria. He knew it was because she'd already been so emotionally battered today. He gripped her arms, trying to slow her down. ''I know it doesn't matter to you, I'm just a naive little—''

''Jamie,'' he cut in, his voice thick, ''if it didn't matter, do you think I would have said all those rotten, contemptible things to you?''

She stopped then, her gaze fastened on him. ''I thought... you said...''

''I said too damned much. I was hurting, Jamie.'' He shook his head as his mouth twisted in a pained grimace. ''I thought you were ashamed. Of me. Of what you'd done with me.''

''Oh, Trey, no. Never,'' she insisted.

''And I felt so damned guilty!'' A touch of the torment he'd been living with crept into his voice. ''God, Jamie, why didn't you tell me you were... that you'd never...''

"I was afraid you would stop. And . . . I didn't want you to stop." Her cheeks were flaming, but her head was high.

"Stop?" He laughed harshly. "I couldn't have stopped by then if you'd put a gun to my head. I wanted you too much."

Her color deepened. "Then it wasn't just because I was . . . handy?"

He moved then, pulling her hard against his chest, groaning as he tightened his arms around her.

"Jamie," he said against her hair, then said it again. "Jamie, I didn't mean any of it, any of those lousy things I said." He felt her tremble and held her tighter. "I was just . . ." He trailed off, shuddering. "First I felt guilty, when I realized what I'd done. That you'd been a virgin."

"I wanted you to be the first," she whispered, and it was he who trembled this time.

"That's what scared me," he said tightly. "When I thought about . . . what you'd given me . . ." He shook his head. "And I was too stupid to know it. I was too rough with you—"

"It wasn't your fault." The words came on a little breath that tickled his chest. "You said you weren't sure you . . . could, after—"

His low groan cut her off. "Damn it, Jamie, that was just another cheap shot." He gave a grimly rueful laugh. "I knew I was functioning just fine the first time I ever saw you."

Her head came up, her eyes wide as she looked at him. He took in a deep breath. He was going to need more nerve for this, he thought, than he'd ever needed to go up against enemy guns. He went on, knowing he owed it to her. "You came into the dining room that first morning, in that gold thing that slid over you like it was poured on, with your hair all silky and loose. That was enough, but when I saw those eyes of yours, I knew I was in real trouble."

"I never guessed." She'd said it shyly, wonderingly, and he lifted his hands to cup her face, smothering the qualm he felt. How could he not have recognized that innocence for what it was?

"Jamie, I..." He struggled for words, battling the impossibility of it all. Nothing had changed; she was still far, far out of his league, but he couldn't seem to care about that, not now. Nor could he find the words for his tangled emotions. At last he shrugged helplessly.

"Oh, Trey." She fell forward, her arms going around him in a fierce embrace. "It's been so horrible. I didn't know what had happened. I just thought...it wasn't any good for you, that night. That I wasn't ... any good."

"Not any good? You tore me apart! Why do you think I...lost control like that?"

"I didn't realize ..." She blushed. "I don't know anything about it. I just knew that...I was so happy that morning, and then..."

"Tell me about it." His mouth twisted wryly. "I wasn't exactly thrilled with the idea that you hated me."

"I could never hate you." She let out a little breath before adding quietly, "Even when I wanted to."

"Oh, Jamie." He hugged her close. "I know. Lord, do I know. I couldn't understand why I kept thinking that you were the one suffering. I guess maybe I knew, even then, that there was something wrong, that something didn't add up."

He pressed his lips softly against her hair. She let out a long sigh. "Why didn't you just ask?"

"Stubborn?" He sighed. "No. Stupid. Embarrassed. Too damn much pride."

Jamie lifted her head then, and the smile he saw there was worth everything. He smiled back, soft and warm, but he was quietly serious when he spoke again.

"I haven't had much practice at...sharing myself, Jamie. My first reaction was to strike back. But I guess you know that now."

"It doesn't matter. Not anymore."

She snuggled closer, her breath soft and warm on his skin. Her hand slid over his chest to rest in the center, her fingers moving slightly in a caress much too light to cause the ripple of sensation that went through him. When he moved his own hand over hers to still it, she defeated his purpose by pressing her lips against him in a soft kiss.

"Jamie..."

He'd meant it to be a warning; it sounded like a plea. She responded to the sound of it, not the intent, and kissed him again. His hands shot to her shoulders, and he lifted her up so he could see her face.

"Jamie?"

"Please, Trey," she whispered. "I...I need to feel alive again."

He sucked in a deep breath. He knew what she meant. He'd felt alive for the first time in months when he'd spent those glorious moments in her arms. When death struck so closely, the drive to know you were still alive was powerful. And Chuckie's death had struck very, very close.

"Jamie, I understand, but that can't be why. You'll only regret it."

"It's not. But even if it was...I'll never regret anything with you."

"I don't want to...hurt you again."

She looked at him, two spots of color staining her cheeks. "It won't, will it? This time, I mean?"

He shuddered under the power of the images her shy words sent racing through his mind, and in that moment he surrendered.

"No," he said huskily. "It won't hurt. I'll make sure of that."

He threaded his fingers through her hair, drawing her head down to him. He brushed his lips over hers lightly, but she wasn't content with that. She kissed him hungrily, deeply, her lips moving over his insistently. His fingers tightened, and he traced the delicate shape of her mouth with his tongue. He let out a startled sound of pleasure when her lips parted and seized his tongue, drawing it into her mouth.

He couldn't resist the lure, and he thrust forward into the honeyed depths. Tasting, probing, he searched, finding the sweetness he remembered and feeling his body react with the same fierce swiftness he'd known from the day he'd first seen her.

She returned his eagerness tenfold, her tongue mating, dancing with his, sending his pulse pounding in hot, heavy beats. Her fingers moved over his chest, stroking, caressing, and leaving fiery little trails of sensation in their wake. When they reached and brushed over the flat nubs of his nipples, he groaned and deepened the kiss, his tongue delving into every secret corner of her mouth.

On fire now, he tugged at her shirt, and she lifted her arms so that he could pull it over her head. He reached for the front clasp of her bra, flicking it until it gave, pushing at the silky fabric until one side slipped away, revealing one full, perfect breast. He groaned again and lifted a hand to tenderly cup and lift the firm, rounded flesh.

Jamie gasped when his fingers found her nipple, tugging gently, sending currents of fire blazing through her to settle hotly between her thighs. She arched to him, her hands going to grip his shoulders, then his back, before she remembered and pulled her digging fingers quickly away.

He stopped at her sudden movement, lifting his head to look at her.

"Your back," she said breathlessly.

Something flickered for a moment in his eyes, then was gone. "It's all right," he said quietly. "I know it's...not easy to touch."

"No!" she cried out, sitting up suddenly beside him, careless of the bra that slipped away, baring her to him. "It's not—I was afraid of hurting you."

He stared at her, remembering that moment when she had done the same thing in the solarium. While he had been blithely oblivious of what should have been so apparent, while he had been heedlessly causing her pain, she had been worrying about him.

"You didn't," he said hoarsely. "You couldn't. Not like that. Not touching me."

Stunned anew by her capacity for tenderness, he renewed his resolve. When he turned to her again, stripping away the last of her clothes and pressing her gently back against the sofa cushions, it was to stroke, tease and caress every gentle curve, every tender, secret place, until she was making tiny little sounds of pleasure at every touch. He followed the path made by his hands with his mouth, kissing, nibbling, suckling, until she was gasping.

He clenched his jaw, ordering himself to ignore the aching cry of a body that was demanding release, straining against the zipper of jeans that were rapidly becoming intolerably tight. He kissed her deeply, then once more let his mouth follow the path his hands had blazed. He felt her tense when he pressed a soft, tender kiss on the sandy curls at the top of her thighs.

"Please, Jamie," he whispered, "let me make up to you for the first time. Let me make it what it should have been, what it should be."

She made a small, low sound he took for assent. His lips and tongue resumed the stroking caress his fingers had begun; her body bucked and a shocked cry of pleasure broke from her. He slid his hands beneath the slender hips that had arched at his first touch, lifting them and holding them for even deeper caresses.

Jamie was quivering now, little ripples of her body echoing the ripples of heat and sensation that were racing through her. An exquisite pressure was building beneath his mouth, a pressure that made her moan for more even as she knew she couldn't bear it. And then, just as the pressure threatened to overwhelm her, she felt the beginning of an incredible explosion unlike anything she'd ever known.

"Oh, Trey!"

"Go with it, honey," he urged against her throbbing flesh, just before he made it impossible, with a loving stroke of his tongue, for her to do anything else.

She was writhing now, her hands clutching at the cushions beneath her as her body shattered into a thousand pieces that seemed to swirl in the silver moonlight. She cried out, then cried his name once more before she came tremblingly back to rest in the strong arms that were there to catch her.

When at last her breathing slowed, she became aware that he had moved up to lie beside her on the couch, pulling her close as he lay on his side. She reached for his hand, stilling it as she looked at him with eyes that were wide with wonder.

"Is it... Was that..." Words to express what she was feeling failed her, and she said simply, "I didn't know."

Trey hugged her fiercely. "I know. And that's my fault."

"Is that why you said...you were sorry, then? Because I didn't..." She broke off with a blush.

He nodded. "I should have realized. It should have been...special for you. If I'd known—hell, if I hadn't been so damned wrapped up in myself—I would have realized," he said sourly, but she hushed him with a gentle finger against his lips.

"No. We're past all that."

He sighed, then nodded in acceptance. "Maybe it wouldn't have mattered. I never..." He smiled ruefully. "I don't have any experience with virgins."

"You do now."

Startled, Trey stared at her. He saw her mouth twitch at the corners, and a joyous laugh burst from him. "Yeah, I guess I do."

"Would you...like some more?" she asked shyly. "I think it's your turn, isn't it?"

His throat tightened, and he shivered at the effect of those soft words. "Jamie..."

Her name faded into a groan when she shifted on the sofa, bending over him to trail soft, warm kisses over his chest. The ache that had never really receded resumed with even more strength, tightening him with a need he'd never felt before. He'd had a taste of her sweetness, a taste his body remembered so very well, and it rose to the thought of more with stunning force.

She was all over him, stroking, caressing, her tongue tasting his skin, flicking over his nipples, until he was twisting beneath her tender ministrations.

When her hand slid down his belly to the button of his jeans and then paused, his lashes lifted.

"Yes," he muttered thickly, "please."

Her fingers trembled slightly as she fumbled with the unfamiliar task, and he felt a rush of tenderness that strengthened his determination to make certain that she felt nothing but pleasure from now on.

The button freed, she tugged at the zipper. He couldn't stop the groan that broke from him when her fingers brushed over the swell of his hardened flesh. Her fingers jerked away.

"No," he choked out, reaching for her hand. He turned it in his and pressed her palm over him. She blushed furiously, but left it there. When her fingers curled reflexively, unintentionally stroking him, his hips jerked convulsively. She froze, looking down at him.

"Please, don't stop now," he gasped. After one moment of staring at the quickened rise and fall of his bare chest, Jamie moved, tugging the zipper down the rest of the way.

He lifted himself up and shed jeans and briefs in one swift movement. Every muscle in his body seemed to quiver as she looked at him, as if her gaze was a caress. Before he could reach for her she was touching him again, her hands sliding over him. Heat flooded him, growing from every place she touched until it all came together in one searing, fiery pool deep and low inside him.

Something knotted in his chest when, with pink tingeing her cheeks, she bent and pressed a soft kiss over the scarred indentation that marked his thigh. He pulled her down on top of him, his mouth taking hers with fierce passion. The feel of her slender, naked body stretched out over his fired his blood, and he raised his hips convulsively, pressing himself against her.

She twisted against him, sinuously, voluptuously. His hands slid up her arms to her shoulders, and he lifted her from his chest. She didn't understand until he lifted his head, seizing one taut, coral nipple between his lips. She gave a soft little moan, arching her back to give him more; he took it hungrily. Then he moved to her other breast, until she was writhing atop him.

"Trey," she moaned, "please. Oh, please."

Gritting his teeth against the heat that lanced through him at the pure, sensuous need in her voice, he slid his hands down her sides, down to her trim thighs, then pulled her legs forward so she was straddling him. He could feel her heat, radiating from her slender body, washing in waves over his rigid flesh, and he groaned aloud.

"Trey," she pleaded, unable to hold still.

"You do it," he said hoarsely.

Jamie looked at him, doubt clouding her expression. Then she realized what he was doing—giving her control, making sure he kept his promise that she wouldn't be hurt this time. A rush of love so strong it left her breathless swept her.

"Help me," she gasped, letting every ounce of what she was feeling into her voice.

His hands went to her hips, lifting her and centering her over his erect, throbbing shaft. She saw the tremor that went through him, that tightened the muscles of his belly, of his thighs, but still he left it to her. She hesitated, uncertain.

"You're the rider," he whispered thickly. "Ride me. Now."

Shivering at the sound of those words, at his voice heavy with need, she lowered herself slowly, tentatively, until the tip of that probing, hardened flesh began to slide into her. She looked at him, wonder and doubt in her face in equal measure.

"Jamie," he grated out, "if you don't take me now I'm going to die right here."

She moved swiftly then, taking him in with breath-stealing suddenness, drawing a sharp cry from him as she dropped her body down to his, driving him deep inside her. She gasped in turn at the wonderful discovery that, after the first twinge, it didn't hurt at all. Far from it; it felt wonderful. He felt wonderful. He was inside her, so full and deep and hard....

A look of surprised pleasure crossed her face as she rocked on him, a look he couldn't help smiling at through a haze of pleasure; he obviously wasn't hurting her. He savored the feel of her, the pressure of her full weight pressing down on him, making her body's grip on him even tighter. He watched her above him in the silver light, watched the flow of her hair as she let her head fall back, the sway of her out-thrust breasts as she moved.

Those tempting twin spheres were too much to resist, and he grabbed her shoulders to bring her closer. She protested the halt of that lovely motion, until she realized he was again holding her so that her nipples were within easy reach of his seeking mouth. His tongue flicked up and over them, teasing them to exquisite hardness. She arched her back, wanting more, thrusting her breasts toward him, silently begging for his mouth on her.

It took all his concentration to continue the hot, wet caress; he had to try to ignore what it was doing to the satin flesh that was surrounding his own. Her body stroked him, told him beautifully of the connection between them as he felt her tighten around him a split second after each suckling motion of his mouth.

Her hips began to move once more, rocking on him in a sweet rhythm that drove him crazy. Each time, she pressed herself against him, as if to savor every hard, solid inch of him. At last he gently pushed her back, and her protest at the loss of his mouth on her breasts changed to a breathless gasp as she sat upright and felt the increased pressure of his surging fullness inside her.

He heard it, urged her knees farther apart as she straddled his hips, bringing her down harder atop him, driving him deep and hard into her slick, heated body. She moaned and arched backward, her head thrown back, her breasts thrust upward, the curve of her body, supported by her hands braced behind her, bared and open to him.

To have gained such trust, so quickly, made his heart hammer in his chest, and he knew in that moment how much he loved this golden-eyed sprite. He had to clamp his teeth on his lip to keep from surging to completion just at the sight of her.

He slid one hand down from her hips to where their bodies joined, probing into the wet heat, his thumb parting dark and sandy curls until he found that tender spot. He began a steady, rhythmic stroking that soon had her rocking on him at a matching pace. And then she began to move faster, her hands clutching at him as small cries began to break from her throat, every other one his name.

He knew he was losing his grip; he could feel his control start to slip. He couldn't hold back, not when she was taking him so deep, not when he knew she wanted it, wanted him. Involuntarily his hips bucked upward, lifting her, burying himself in her until he couldn't tell where the boundary between them was anymore.

"Oh!" Jamie cried, loving the fierceness of it so much it startled her. "Oh, yes!"

Again he thrust upward, and again. Then he felt it begin for her, felt her body clench around him, stroking him, drawing him up with her. She cried out his name again, high and sweet and clear, and the sound of it sent him tumbling after her with a hoarse, choked shout of her name.

She collapsed atop him, quivering, little echoes of her moans vibrating against his chest. He held her close, feeling echoes of his own fiery eruption sizzling along his nerves.

He hugged her, letting his hands drift down to her waist, loving the feel of her slight weight pressing down on him. His fingers lingered over a tiny, thin ridge that ran for an inch and a half along her spine well below her waist. He recognized a surgical scar and guessed they had had to operate at least once. He caressed it gently, pressing another kiss against her hair. Then he pulled the brightly colored Navajo blanket from the back of the sofa and covered them both with it.

They lay in quiet, peaceful silence for a long time. So many things were tugging at the edges of his consciousness, demanding entry; he slammed the door on them. Except, at last, for one.

"Jamie?"

"Hmmm?"

"I'm sorry about Chuckie. So damned sorry."

He felt her tense atop him and tightened his embrace. Gradually her taut muscles slackened, except for her arms where she clung to him. He felt the ripple go through her as she fought not to cry again.

"God, Trey, it's just not fair. He was in remission, he was so close to being cured—"

"Remission?"

"He had leukemia."

So that was it, Trey thought despairingly. That was the silent killer that had—

"But he'd had a bone marrow transplant," Jamie explained, with an obvious effort to steady her voice. "He was doing so well, he'd had his three-year checkup.... He was so happy that they had stopped most of the drugs, so he wasn't all fat and pudgy anymore." She gulped back tears once more, and her voice rose with emotions. "And then this happens. God, it's so stupid!"

Trey's brows lowered. "You mean...it wasn't the leukemia?"

She lifted her head and he saw the pain in her eyes, which he'd expected, and the anger, which he had not. "No," she said flatly. "It was a truck. A racing, careless truck that came out of nowhere and knocked him off his bicycle."

Trey sucked in a shocked breath. After a moment he let it out slowly. "My God."

He felt a shudder ripple through her in the same moment he saw the pain rise up to vanquish the anger in her eyes.

"He was so brave," she whispered. "He just held my hand and told me how glad he was that Scout had won a ribbon. He could hardly talk." She shuddered. "He made me promise to take care of his horse. And five minutes later, he was gone."

He crushed her against his chest. "God, Jamie, I'm sorry. I didn't know...you'd been there."

"They called me. He...wanted me."

"Oh, honey, and then I was such an ass—"

"You didn't know."

"That's no excuse."

"Please, Trey. No more guilt."

After a moment, and with difficulty, he nodded. Letting her slip to his side, he held her close for a long time, until he felt her yawn. Then he tucked the blanket closer around her. She made a little sound of protest when she felt him begin to move away.

"Stay," she said sleepily. "Please?"

"Jamie," he said reluctantly, "I want to. God, I want to. But I can't. You know that. Jean is liable to be checking on you." *Make that* likely, he thought; she worried as if Jamie was her own. And if she found Jamie's room empty, she wouldn't stop until she found her.

"I don't care," she said stubbornly.

"You will if you end up having to explain what we're both doing here, naked on the couch."

"I'll tell her. I'm not going to hide it."

Pleasure surged through him at her words, wiping away any lingering remnants of the pain he'd felt when he'd thought her ashamed of having slept with him. But he knew he was right in trying to spare her the kind of scene that would ensue. She might not care now, but she would then. Especially when she realized how impossible it was. How impossible *they* were.

"Please, Trey. Don't go."

His resolution melted at the tremulous undertone of her voice. He couldn't do it. He didn't want to do it. He wanted to hold her through the night, he wanted to be there when she woke up remembering the horror of a young life lost; he wanted to make love to her, to make her feel beautifully alive in the morning light. He wanted it, and he couldn't have it.

But he could hold her now, for a while. He could have the pleasure of her falling asleep in his arms, before he had to leave her. He lifted the blanket and slipped back down beside her. She gave a glad little cry that thrilled him, and then settled down into the curve of his body as if she'd been waiting all her life for him to be here. He buried his face in the cloud of her hair, swallowing heavily against the tide of emotion that engulfed him. And in that instant, La Selva, Lucero, revenge, none of it seemed quite so important. Even the pain of young Chuckie's death was bearable, as long as he could hold her. He knew it wouldn't—couldn't—last, but for the moment, he wanted to cling to the feeling.

He savored the silken warmth of her as he held her, waiting for the signs that she had slipped into sleep. She felt so good, pressed against him like that, he was going to hate to leave her here alone. She snuggled closer, and a warmth that was far more than physical engulfed him. Lord, he'd never known it was possible to feel like this....

He came awake with a start, the realization that he'd been awakened by a noise in the hall coming at the same time as the knowledge that the light streaming in the window had gone from silver to gold. Sunlight. Morning sunlight.

Damn, he swore silently, his body tensing to dive for the cover of the bathroom, out of sight, before Jean came in.

He didn't get the chance. The door swung open, and he heard the voice calling out to Jamie. And he knew in that moment that the scene he'd envisioned saving her from would have been a snap compared to what faced them now. For in the doorway, staring at them, stood James McCall.

Chapter 10

Jamie sat up groggily, rubbing at her eyes. Strange dream, she thought, with her father shouting—

"What the hell is going on?"

Oh, God. Her eyes snapped open. It wasn't a dream. She could feel the warmth of Trey beside her on the couch, but she didn't dare look at him. Not when her father was standing there, glaring murderously. Instinctively she tugged at the blanket, but she knew it was far too late, it was already in a tangle around their naked bodies.

"Daddy—"

"I'm not asking you, I'm asking him!"

She'd never heard that voice from her father. Nor had she ever seen his eyes like this—cold, icy blue.

"Daddy—"

"No, Jamie." Trey's voice was quiet, steady as he hushed her. "Not now."

"I want an answer, Logan! What the hell do you think you're doing?"

From the corner of her eye, Jamie saw Trey draw himself up straight, his gaze fastened on her father unflinchingly.

"You bastard!" It burst from James McCall in a rush of fury. "You son of a bitch, I trusted you! I brought you into my home, because I owed you! You were my guest!"

Trey winced, but never looked away. Jamie tried again.

"Daddy, please—"

"I took you in!" He cut her off without a glance. "I trusted you, you worthless scum, and you—you seduce my own daughter under my own roof!"

Why was Trey just taking it? Jamie wondered, her stunned gaze flicking to him. Her father was so wrong, but Trey just sat there, letting the man insult him, not even letting her explain.

This didn't make sense. She would have expected him to be upset, even angry, but this raging man wasn't her father. She tried again. "He didn't—"

"Get out." James McCall's voice was a chill blast. "Get out of this room, and out of this house."

"Daddy, stop—"

"Be quiet! You're too foolish to know when you've been used. I'll deal with you later."

Jamie jerked back, stunned. Never in her life had her father used that tone with her. Never had he looked at her with such anger, such distaste. She stared at him, shivering.

Trey reached for her hand, giving it a reassuring squeeze. James moved swiftly, his hand swinging in a fierce, backhanded slash across Trey's face.

"Get your filthy hands off her!"

Trey's head snapped back under the force of the blow as Jamie let out a cry of distress. His hands clamped around the cushions beneath them, his knuckles whitening with the strain of his grip. Jamie stared at those hands, thinking of the night he'd clutched at the mat to keep from screaming. She'd seen him stand much worse than her father's blow without—

It came to her then, with her first look at his eyes. His grip was not in reaction to the pain of the blow. He was a trained fighter, and it was the only way he could keep himself from striking back. Her heart knotted with pride in him.

"You're wrong, Daddy," she said, her voice low and tight.

"You're in quite enough trouble already, Jamie," her father said coldly. "I suggest you keep your mouth shut." The pain that showed in his face for a moment stilled her.

Turning back to Trey in rage, James snapped, "I gave you an order. Get out of here."

Trey's head came up, steady even under the icy blue glare, unflinching despite the tiny trickle of blood that trailed from the corner of his mouth. As if knowing there was no point in trying to hide his nudity, he freed himself from the tangle of the blanket and Jamie and got up. He reached for his jeans and began to pull them on.

James McCall watched him, obvious loathing glittering in his eyes, and Trey's steadiness, his control, seemed to infuriate him even more.

"I'd like to blow your head off." He bit out the words as his gaze lowered to where Trey was zipping his jeans, making it clear that he actually meant a totally different part of him. "But I won't. I owe you that much. But no more. I want you out of this house. Pack your bags and—"

"I already packed. Last night."

Uttering the first words he'd spoken since he'd tried to halt Jamie's impassioned defense of him, Trey's voice was cool and steady. Then Jamie made a tiny sound, and he realized what she was thinking.

"*Early* last night," he said, his gaze flickering to her, willing her to understand. The golden eyes locked on his, then lowered, and he knew she had.

"Then you have exactly ten minutes to get out of my home. Any longer, and I might forget my promise not to kill you."

"Stop it!" Jamie cried out sharply. "I am not a child. You can't—"

"You are my daughter, and as long as you live under my roof you will do as I say."

"I will not!"

"Jamie."

Trey's voice was gentle, but rang with warning. She subsided, staring at him wide-eyed, not understanding. Why wasn't he fighting? What he'd said last night... hadn't he meant any of it?

James's anger, already intense, seemed to soar at the sight of the daughter who had always been so dutiful defying him, yet yielding to one soft word from the man responsible for this outrage.

"Get out. Now. And with only what you brought with you."

Jamie gasped at the insult, but Trey never even blinked. He held the older man's gaze steadily for a long, tense moment before he walked silently out of the room.

Jamie was quivering, tiny sounds of shock breaking from her with every tortured breath. She was staring at the doorway, unable to believe Trey had just gone. He'd never said a word in his defense, hadn't let her say a word. He'd just taken it, all the abuse her father had heaped on his head....

Her gaze shifted to the man she had adored all her life, trying to comprehend the change in him. Or had he been like this all the time, and she just hadn't seen it? Was this how he'd built the McCall Corporation, with cold, unbending ruthlessness? The words broke from her on a moan.

"Daddy, please—"

"Don't. Not a word."

"But—"

"I said not a word. I don't want to speak to you until that... man is out of here."

"I—"

"I said be quiet! Go to your room and . . . clean yourself. I'll see you back in this room in an hour. When I can look at you and not feel sick." He turned on his heel and strode out.

Jamie sat huddled on the sofa, shaking. She didn't understand any of this. She didn't know either of these men. Trey, refusing to defend himself in the face of the most vile of accusations, and her father, who had turned into a furious, vicious stranger.

In a sudden burst of emotion she leapt from the sofa, grabbing her stable clothes with quick, choppy movements. She ran from the library, racing silently up the stairs on bare feet. When she reached her room, she grabbed better clothes and pulled them on, ignoring her father's disgusted order to "clean" herself. She wouldn't, she thought. She wanted every memory she could hold fast to, she wanted the feel and scent of Trey to cling to in this confrontation she'd never anticipated, as if those things could invest her with some of his strength. Dressed again, she started back down the stairs to look for Trey. She halted on the landing at the sound of her father's still-angry voice.

"—but I owe you nothing now. If I ever see your face again, anywhere near me or my daughter, I guarantee I will make your life so miserable you'll wish you had died in Central America."

Jamie's hand flew to her lips, smothering a cry of dread. She couldn't see her father, but she could see Trey, standing in the entryway, holding the one small duffel bag that held all the meager possessions he'd brought with him. His face was as cold and shuttered as it had been the first time she'd seen him, and when she remembered how his laugh lit it up, how it went taut with passion, she could barely stifle the moan that rose in her.

"You're right," he said flatly to the man who was out of her line of vision. "I took advantage of your hospitality, of

your sense of obligation, and of your daughter's innocence.''

No! Jamie's mind cried out in protest as she stared at him
from the stairs.

"I betrayed your trust, and you have every right to hate
me for it."

He meant it, Jamie thought, stunned anew. That's why he
hadn't fought back. No matter how she tried to tell him
otherwise, he still felt guilty. He hadn't defended himself
because he thought her father was right.

Of course he did, she thought suddenly. How could he
not? The only kind of father he knew was the kind who
would blame his own son for the accidental death of his
mother. Why should he expect any different from hers?

She reached for the banister, ready to sail down the stairs.
If he wouldn't—couldn't—defend himself, she would! Then
his next words froze her in midstride.

"I'm everything you said I am, and probably worse. But
you're wrong about one thing." She heard the first undertone of emotion in his voice. "I didn't use her. Not like
that." He took a deep breath, and she had the oddest feeling he knew she was there. "It was never like that. It
was...the most honest thing I've ever known."

Jamie's heart soared, but as it rose it quivered in pain at
her father's reaction to that fervent declaration.

"How dare you?" James's voice quivered with rage.
"You're not fit to—"

"I know that. But your daughter is...remarkably free of
prejudice. She doesn't seem to think a broken-down ex-
ranger is beneath her."

"You bastard!" James McCall's exclamation echoed off
the walls and tiled floor of the entry. "She's a child! She
doesn't know anything about men like you, and you used
that."

Jamie wanted to scream, wanted to run down the stairs and beat sense into both of them, but she couldn't seem to move.

"Is that your game?" James said, a different kind of sharpness in his tone now. "You seduce her, convince her she loves you, then expect to sit back and reap the benefits? Do you really think I'd let that happen? You may have fooled her, but I know a true mercenary when I see one. They were right when they called you a soldier of fortune, weren't they? Well, you can forget this fortune, and get the hell out of here! You'll get no payoff from me!"

"No!"

Jamie had found her voice and her legs at last, and she came down the stairs in a rush. "Stop it!" she screamed at her father. "It isn't true, any of it—"

"Go back to your room!" James thundered.

"I am not a little girl you can send to her room anymore," she cried. "And I won't listen to this any longer! You have no right to talk to him like—"

"I'm your father! I have every right!"

"No! I won't—"

"Jamie."

Trey's low, near-whisper of her name stopped her dead. She turned to him.

"Jamie, no. Not over me. He's your father."

"No, he's not. Not this man. I don't even know this man."

"You've said all you're going to say," James spat out. "Get out now, or I'll call the police."

Trey moved toward the door. Jamie started to follow him, but James took one long stride toward her and grabbed her arm. Jamie shook it off and ran to Trey, throwing her arms around him.

"Trey—"

"Jamie, you can't. Not now. We'll work it out—"

"You'll work nothing out." James crossed to the phone and quickly dialed 911.

"No!"

Her cry was anguished, her eyes wide with pain and panic.

Trey dropped his bag and pulled her to him. "Please, Jamie, don't! I can't stand this."

"Let go of her," James ordered, then quickly spoke into the phone.

"He's your father, Jamie," Trey said, ignoring the command, "and you love him, no matter what you feel now."

"No," she protested, trembling in his arms.

"Jamie, you don't mean that. I know how close you two are. I never had that. I can't be the cause of your losing each other."

"You aren't," she moaned. "He is."

"Damn," Trey groaned, "this is my fault. I knew I should never have stayed last night. I meant to leave, I never meant to fall asleep—"

She jumped at the sound of the phone being slammed down.

"The police are on their way. If you think I won't have you arrested for trespassing when you are no longer welcome, you're wrong. Now let go of her."

"Damn it," Trey said desperately, "can't you see we're tearing her apart?"

"She brought this on herself."

Jamie made a tiny little sound, and a tremor rocked her on her feet. Trey led her gently back to the stairs and eased her down on the bottom step.

"Jamie, I have to go," he whispered, kneeling beside her. "It will only make it worse if I don't. Let it cool down. Let him cool down."

Jamie's hands gripped her elbows as she wrapped her arms around herself, rocking back and forth. She didn't answer, just sat there, trying to control the shaking with a tighter grip.

Trey straightened, giving her father a long, hard look. "I don't know who's the worse bastard," he said tightly, "me...or you."

And then he turned, picking up the duffel bag with a sweeping motion, and strode out the front door.

Exhaustion finally overtook Jamie and blotted out the horror of the past thirty-six hours. Her world had caved in on her for the second time in her young life, and she was too weary to fight it anymore. She curled up in her lonely brass bed, shivering helplessly until at last sleep claimed her.

A suitcase also lay on the bed, stuffed haphazardly with tossed clothes and other items. That case had been the cause of another angry confrontation, one that had so battered her emotions that she'd had to sit down to stop shaking.

She had left her father in the entry the second the door had slammed shut after Trey, ignoring his orders to stay. She had been angrily yanking clothes out of her closet, tossing the first things that came to hand on the bed, when her father had come into the room to glare at the open bag.

"Just what do you think you're doing?"

She had folded another pair of jeans with little care for neatness and dropped them in the case.

"I asked you a question!"

It was a blouse this time, the hanger hitting the floor as she yanked it free. James crossed the room and slammed the half-full case shut.

Carefully she picked up the next piece, the shimmering gold caftan. She clutched it close to her, remembering what Trey had told her about the first time he'd seen her in it. Somehow it gave her strength.

"I want an answer."

"Oh?" She looked at him coolly. "I didn't realize. You haven't been interested in anything I've had to say all morning."

"Watch your tone, Jamie."

"Then you don't want my answer."

Angrily he reached out, as if to grab the caftan she was holding as if it was the most precious thing she owned. She backed away.

"Where do you think you're going?"

"Does it matter? You've made it clear I'm not welcome here."

"I said no such thing. It was that— It's Logan who's not welcome."

She looked at him steadily for a long moment. "You don't get it, do you? There's no difference. If he's not welcome, then neither am I."

He stared at her, and she saw him draw in his breath in an effort at control.

"My God, he's really done it, hasn't he? He's conned you completely."

"No. What I feel for Trey is the most real thing in my life."

"Oh, child, how can—"

"I am not," she said, enunciating each word with exquisite care, "a child. I am twenty-four years old, and even the law considers me an adult, Daddy." A fleeting look of pain flashed across her face. "Or whoever you are."

"I am your father, Jamie. And I know what's best for you."

"You are not the father I grew up with. He would never turn on me like ... like ..."

"What did you expect? I came home early because I heard about Chuckie, and I was worried. Then to find you ... with that con man ... I should have known he'd betray my trust, he's no better than—" He broke off, as if he'd caught himself about to say something he didn't want to say. Then he went on, his voice slightly softer now. "I just want the best for you, Jamie. I always have."

Something flickered deep in the blue eyes, and Jamie was determined to pursue it. Somewhere in this cold, unrelenting man was the father she had loved all her life, and she had to find him again.

"I'm sorry if you feel you've lost your little girl, Daddy," she began quietly. "Maybe that's my fault, for not striking out on my own when most children do. Maybe I stayed here too long, made it easy for you to think of me that way. But I'm not a child anymore."

"You think that ... this makes you an adult?"

She sighed. "I love him, Daddy. I love him, and even if it hurts for you to say it, I slept with him. I made love with him. It was the most beautiful thing that's ever happened to me. And if you can't be happy for me, if you can't live with that, then you can't live with me."

For a moment, one brief, frozen minute in time, she thought she had gotten through to him. He wavered, pain, love and anger warring in his face. Then the chill, bitter anger won, and he asked coldly, "Just how long has this been going on? Did you fall into bed with him the first time he asked?"

Jamie shuddered, knowing she'd lost. She drew herself up once more. "That is none of your business. But I will tell you this—he didn't have to ask."

"Damn you! You've turned into a lying, sneaking little slut, just like—"

He broke off. Jamie flinched, but didn't look away. She didn't understand any of this—his words or the fury that had taken hold of him. But Trey had faced him, had taken it for her sake; she could do no less.

"If you ever find the man who was my father," she said softly, "tell him I still love him." Then she reached for the suitcase, only to have him yank it out of her reach.

"You're not going anywhere."

"Going to lock me up, Daddy?"

"I won't have to. You can't go anywhere without money. I'll freeze every account you have."

"I have my own money."

He laughed harshly. "Not for the way you're used to liv
ing, you don't. You think your fortune hunter is going t
help? You think he'll have the slightest interest in you onc
he finds out my money doesn't come with you?"

Jamie paled. "My, God. Is that what you think? That I'r
so horrible, so unlovable, that I have to buy love with you
money?"

"That is not what I said. I said that is all Logan is after.'

"This is the man who saved your life! And who nearl
lost *his* doing it. He went through months of hell for you
My God, Daddy, he was chained up and whipped for you!"

"Whatever I owed him," James said icily, "he's mor
than destroyed."

"I suppose you'd like to see me with someone admirabl
and upstanding, like Edward."

Her sarcasm seemed to go unnoticed. "Edward is a fin
young man."

"Edward," she said tightly, "is a drunk. An arrogar
drunk."

"He's from a good family—"

"Your precious Edward got into a bar fight at some sleaz
dive last week. He started a brawl and got himself arreste
and thrown in the drunk tank. So much for good family."
She shook her head wearily, her expression sad as she looke
at her father. "Trey was right. When he came here, he as
sumed there was a spoiled, rich snob in this house. He jus
thought it was me. And all the time it was you, and I neve
knew it."

She was saying it to empty air; her father had stalked an
grily out of the room.

It had all hit her then. Everything that had happened i
the past week crowded in, weighing her down. Finding suc
sweetness in Trey's arms, only to have it destroyed by wha
had seemed at the time to be his betrayal. Then Chuckie
taken from her and from this world despite his valiant spiri
so many years too soon. Only the precious, honeyed hour

of last night had been able to soothe that wound, hours that had been followed so closely by disaster, by the realization that her father had become a virtual stranger to her. It all rose up to swirl around in her dazed mind, sapping her strength.

She would rest a minute, she'd thought as she sank down on the lounge. She would rest just for a minute, and then she would deal with it all.

She awoke to the first gray light of dawn, shocked that she had slept for so long. She felt sore, aching, as if she'd been ill for days. But her first thought was of Trey, and life flooded through her again.

Where was he? Where had he gone? She knew he'd been planning to leave before, but she didn't know where he'd planned to go. Maybe Uncle Hank would know, or someone in his office, she thought.

She got up, straightened her robe and went swiftly toward the stairs. She met Jean outside the library and knew immediately from the housekeeper's troubled look that her father had already spoken to her.

"I gather you know I'm in disgrace," she said wryly.

Jean sighed. "I feel so terrible, baby. It just breaks my heart—you two were always so close."

"It breaks mine, too. But I don't know him anymore, Jean. I could understand his anger, but this..."

Jean nodded, opened her mouth to speak, then looked away. When she did go on, Jamie was certain her words were not what she had been planning to say.

"I feel so responsible," she said.

"You? Why?"

"I...practically sent Trey to you last night."

"You...what?"

"He looked so devastated when I told him about Chuckie. And he was so worried about you. I could tell how he felt about you, but I shouldn't have encouraged—"

"Yes," Jamie said quickly. "Yes, you should have. I love him, Jean."

"I know, baby. I've known for days."

"Well, my father had better know it, too. I've learned stubbornness from an expert lately, and I'm not taking this without a fight. And first I have to find Trey."

"Yes. You do."

They both whirled, Jean letting out a startled little cry at the unexpected sound of James McCall's voice.

"I'll see you in the library. Now. Jean, you must have something else to do."

Jamie felt the older woman stiffen, and knew she would stay if she wanted her to.

"Go ahead, Jean," she said quietly. "I'll be all right."

"I see," James said as he shut the library doors behind them, "that I can't trust you to obey my orders."

"I take orders," Jamie said as she turned away from him, "about as well as you do."

"That's not true. He's done this to you. You always did as I asked before."

"Yes." She whirled back to face him. "Because you asked, not ordered!"

"And if I asked you never to see Logan again?"

She walked past him, dropping into the chair Trey had always used. She closed her eyes, drawing the warmth of his image around her like a cloak of armor. Only when she sensed her father standing before her did she open them again.

"I would say no. I would have to. You're my father, and I love you. At least, I love the father I remember, not the one I met yesterday. But I would say no." She sat up in the chair, driven by some spirit in her that wouldn't die, wouldn't let go of the father she'd always known. "I love him, Daddy. I didn't think I could love anyone like this. I was afraid there was something wrong with me, that maybe somehow that had been killed when I was hurt."

It was there again, that brief flash in his eyes, that fleeting glimpse of the man she'd grown up with. "You never told me that."

"I didn't know that's what it was. I didn't put it into words, until I met Trey. I didn't understand the feeling until he proved it wrong. All I knew was that I was afraid that something inside me wasn't working right, that I would never have what I wanted because I wasn't capable of feeling it. And that because I couldn't settle for less, I would be alone forever."

"Less?"

It was still there, that trace of warmth, and Jamie leaned forward eagerly. "Less than what I feel with Trey. Less than what you had with my mother."

Her father went suddenly still, and the warmth she'd seen vanished. So swiftly it stunned her, the icy chill was back, and the blue eyes frozen and hostile. She didn't know what had happened, or why, but she knew she had lost again. And she knew as well that her exhausted spirit wouldn't try again.

"You give me no alternative, Jamie." He reached into his pocket and took something out. "Here."

She took the piece of paper he held out to her, and read the phone number written on it in her father's precise hand. She looked at him quizzically.

"Call him."

Her eyes widened, and she looked at the number again.

"Trey? You *want* me to call Trey?"

"Yes. Call him and tell him you want to see him. Tonight."

Suspicion bit, hard and deep, and she drew back in the comfort of the chair that had held his body so often.

"Why?"

With a hard, cold look, he told her.

Chapter 11

"It is the way of things here," Miguel said patiently in the face of Trey's frustration as they made their slogging way to the rendezvous point. "The rains come, and all creatures take shelter. Including Lucero."

Trey swiped at a trickle of water that was making its way down the back of his neck, then wondered why he bothered—he was already soaked to the skin, not that he cared. He hadn't cared about much of anything since Jamie McCall had quietly blown him to pieces that night two months ago. Yet, he marveled at Miguel's forbearance.

The only thing harder for Trey than accepting that the weeks of cutting their way through the fierce growth along barely discernible paths had been for nothing was accepting Miguel's generosity. Even when Miguel had been proven right, he hadn't once tossed a well-deserved "I told you so" Trey's way. Trey eyed his wiry, dark-haired companion ruefully.

"You knew this would happen, didn't you?" Miguel merely shrugged, but Trey knew what he'd said was true. "So why did you come with the 'crazy American'?"

"Because," Miguel said, flashing a smile that for a moment lit dark eyes weary with the endless months of war that threatened to destroy his homeland, "we owe you. Had it not been for you, we would never have found Lucero's stronghold. If he had had the entire wet season to 'dig in' there, as you say, we might never have gotten him out."

The stronghold. Trey suppressed a shiver as the image of the place rose before him. They'd passed it on their trek, and he had looked down into the deserted compound from the hillside trail. The sight of the post in the center of the open yard, chains still dangling from it, made his stomach knot and his wrists ache in vivid memory. If he hadn't been able to break loose that night, as they'd been dragging him back to his cell . . .

By comparison, Trey only vaguely remembered that day in the hospital, fighting through the mists of pain, trying to pinpoint, on the map Miguel had had to hold for him, the hellhole where he'd been imprisoned. It had taken him hours, it seemed, trying to fit what little he'd seen, what he could remember, with the wavy, concentric lines on the topographical map. But at last the two peaks that had hovered over the encampment, and the memory of a chilly morning sun appearing between them, oriented him enough to point with a shaky finger to the narrow, high valley where he had nearly died.

A small thing, he thought, especially since Lucero had still managed to escape into the jungle when Miguel's men stormed the camp. But Miguel was not one to forget a debt, of any size. So he had come with Trey on this useless, weeks-long trek through the jungle.

When they broke through to the rain-soaked clearing and Trey saw the waiting helicopter Miguel had arranged, he let out a soft sigh he hadn't been aware of holding back. Only then did he realize he'd been half-afraid of being stranded here once again.

"You are a brave man, amigo, to come back to the place where you so nearly met death."

"Or stupid," he muttered. Miguel was a very observant man.

"I believe *obsessed* might be the better word," Miguel said mildly, as they clambered aboard the waiting craft.

At the unexpected statement, Trey shot Miguel a sharp glance as they strapped themselves into the seats. "I thought you wanted Lucero as much as I do."

"True," Miguel agreed as he gave the pilot the signal to lift off. "But I wasn't speaking of Lucero."

Trey's brow furrowed. "What?"

"I recognize a man who has substituted one obsession for another, my friend. Resolving one will do you no good unless you resolve the other, as well."

Trey stared at the whipcord-tough man he'd come to know and admire in the past weeks, then looked away. "You're *too* damned observant, amigo," he muttered. Miguel obviously hadn't forgotten the night he'd caught Trey studying, by the light of their small campfire, the photograph he'd pilfered from the McCall library in the moments before that final, ugly confrontation with Jamie's father.

"She is very beautiful" had been Miguel's only comment then, and his expression had been unreadable as he watched Trey carefully tuck away the reminder he hadn't been able to bring himself to part with.

Trey was saved from having to say any more by the increased noise as the helicopter lifted off, and he retreated into his own weary thoughts. Deep down, he'd known this trip was useless. Miguel had tried to talk him out of coming at all, telling him they had little chance of finding Lucero in the few weeks before the rains set in and made further searching impossible for at least a month, if not two. But

Trey had been desperate. After nearly a month of trying to go on as if nothing had happened, he had needed something—anything—to distract him. Even if it meant inducing the old nightmares of the jungle to replace the images of Jamie.

By the time they arrived back in Jardín, the capital, Trey was feeling no more settled than before. And no more at peace.

"Send word when the weather breaks," he told Miguel. "I'll be here within forty-eight hours."

Miguel studied him for a moment, rubbing a hand over his stubbled chin in a gesture Trey had come to know. "Do not mistake me, my friend," the man said at last. "There is no one, even among my own men, who I would rather have at my back. But this is not your fight."

"Lucero made it my fight when he chained me to that post and turned that lieutenant of his loose on me with a whip."

"You have suffered much," Miguel agreed. For a moment Trey thought he wasn't going to go on, and then he did, seemingly incongruously, in a flat, unemotional voice. "There was a woman, Lupita. From my village. I loved her deeply. We were to be married. She was killed, early in the war."

He stopped, and Trey felt those dark observant eyes on him. He didn't know what to say. He wasn't at all sure why Miguel had told him this personal thing, or what that long, intense look meant. Then Miguel said softly, "I will send word, my friend, if you wish it. But when I do, if you do not come, I will understand."

"I'll come," Trey insisted.

But the memory of that look stayed with him on the long flight home.

After he'd unlocked the desk, Trey dropped his keys on top of it wearily, hung up the leather jacket he'd peeled off and ran a hand through his hair. He needed a haircut, he thought idly as he dropped down into the chair behind the desk. And a shave. But then, he'd needed both before he'd left La Selva. He ran his hand over his stubbled chin and tried to ignore his exhaustion. And the queasy feeling that had overtaken him the moment he'd gotten off the plane, unable to stop himself from looking for a pair of amber eyes amid the crowd at the airport gate.

His mouth twisted ruefully at his own thoughts. You are one sick puppy, Logan. It's been over two months, and you're still mooning over that little golden-eyed witch, hoping for a miracle. Over two months since Jamie McCall had quietly blown him to pieces.

Forcing his mind off that worn, ugly track, he leaned back in the chair, staring out the window, not really seeing anything except the sunlight glaring off the reflectorized windows of the building across the street. Sunlight. Such a simple, natural thing. Yet the lack of it had sent him home from La Selva having accomplished nothing more than making his leg ache and renewing his distaste for the jungle. And, he amended, increasing his respect and liking for Miguel Cárdenas, a wise, honest man caught up in a civil war not of his making. A man who saw too damned much. Like Hank.

Hank. Did he know by now, know what Trey had done to his precious niece? He'd been sure Hank hadn't known before he'd left for La Selva, or he would have tossed Trey out on his butt right then. As it was, he had half expected Hank to be waiting for him today, in a cold-eyed ambush planned the moment Trey had called the office with his return time. But it was early yet, he told himself wryly. He'd only been back a few minutes.

He wondered again, as he had so often before, why James hadn't immediately told his brother. Sometimes Trey almost wished he had. It would be over then, and at least he wouldn't have to look at that damned McCall name on the front of the building every day.

Maybe James considered the problem solved. And why shouldn't he? He'd obviously gotten Jamie to see the... What had she said that night? The truth when it was pointed out to her?

Right, Logan. Quit kidding yourself. You remember every word she said to you. He propped his elbows on the desk and let his head fall forward into his hands.

She'd looked so damned beautiful that night. She'd been wearing a simple silk dress in a bronze color that made her hair look even more golden and lit her eyes with oddly metallic glints. She had run to him, throwing her arms around him fiercely, smothering the doubts that had been swirling around inside him while he'd waited, pacing, in the park where she'd told him to meet her.

"Jamie," he'd breathed, holding her close, "God, Jamie, are you all right?"

"I..." She had broken off, burying her face in the softness of his sweater.

"Did he... Did your father calm down?"

She'd made a small sound, unintelligible against his chest.

"I've been worried. I was going to break into the damned house tonight if you hadn't called."

"Oh, Trey," she moaned, her embrace tightening. He waited, but she didn't go on.

"Does he know where you are?" She shuddered, and his arms tightened around her. "Does he even know you called me?"

When she still didn't answer, the doubts that had faded when she'd run to him returned, heavier, darker. They boiled up inside him until he gripped her shoulders and held her away so he could look at her closely.

"Are you all right?" he asked again.

"I... Yes. I'm fine."

"Are you sure? You look like..."

"Like hell?" She laughed, an odd, tight little laugh that made those fears expand and take a firmer grip on his already strained nerves. "I could say the same for you."

"I've been worried sick. I went to the stables, but they said you hadn't been there. They thought it was because of Chuckie, but it wasn't, not completely, was it?" He said it with a certainty he wasn't sure he felt.

"Trey, please."

His gaze had gone over her again, worriedly. Her eyes were wide and dark, shadowed with circles of fatigue. And she was, he realized the moment he'd touched her, strung as tight as an overwound mainspring. She seemed to go paler even as he looked.

"Jamie?"

"Don't talk," she whispered. "Just hold me. Please."

He pulled her hard against him again, his arms tightening around her until he was afraid he would hurt her. She hugged him back long and hard, and then pulled away and moved back one full step. Her head came up, her shoulders squared, and something changed in the golden eyes. It was as if a shutter had closed, or a wall had risen. It was, he realized with a little shock, like looking at himself, before this honey-sweet woman had torn down all his barriers.

"Jamie," he began, reaching for her.

"No." She moved back another step. "Don't touch me."

His fingers curled into fists as he stared at her, the dread that had come rumbling back the moment he'd heard that tight, nervous little laugh growing.

"I have something to say to you."

That dread was blooming, mushrooming into a black, hovering cloud.

"I can't ever see you again."

The cloud lowered, its cold shadow enveloping him.

"I made a horrible mistake."

The words were mechanical, totally without emotion. The shadow was icy now, chilling him to the bone.

"My father was right. I have a certain...position to maintain. A certain status in the community."

"What the hell did he do to you?" His words were low, grating and furious.

"He made me see the truth. That I was being foolish. That...it would never work."

"It?" The single word broke from him harshly.

"Us." Her voice was steady, and utterly flat. "There is no room for someone like you in my life. I'm sorry. You must never try to see me again."

He stared at her, his heart hammering in his chest; he could barely stop from shivering, he felt so cold. "Someone...like me?" He shook his head, trying to brush off the pain that was starting to beat at him, despite the fact that what she was saying were things he had told himself time and time again. It made no sense. He had believed those things but she never had. So why was she doing this?

"What the hell did he do?" he asked again. "What did he use on you?"

The mask faltered for a moment, then steadied. "Nothing. I merely saw the truth when it was pointed out to me."

"I don't believe it. How could anybody who could stand up to me like you did, who had the guts to go through what you went through when you were hurt, cave in like this? Damn it, Jamie, what's going on?"

"I don't consider acknowledging a mistake caving in," she said coolly. "Goodbye, Trey."

She had turned to go then, but he grabbed her arm and spun her back to face him. "Just like that? 'Goodbye, Trey,' and you walk out of my life?"

"No."

Despite the difference in their heights, she drew herself up and managed to give the impression of looking down her nose at him. It was the kind of look he'd expected before he'd ever met her. She was acting like the rich, spoiled woman he'd thought she was in the beginning, and he knew it wasn't true. He knew it.

"No?" he echoed.

"You walk out of mine," she said imperiously. "And you don't come back."

Stung, he let go of her arm. He backed away this time, studying her. He knew something was wrong with this whole scene; none of it rang true. But why couldn't he get through to her?

"Jamie, don't do this," he said, knowing he had to try one more time. He knew the strength of this woman; whatever her father had done to her, it had to have been overwhelming. "Tell me what happened. We'll deal with it, whatever it is. Did he threaten you?"

For a split second he thought she had winced, but the expression was gone so quickly he couldn't be sure.

"It doesn't matter. It's over, Trey. Just accept it and get on with your life."

He let out a harsh, muffled breath. He'd never before revealed himself so completely, but, as always with Jamie, all holds seemed to be off. Just for a second his control faltered, and pain crept into his voice. "What life?" he whispered.

She paled, as if reacting to his anguish. "I—" She stopped herself. "Goodbye, Trey."

She turned and began to walk away. He didn't understand this, any of it. He, who had always expected the worst out of life, was suddenly unable to deal with it without striking back.

"Jamie."

She stopped, but didn't look back. When he went on, his voice was ragged, like something pulled over broken glass.

"Tell Chuckie goodbye for me."

A smothered little cry had floated back to him, but she didn't turn, didn't look. She began to walk again, then to run. He had turned away, unable to watch her go out of sight.

He didn't remember much of that weekend. For the first time in longer than he cared to remember, he had gotten drunk. Very drunk. He didn't know where he'd gone, or how much he'd had, but the size of his head Monday morning told him it had been a lot. It was the perfect condition, he'd thought hazily, to go in and be officially fired.

Instead, he had been confronted with cheerful "Welcome back's" that echoed painfully in his aching head, solicitous inquiries about his health that made him snarl that that should be obvious, and several salutes to what they called his heroics that made his touchy stomach want to give up the battle to stay inside in.

They just didn't know he was a lame duck yet, he'd thought, with a sourness of disposition that matched the sour taste in his mouth. When the colonel showed up, he'd be out so fast it would make his head spin. Or at least spin faster; it was doing a fine job already.

But it hadn't happened. Hank had strolled in, ignored his obvious hangover and slapped several files on his desk.

"These should keep you busy until the doc gives you the all clear. Security reviews on all the plants. I'll need your recommendations by Friday."

And then he was gone, leaving Trey more confused than his alcohol-befuddled brain could handle at that moment. For days he'd waited, certain that at any minute the ax was going to fall. Just as he'd waited for Jamie to call, to come to him, to tell him the truth. Neither had happened.

He'd stood it for nearly a month. The very hour the company doctor had pronounced him fit—with only a little coercion on his part—he had gone to Hank and told him if he didn't get out of that office he was going to leave by way of the twelfth-floor window. And he wasn't totally sure he didn't want to be turned down.

"So what do you want to do?" Hank had asked with maddening calm.

"Go after Lucero." Trey knew that was the only thing that had the slightest chance of blunting the pain he'd been walking around in lately, pain that made his lengthy healing seem effortless.

Hank lifted a brow. "Revenge?"

"I prefer to think of it as pest control."

"Hmm." Hank had tapped a pencil on his desk blotter, studying Trey without giving a hint of what he was thinking. "All right," he said at last. "I guess you've earned that much. Under one condition. You work with Miguel Cárdenas to bring Lucero in to the legitimate La Selva authorities. No loose-cannon stuff."

Trey had agreed without hesitation. He didn't need to kill the man himself, although he wouldn't deny the attractiveness of the thought. But if the government wanted the honor, he'd settle for turning the bastard over to them.

But after weeks of futile effort, he was back. And now, after less than an hour in the office, he was feeling the walls close in again.

Pack it in, Logan. You can't live like this. You've got to get away from here, away from everything that reminds you of her. She's always there, eating away at your peace, anyway, but you don't have to aggravate it by working for her damned uncle, in the company her father owns.

He opened a drawer and took out a sheet of McCall Corporation letterhead and a pen. He rolled the pen between his fingers, wondering what to say. Personal reasons, he supposed. His mouth quirked at the corners. Real personal.

He dropped the pen, leaning back in his chair and rubbing at his tired eyes. *Damn it, Logan, you're acting like a lovesick teenager. Hasn't she made it clear enough for you? Not a call, not a note, nothing, for two damned months. What more do you need to get it through your thick head that she meant what she said? That she was going to live by her father's twisted view, whether she believed it or not? God, haven't you been a big enough fool already?*

Apparently not, he thought grimly, *considering how much time you've spent trying to convince yourself that something doesn't add up, that something was missing from that pleasant little scene that night. Give it up,* he told himself; he'd lost track of how many times he'd said it.

He picked up the pen again. *I quit,* maybe. Short and sweet, he thought. There was no way he could put into words what he was feeling, how much he hated to leave the man who had given him a chance to turn his angry departure from the service into something positive. How much his good opinion meant to him.

I should just tell him, he thought sourly. *That'd get it over quick. Hey, Hank, while I was staying in your brother's house, while he was giving me a home, a place to heal, I helped myself to his daughter. You know, your innocent, virginal niece? Sorry about the virginal part, but—*

"Trey?"

He dropped the pen as the tap on his door and the voice of the security department's secretary startled him.

"Yes, Sherry?"

The door came open to reveal the petite, plump blonde's surprised face.

"You *are* here! He said so, but— Oh, dear, I have a stack of messages for you, and—"

"Sherry," he said, not at all up to dealing with her boundless cheer, "what did you want?"

"Oh! Mr. McCall is here to see you."

His brow furrowed. Hank never stood on ceremony with him, he just barreled right in and said whatever he had to say. He never even knocked, let alone had Sherry announce him. Why the formality all of a sudden? Unless . . .

It hit him then. The ax he'd been waiting for was about to drop. *It figures,* he thought ironically. *Your timing has been the pits lately, Logan. You finally come to your senses and*

realize you've got to get out of here, and that's when he de-
cides to pull the plug on you.

"Trey?"

Sherry was looking at him rather oddly, and he realized
she'd been waiting for several seconds. *C'mon, Logan, get
it over with.* "Send him in."

He picked up the ring of keys he'd dropped on the desk
and flicked through for the keys to the building, and his
desk and file cabinet. Hank would want them now. Maybe
he would just quit before Hank could say a word. Beat him
to it.

When he heard the footsteps approaching, he took a deep
breath and steeled himself. He could stand this, he thought.
If he could stand Jamie turning her back on him, he could
stand anything. Even seeing contempt in the eyes of one of
the few men in the world he respected.

But when he looked up, keys still in hand, the eyes he met
were those of James McCall.

Chapter 12

Trey threw the keys down on his desk with an exhausted sigh. "I should have known you'd want the pleasure yourself."

"Believe me, this is no pleasure." James McCall's voice was stiff, yet strangely tired.

"Let's just get it over with, then." Trey picked up the keys again, sorted out the building key and began to work it off the ring.

"May I sit down?"

Trey stifled his surprise. James McCall ordered, not requested. Then he shrugged, nodding toward the empty chair across the desk from him.

From the chair, James looked silently around the office for a moment, his gaze lingering briefly on the framed photograph of his brother, in camouflage uniform, with his arm around the shoulders of Trey Logan. His brother looked several years younger. Trey looked a century younger, the difference all in the weary, red-rimmed gray eyes.

As Trey tossed the key down on the blotter, the older man's gaze caught and held on the airline boarding pass that protruded from the pocket of Trey's jacket, which hung on the back of the door he'd closed behind him.

"It's true, then? You've just come back?"

Trey raised an eyebrow, then it came down in rueful realization. It was James's company; if he ordered someone to report on an employee's whereabouts, it would get done.

"Yes." He went to work on the key to his desk.

"Then she didn't come to you."

Trey's fingers halted. "What?"

"I thought . . ."

Trey looked at him sharply; that hesitant, weary voice was not the voice of James McCall.

"The letter said no, but I still hoped that she had gone to you."

Trey dropped the keys again. He didn't waste time by pretending not to understand who the older man meant.

"She's gone?"

"She . . . ran away."

Trey grimaced. "Children run away. She's twenty-four years old, despite your unwillingness to admit it."

James gave a slow nod, and Trey suddenly realized what had changed about him. He looked old. And he moved old, as if every motion was an effort.

"Where?" Trey snapped.

"I don't know. That's why I thought . . ."

"You thought I knew? That she was with me?" At the next weary nod, Trey leaned forward and stared at him. "Why in hell would you think that? She made it quite clear that she wants nothing to do with me."

"No."

"You know she did. You probably coached her."

To his amazement, James winced as if in pain. "I meant—"

"I don't care what you meant. It's none of my business. She's none of my business." He was swearing inwardly. If he'd been here, would she have come to him? Where had she gone? Damn—was she all right?

Then he nearly laughed at himself. Of course she was. Little rich girls were always all right. It was idiots like him, who couldn't see the truth when it was staring them in the face, that had the problems.

"Can we just get on with what you came here for?" Trey reached for the keys again.

"All right." For a moment, the old James McCall was back, brusque, commanding. "I want you to find her."

Trey barely heard the clatter as the keys went down again. "You what?"

"You heard me." James's voice was sharp, even testy.

Trey couldn't stop the bitter chuckle that broke from him. "You are really something, *Mr.* McCall. I'm good enough to find your daughter, but not to touch her, is that it?"

James made a stubborn effort at command. "I can order you, you know. You may work for my brother, but this is my company."

Trey smiled, a slow, lazy smile that never reached his eyes. James shifted uncomfortably in the chair.

"True," Trey said. "But I don't work for it anymore."

"What?" James looked startled.

"I quit. I was about to write it up, but you saved me the trouble."

"You can't do that!"

"I just did." He chuckled again, mirthlessly. "Sorry to deprive you of the gratification of firing me."

"No, damn it!" James came out of the chair explosively.

"Easy, Mr. McCall." Trey never blinked at the eruption. "You're losing your cool, and you do have a ... social position to maintain."

James sagged back in the chair, rubbing at his temples. Trey didn't look at him. He opened the top right-hand drawer of the desk and took out his personal list of phone numbers, a few loose business cards and some other papers. Tossing them on the desk, he opened the next drawer down.

"Logan..."

Trey ignored the odd, pleading note that had come into the older man's voice. He lifted out a zippered leather case and opened it to check the lethal-looking .45 automatic pistol that nestled in the sheepskin lining. He made sure that the clip was out, that the chamber was empty, then zipped the case and set it on top of the stack he was making. Then he shut those two drawers and opened the center one and took out a few papers.

"Trey, please..."

He slammed the middle drawer shut. James jumped at the sharp sound, and drew back from the look Trey fixed on him.

"What the hell do you want from me?"

"I told you. I want you to... find my daughter."

Trey let out a short breath of pure exasperation. "Your daughter," he said carefully, "wants nothing to do with the likes of me. You made sure of that. And I don't work for your brother—or you—anymore. So what the hell makes you think I have the slightest interest in finding her?"

"Because... you love her."

Trey leapt up. "Damn you! Damn all of you high-and-mighty McCalls." He strode around the desk, furiously yanking his jacket off the hook on the back of the door.

"You don't know what you're doing—"

Trey whirled, cutting him off with a scornful snort. "This is the first time in six months I've known what I was doing. I am, as they say, outta here." He pulled the jacket on with short, jerky motions.

"Logan, stop—"

"With all due respect, *Mr.* McCall, go to hell."

"Damn it, maybe I deserve this, but she doesn't! She loves you!"

Trey's face went pale, his eyes even icier. "You don't really expect me to believe that?" He reached for the small pile of belongings on the desk.

"She loves you more than you know."

"Excuse me," Trey said coldly, "but I was there the night she told me how much she loved me."

"But you haven't heard why she did it." James sank back down into the chair, looking every year of his age and more. Trey leaned forward, bracing himself with his hands on his desk as he pinned the older man with a chilly glare.

"She did it," he said carefully, "because her father convinced her he was right. She did it because I don't fit into her perfect little life. She did it because I'm damned well not good enough for her. She did it—"

"—because I forced her to."

"Forced?" Trey straightened up, moving with rigid control. "She's too tough to be forced."

"Not when— She did it for you."

"Me? That's rich." He laughed bitterly. "No pun intended."

"She did it," James said brittlely, "because I told her if she didn't, I would see that you were fired."

Trey froze in the act of shoving the leather weapon case in his jacket pocket.

"I told her I would see to it that you were blackballed everywhere that I could contact. That you wouldn't find a job anywhere west of the Rockies."

Trey sagged against the edge of the desk. James went on methodically, as if now that he'd begun, all he could think of was getting it all said.

"I told her I could start a rumor that you had been dishonorably discharged from the rangers. A rumor strong enough that no one would bother to check first. A rumor that would dog you for the rest of your life."

"You bastard," Trey breathed.

"Yes." He said it flatly, without apology. "And I would have done it. Then."

Blindly, Trey felt for his desk chair, his muscles gone sickeningly slack. He sank into it, his mind reeling. Jamie, he thought numbly. God, Jamie. He'd been right all along. Right about the clean, pure strength of her. *You should have known,* he told himself raggedly. *You're the one who runs away from things, not her. Never her.*

She'd done it for him. No wonder that scene hadn't felt right, no wonder it had been nagging at him ever since. God, he should have gone to her, forced her to tell him the truth. He shuddered, thinking of what that night must have cost her....

"Now will you listen?"

Trey's head came up sharply, and he didn't bother to try to hide the loathing he was feeling. James McCall shifted in his chair uneasily, as if he were seeing again the man he'd seen in that Central American jungle, and having those deadly gray eyes pinning him to the chair was not a feeling he relished.

"How long has she been gone?"

James looked away.

"How long, damn it!"

"A month."

"A month— And you haven't done anything?"

"I called the police," James said defensively. "They said that she's over twenty-one, and since she left on her own..."

"You're certain of that?"

"Of...what?"

"That she left on her own. No one's contacted you? For money?"

"No. She wasn't kidnapped."

Trey looked at him coldly. "Which I'm sure you would have preferred. It would have been better than coming to me, wouldn't it?"

James made a small sound of protest, but he didn't speak. He was thoroughly chastened, but Trey didn't find much pleasure in the sight. After a moment the man pulled a folded envelope from his pocket and handed it to Trey. "I got this two days after she left."

Trey took out and unfolded the page, his throat tightening as he saw Jamie's vigorous writing ravaged by a shaking hand. There was no salutation and no signature, just a formal statement that she had kept her promise by not going to Trey. And a fervent guarantee that, if her father did not keep his end of their "nasty little bargain," she would solve all their problems by parking the Rover—with her in it—at the bottom of the nearest cliff.

The words jumped, blurred, and Trey found himself looking down at a crumpled piece of elegant stationery through stinging eyes.

"I hope you're very happy," he choked out.

"Never mind that now. There isn't time. You've got to find her. I hired an investigator, but he didn't have your motivation. He traced her to Oxnard, but then lost her."

Trey grimaced, looking at the envelope. "I could have told you that from the postmark. What the hell else did he find out?"

"Not much. Nobody saw her go. She didn't contact—"

James broke off as the door to Trey's office swung open without warning. From the doorway, Hank McCall's gaze swept over his brother without stopping, then came to rest on Trey.

"I need to talk to you," his boss—former boss, Trey thought, although he didn't know it yet—said. "Now." He glanced at James. "In private."

James looked startled. "Listen, Hank—"

"Don't be more of a mule's hindquarters than you already have been, Jimmy." He jerked a thumb toward the door. "Out."

He went. Trey stared at Hank.

"My brother," he said in irritation, "can be an idiot. I could slaughter him for not telling me sooner." He turned to Trey. "So what are you going to do?"

"Sir?" The question was reflexive, the designation one he gave to few, the respect to even fewer.

"About Jamie."

Trey paled. This was what he'd been dreading, but somehow it didn't matter now. "I..." He let out a long breath. "Save it. I already told your brother I quit."

"Quit? What are you talking about? You can't quit!"

Trey gaped at him. "I thought...you..."

"Stop looking like a fish, and tell me how you're going to find Jamie!"

He'd had about enough of McCall arrogance for one day. "I'll find her," he said tightly, "and I don't need any help from either of you. I may not be in the social register, but I'll find her."

Hank grabbed his arm as he tried to walk past. "What the hell are you—" He broke off and swore, low and swift. "Damn that brother of mine. I swear I'm going to—" He stopped, shaking his head. "That's bull, and you know it. And so does Jamie. Or do you expect me to believe that she subscribes to that ridiculous class system of her father's?"

"No," Trey whispered. "And she went through hell because of it." His head came up. "He blackmailed her. Over me. That's why she left."

"Damn," Hank swore again. "This doesn't make sense! He's crazy about her, always has been! Maybe too crazy. He didn't want to give up his little girl." Hank had been pacing the room, but he stopped now. "What happened, Trey? He told me he'd been pretty rough on her, but he wouldn't tell me why."

God, James hadn't told him. And now it was up to him. Trey drew himself up straight, knowing he was about to destroy any support he might have gotten from this man.

"He found us together. In...a very compromising position."

Hank's brow lifted, then lowered in understanding. "I see."

"I thought you might," Trey said stiffly. "Now you know why I'm quitting. It will save you the trouble of firing me."

"Will you quit feeling sorry for yourself? That's not what I meant. Now sit down."

"You're not going to—"

"Fire you? For sleeping with my niece, who happens to be an adult and perfectly able to make up her own mind? No. In fact, I'm glad. I was starting to worry about her, she's been alone for so long. I'm glad she had the sense to pick you."

Before Trey could react to the spurt of relief that shot through him at the words, Hank's gaze narrowed. "Is that what he blackmailed her with? That you'd be fired?"

Trey nodded wearily. "Among other things."

He handed Hank the crumpled note that, he noticed with surprise, was still in his taut fist.

"Damn," Hank repeated a third time when he'd read it. 'I swear, if anything happens to that girl, I may kill him myself. It's time he let the past rest."

Trey wondered what Hank meant, but the words had fired him to a new urgency. "I've got to go."

"I know. But sit down for a minute first."

"But—"

"It's been a month. Another minute isn't going to make a difference. There's something you need to know."

Hank's tone was that of the colonel, and Trey sat back down. Hank seemed to hesitate, and when he spoke again, he seemed uncharacteristically ill at ease.

"It was...a couple of years before Jamie was born. James...found his wife. In bed."

Trey caught his breath. "With someone else?"

"With a man he'd brought home as a guest." Trey winced, and Hank nodded. "He reacted almost violently. He never trusted Vivian again, although she tried to make it up to him, never even so much as glanced at another man. Hell, she barely set foot out of the house." Hank let out a long breath. "I think she thought a baby might heal the breach, but when Jamie was born and it made no difference, I think she just . . . gave up. She presented James with a daughter to atone, and then gave up and died. James never trusted a woman again, except Jamie. He swore she wouldn't grow up to be like Vivian, that he'd see to that."

"And then he walked in on us . . ."

"Yes. And probably felt that the daughter he loved had turned out just like the woman he'd loved, despite all his efforts. Or maybe because of them."

And Jamie was paying the price for her father's painful memories, Trey thought grimly. And she was doing it alone.

But something still didn't make sense, Trey thought as he left his office after Hank had gone. Why, after weeks of sticking it out after her father's manipulation, had she suddenly cut and run? There was something that didn't add up, just as there had been something in that brutal parting scene that hadn't rung true. He'd not trusted his instincts about Jamie then; he wasn't about to make the same mistake again.

"Trey?"

He stopped, looking back over his shoulder at Sherry. "What?"

The petite receptionist hesitated, then asked, "Is all this . . . about Jamie?"

He was suddenly alert. "Why?"

"I just wondered. I mean, I talk to her a lot on the phone, and she's always so nice. . . . I've been worried. I wish I'd known something was wrong when she called for you."

Trey froze, then slowly, very slowly, turned around to face her. "When she . . . what?"

"She called, looking for you, while you were gone."

Trey felt every muscle tighten. "She called here? And asked for me?"

"Yes. About the time that the colonel says she...left."

She tried to reach me. She did try, in spite of everything. The words echoed in his head, and he closed his eyes against the sudden pain that knifed through him.

"I didn't leave you a message," Sherry was saying, "because I knew you'd still be gone for a long time, and she said..." She trailed off.

"She said what?" His voice was tight and hoarse.

"That if she couldn't find you that day, it didn't matter."

Oh God, Jamie....

Trey found James in his top-floor office. His hair was tousled, his eyes red rimmed and glassy. He was a pitiful sight, but one that stirred no charity or leniency in Trey Logan. He strode into the room, coming to a stop a foot away when he realized something else.

James McCall was drunk. Very drunk, if the nearly empty crystal bourbon decanter on the table beside him was any indication. He must have started the moment Hank had kicked him out of Trey's office. The glass in his hand was empty, and it fell from clumsy fingers as the older man looked up and realized he wasn't alone.

"That won't help," Trey said coldly. "Believe me. I know."

The bleary eyes strained to focus. "Logan."

Trey bent to pick up the glass. His fingers tightened around it, wanting to throw it back in the face of the man who had caused such havoc in his life. James reached out for the glass. Trey jerked it out of his reach.

"You can have it in a minute. In fact, you can drink yourself to death. I don't give a damn. But you're going to tell me something first."

"I di'n't—" He coughed. "Never meant for her to go."

"Damn you! She loved you, and you made her take the punishment you couldn't give to the one who really deserved it. Can't you see—"

He broke off, reining in his soaring temper. *He's just a pitiful old drunk, Logan. Remember why you're here.* James looked away, picking at the arm of the chair. Dropping the glass, Trey grabbed his hands, yanking the older man up out of the seat.

"Damn it, what aren't you telling me? Why did she wait? And why did she try to reach me after all that time? Why?"

James drew back, huddling in the chair as if he could hide himself. It brought back raw, bitter memories of Jamie, huddled into herself the day Chuckie had died.

"You son of a bitch," Trey ground out. "She's got more courage, more guts, than you'll ever have. That's why you're so hung up on this class thing, isn't it? Because you haven't got an ounce of it. Jamie's got more in her little finger than you—"

James muttered something unintelligible under his breath, cutting him off.

"What?"

James lifted dazed eyes. They were the eyes of a beaten, broken man. The look in them was echoed in his voice when he said those two words again.

"She's pregnant."

Armed with the information he'd finally pried out of Greg and Henry Doyle, the old man who owned the stables, Trey found himself driving from ranch to ranch on a twisted, tangled trail that seemed endless. At each stop he met with a protective wall that frustrated him even as it made him glad she'd had so much help. The horse world, it seemed, had a grapevine to rival that of the rangers, and Jamie McCall's prowess with horses was well-known. And welcomed, wherever she went.

At each place the surroundings tugged at him. He could feel the peace of this life reaching out and enfolding him. He could sense the magnetic pull of it, of the open fields and the cavorting horses. He even found himself smiling, in spite of everything, at the foals as they tested their gangly legs, only to go tearing back to their placidly grazing mothers when they reached the end of their invisible tether. *No wonder she loves this life so,* he thought.

God, he wanted to hold her, to tell her everything was going to be all right. He wanted to tell her he knew what she'd done, what she'd gone through to protect him. Never had anybody done anything like that for him; that it had been done by this fiery, determined woman filled him with an aching longing, a physical pressure.

Dawn three days later found him in Arizona, outside Scottsdale, headed for a distant ranch that would no doubt be, he guessed, at the end of miles of lousy road unfit for anything less than a tank. The foreman of the last ranch he'd been to had reluctantly parted with the directions, yielding, Trey thought, only to the desperation he knew must show in his face.

He'd been right about the road, he thought as he at last pulled to a stop, but the sight that unfolded at the end of it surprised him. Nestled in the cool shade of a hillside and a grove of tall trees, the wood-and-glass house was an unexpected sight. He heard the nicker of horses, the calls of birds, and somewhere the unlikely sound of splashing water, and felt as if he'd stumbled onto a little slice of Eden.

But before he had time to notice much else, before he even had time to take a step away from the car, he was pinned to the spot by the sight of a large and obviously angry dog racing toward him. What wasn't German shepherd was probably wolf, he thought wryly before it occurred to him that he'd better do something about getting out of the animal's path.

He had backed up a step when a piercing whistle sounded. The dog skidded to a halt, growling, but looked back the way he had come. The object of the dog's attention, the wielder of that rather amazing control, came out of the house.

This figure, clad in jeans and a plaid shirt, was female, but had the same outdoor look as the others he'd met. Her skin was tan and creased, but her eyes were young and alive, and Trey guessed she was about fifty. She was thin and wiry and fit, and she looked him up and down assessingly, her hand trailing over the back of the still-hostile dog in a gesture that he supposed could be either reassuring or threatening, depending on your viewpoint.

"Don't get many people out this far," she said in a rather gravelly voice. He wasn't sure if it was an explanation for the dog's behavior or a question.

"Have you seen—" *Whoa, Logan. Use your head here.* "I'm Trey Logan. John Shanks at the Double Q gave me your name...Mrs. Kelsey?"

The woman seemed to relax a little, although the dog didn't appear convinced. "You must be Logan. John called, said if a man showed up with eyes that looked like the back side of hell, it'd be you." She sounded gruff, and still decidedly unhelpful.

"I'm looking for someone who...might have come to you."

"Oh? Come to me for what?"

It didn't matter that he'd been through this time and again over the past two days; something about this woman made him edgy, and it wasn't merely the fact that her dog kept looking at him as if he wore a USDA Choice stamp.

"For a job, maybe." The woman just looked at him. He swallowed. "Or maybe...just for help," he said softly. "It would have been about three weeks ago. She might have used John Shanks's name."

"What makes you think I'd hire—or help—some stranger just because she had John's name?"

Trey studied the weathered face, realizing he would be foolish to underestimate the quick intelligence in those lively eyes.

"How about because you horse people are tighter than a military combat unit?" he said wryly. Amusement flickered in her weathered face, but she didn't speak. "I don't think it would matter. Not if you saw her work with the horses."

"She's good?"

"Better." The corners of his mouth twitched. "She talks, they listen."

"A whisperer." He looked at her quizzically. "It's an old saying. A person who can talk to horses. Whisper them. Get them to do anything."

"That's her," he said softly. The woman just looked at him steadily. He swallowed. "Look, I...I know you don't know me, and you have no reason to trust me, but..."

He swallowed again, heavily. *Damn it, Logan, don't fall apart now.* He lowered his gaze, not wanting her to see him blinking away the sudden moisture gathering in his eyes. He'd had a sudden vision of every lead petering out to nothing, a vision of the rest of his life spent, wondering, searching...

"What took you so damned long?"

His head came up sharply. "What?"

"You should have been here long ago. She needed you."

He swayed on his feet. "Oh, God...she's here?"

"Was." His heart took that too-familiar nosedive again. "I tried to get her to stay. I hoped you would show up."

He paled. "She...told you about me?"

"She didn't have to. Nothing puts that kind of look in a woman's eyes but a man."

He closed his eyes against a wave of pain. "When did she leave?"

"Week or so ago. She just disappeared one night. She'd been looking a little pale for a few days, like she wasn' feeling well. A letter came, a few days later, mailed from town. Said she was sorry, but she had to go."

"Where?"

"Didn't say, or I would have tried to find her myself."

Trey took an unsteady breath. "She . . . has that effect on people."

"If you find her," the woman said, voice suddenly soft, "let me know? I'd like to know she's all right."

"Not if," he said stubbornly. "When."

They were words he repeated over and over again as he drove back to the main road and into town. And each time the sour, bitter truth rose up to mock his determination. She had dropped out of sight as thoroughly and efficiently as any undercover operative. She had faded into the fabric of this tight-knit horse world as easily as Lucero had faded into the jungle. Trey had a feeling she could go forever without running out of protective allies. He would have no more luck finding her than he'd had finding the renegade general. She—

He hit the brakes hard, nearly sending the little coupe into a sideways skid. He wrenched the wheel around and left the car at a crazy angle against the curb, bailing out before it had even come to a halt. And ran across the street to where the green Range Rover, the decal from the stables still in the window, sat gleaming in the sun.

Chapter 13

The room was dim, the old, heavy drapes closed against the brilliant sun. Jamie lay curled up on the narrow daybed, wishing she could sleep, yet afraid to. Each time she did, she had the same dream, and it was a worse torture than the sleeplessness was.

She knew she would never forget the look on Trey's face that horrible night. She knew then that she was delivering a blow worse than any his body had endured, but she had been trapped, caught by her father's vicious, unexpected threats. She'd had to do it; she couldn't let Trey pay the price for her father's inexplicable irrationality. But the anguish in those gray eyes would haunt her forever.

And the images that followed were as bad—the memories of little Chuckie, who had fought so valiantly against a pernicious disease only to lose his young life so pointlessly, followed so closely by memories of the night that had driven her from the sanctuary of Maggie Kelsey's ranch. That hellish, horrible night, and the morning that had followed, when Trey had never seemed so far away, so completely gone from her life.

With a small, smothered gasp, her body drew up into a tighter curl, and sobs shook her slender body. She couldn't seem to stop it, just as she hadn't been able to do anything but try to hang on from day to day. She should be over it now, she kept telling herself, all of it. She had to make plans, think of the future.

Except that the future, which had once loomed so bright and shining before her, stretched out ahead of her in a dull, flat line. Nothing could ever erase the heartache of what had happened, nothing could ease the gnawing pain. Only one thing could have made it easier to bear, only one person, and he was far, far out of her reach. Even on days when he seemed so near, he was out of her reach.

But it had felt so strong today, as if he were close by, as if she could step outside and there he'd be, tall and lean and strong, gray eyes warm with the look he gave only to her.

As if he was right around the corner, as if she could feel the pull of him, drawing her near....

In the worst days of her battle to heal, to walk again, she had never felt so devastated. Or so close to giving up. Sometimes only the fact that it would take some energy to do it kept her from making good on her promise to her father to end all their problems by heading for the nearest cliff.

No, she didn't have the Rover anymore. So she would jump, she thought tiredly. What money she had left from its sale wasn't going to last long, anyway. Shivering, she reached for the thin spread that covered the daybed and pulled it over her. She wished she could pull it over her head and never come out, shutting out the world forever. The world she knew was still out there, even though she hadn't ventured into it for days now.

There was no place for her in that world anymore, and now, no reason for her to stay and fight for a place. She had nothing left. Nothing except her memories, and she wrapped them around her tightly, knowing that they would keep her much warmer than the worn spread ever would.

Trey knew this feeling, he'd had it before. That adrenaline high, when he passed the point of exhaustion, when his body was running on nerve alone, and he felt as if he could go on forever. Eventually, he knew, he would hit the wall, but he didn't care, not if it held out long enough.

She'd sold the Rover, here in Scottsdale. All he knew was she'd gotten twenty-two thousand for it. The paperwork he'd snuck a look at gained him nothing; the address was the Kelsey ranch. But twenty-two thousand was enough money to run on for a long, long time.

That must be what she'd meant to do. If she'd been going to stay, she would have stayed at the Kelsey place. He didn't know how he knew that, but he was certain of it nevertheless. And why would she sell the Rover, if she didn't mean to run again? Unless...she'd needed the cash quickly. Mrs. Kelsey's words echoed ominously in his mind. *She'd been looking a little pale for a few days, like she wasn't feeling well....*

He remembered James McCall's drunken words tumbling out about the mail he'd opened, hoping for a clue to Jamie's whereabouts. And finding the card inserted with a lab bill, reminding her to contact her personal physician for a prenatal checkup. Now, Trey's stomach knotted. He started out on a new trail.

He began with the hospitals, one by one. He stayed up, nursing that unnatural energy, checking phone-book listings against his map, stopping now and then for a cup of coffee when he came across a twenty-four-hour restaurant.

After the first day, expanding his search to the huge sprawl of Phoenix, he fell into a numbed routine, asking his question, showing the picture, saying thank you for nothing. Late one afternoon, after nearly a week of searching, when the deviation from the norm occurred, it took a moment to get through to him.

"—several days ago."

He stared at the nurse. Could this really be it, this small, out-of-the-way community hospital? "Are you sure?"

She glanced at the picture again. "Why, yes. Just a moment...." She turned to a computer terminal that sat on the counter, and made an entry. "I remember...we had no medical information. She hadn't been to a doctor. Ah, here it is."

Trey couldn't help himself; he leaned eagerly over the counter to peer at the blinking screen. The woman frowned. "Are you a policeman or something? Is she in trouble?"

"No. I just...have to find her. When was she here?"

She looked at the screen. "Let's see, she checked out two weeks ago...came in...here it is, four days before that. At least, that's when she moved to a room. The emergency room could tell you exactly when she came in."

He paled. "Emergency room?"

"Yes, since that was where she was admitted."

"Why?" His voice was harsh. My God, she'd been in this hospital for four days? "Why was she here?"

The nurse became suddenly formal. "I'm sorry, but that's privileged information. Unless you are a family member—"

Something snapped in Trey. He slammed his hands down on the counter. "I have been up for the better part of a week. I've driven well over a thousand miles, and I haven't eaten in twenty-four hours. My patience has just run out."

The young nurse backed up a step, fear showing in her face. Suddenly Trey went slack. *Damn, you're as bad as her father,* he told himself wearily. *Turning into a bully when things don't go your way.*

"Look," he said raggedly, "I'm sorry. It's just...I've been looking for her for so damned long. And every time I get close, I hit a dead end."

The young nurse studied him for a moment, sympathy slowly replacing wariness in her gaze.

"I wish I could tell you," she said, "but unless you're related—"

She stopped when his head came up swiftly. "I am," he said suddenly, realization flooding him. "Indirectly. I— She's pregnant."

The nurse's eyes widened. "The baby...yours?"

He nodded, but the movement slowed when he saw the distress that had filled the young woman's face. He went rigid, the blood draining from his face.

"She...lost it, didn't she? That's why she was here?"

"I'm sorry, Mr. Logan. She was under so much stress...."

He sagged against the table, barely hearing the rest of the words. Dear God, how much was she supposed to take? First Chuckie, now this?

"—hemorrhaging, but she was all right when she checked out. The doctor wouldn't have let her go if she hadn't been."

He raised his head, made himself ask.

"Do you know where she is? Did she leave an address?"

"I can't tell you that." A shudder rippled through him, and the young woman said suddenly, "But if I had to go get something and happened to forget to erase the screen, well, that would be an accident, wouldn't it?"

She glanced around, then scurried out of sight behind a partition. Breathing a heartfelt word of thanks, Trey reached for the terminal and tilted the screen so he could read it.

His heart sank once more as he read the now-familiar address of the Kelsey ranch. Then, halfway down the screen, there was another entry, dated nearly a week after her release date. It showed the bill paid in full, and with a pang he realized it was the day after she'd sold the Rover. And that it had taken over half of what she'd gotten for it.

And there, glowing in small amber letters, was an address.

*   *   *

The older apartment building was small and looked rather dreary in the fading light. It didn't improve on closer inspection, and Trey felt that knot of anxiety he'd been carrying around for nearly a week now tighten another notch.

The mailboxes were blankly unhelpful. Or maybe not, he thought after a moment. The apartment number the hospital computer had shown was one of the three that had no names at all, and she was hardly likely to advertise her presence by posting her name in plain sight.

He had to pull himself together when he stood on the small step outside the faded blue, peeling door. He could feel that adrenaline high fading, knew he was pushing the limit. With a hand that was shaking, he tapped on the door.

Nothing. And no lights from inside, despite the fact that it was dusk. He tapped again. The silence stretched out. He considered his next move for a moment, but knew there had really been no question. A quick glance at the old doorknob told him it would be little trouble. A quick flick with the credit card he pulled from his wallet and it was done, the door swinging open on hinges that creaked.

"Jamie?"

He felt a little ripple of shock at, for the first time in so long, being able to say her name and honestly hope he might get an answer. But none came, and he felt blindly along the wall for a light switch to chase away the dimness of the shadowed room.

He found it, and the darkness retreated. The inside was no less dingy than the outside, and that knot clenched even tighter. He froze when his gaze came to rest on the huddled shape on the narrow bed in one corner. For a moment he hesitated, uncertain. If he was wrong . . .

Then he saw it, on the back of the single chair, the battered straw Stetson with an elaborate feather hatband, the hat she'd worn the day of the show.

"Oh, God, Jamie!"

With that harsh cry he strode across the room, gathering that huddled form in his arms. She came awake with a start, fighting with all the fragile strength in her too-thin body.

"Hush, baby, it's all right, it's all over," he crooned, capturing and holding her flailing fists with exquisite care.

She went rigid in his arms, and he thought his heart would rip in half at the dull, exhausted and frightened look in her eyes. She stared at him, and then, in a movement so tentative it was a white-hot talon sinking into his flesh, she lifted a trembling hand to touch him.

"You're...you're really here," she said in wonder, as if she'd had the dream dissolve before her eyes one too many times.

He crushed her to his chest. "God, Jamie! Yes, I'm really here, and it's all over, everything's going to be all right."

"It can't be." Her voice was tiny, still stunned sounding. "It can't ever be right again."

She was in shock, he thought. Carefully, he set her down on the edge of the narrow daybed, then knelt beside her, keeping a careful grip on her hands. They felt far too thin, far too cold. He saw a shudder ripple through her, violent and powerful. She opened her mouth, but no words came. She just began to shake her head, in silent, agonized denial.

"I know, honey," he said, pleading now. "I know about the baby." She went rigid again, the quick, harsh gasps of her breathing her only movement. "God, Jamie, I'm sorry. So damned sorry. To go through that, all alone—"

"You...know?"

He nodded.

"I wanted it, so badly," she choked out. "I couldn't have you, but..."

"Jamie," he breathed, his heart twisting inside him.

"And then I...lost it, anyway...."

She shuddered again, so violently it frightened him. He moved swiftly, sitting on the narrow bed and lifting her onto his lap.

"I know," he said, stroking the tangled silk of her hair. "I'm sorry, Jamie."

"You are? You're not...just saying that?"

"Jamie," he whispered. "It was mine, too."

She quivered against him. "I didn't know...how you'd feel.... I didn't mean to get pregnant...."

"Oh, no you don't. Don't take that on, too. If anybody deserves the blame for that, I do. I should have handled it." He let out a breath. "I should have handled all of it."

"I tried to reach you...."

"I know. Sherry finally told me." He slid his hand up to press her head to his chest. "God, I wish I'd been there when you called."

"I was going to tell you. About the baby, I mean. I thought...you had a right to know, no matter what."

"You could have gone to Hank. He's been great."

"I didn't know. I was afraid he'd gone as crazy as my father had." She shivered. "I couldn't stand it...every time I looked at him, all I could think of was...what he'd done to you, how he'd ruined my life. Then, when I found out about the baby...I knew I had to get out. Get away. Far away from him. For the baby."

Trey hugged her fiercely. She nestled closer against him. He smoothed a strand of hair back from her pale cheek. "God, Jamie, I wish you'd told me what happened. I could have handled it—you didn't have to fight for me."

"I thought...he'd do it. He'd ruin you."

"Maybe he would have. But even if he had, it wouldn't have been worth what you went through." He pressed his lips gently against her hair. "Don't worry about it any more now. It's all over."

She moaned, low and harsh. "God, Trey, that night, what I said—"

"Hush," he said quietly. "I know you did it to protect me. And I should have known something was wrong. Should have known you...wouldn't do that. Hell, I did know, but I was too damn proud to go to you. I kept waiting for you to come to me. I owe you an apology for that."

"No! No, you don't. None of it was your fault! He did it, he did it all, he—"

"Shh," he soothed when her voice began to rise.

She shook her head, like an animal in pain. "I don't know him anymore. It's like he went crazy."

"Essentially, he did." He let out a long breath. "Jamie, it wasn't you, or me, or what we did, that set him off. It wasn't you he was trying to punish."

She looked at him, the quivering of her body finally slowing. "What do you mean? Punish who?"

"Your mother."

She gaped at him. "What are you talking about?"

He hadn't wanted to do this, he thought, not now, but perhaps it would be better to get it all over with at once. So he told her what Hank had told him.

"My God. All these years, I thought he'd never remarried because...he loved her so much. I never imagined..."

"You couldn't have known."

"He never talked about her. I thought it was because it was too painful for him. Like my looking like her was." She gave a shaky little laugh. "I guess I was right."

"He's carried that around inside for a long time. That doesn't excuse what he did, the way he manipulated you, not by a long shot, but..."

"I...can almost feel sorry for him."

"More than I can do," he said tightly. "At least right now. It'll be a long time before I forgive him. Not only did he put you through hell, he...he's responsible for our baby."

Somehow that "our," that assumption of parenthood for the child he hadn't known existed until mere days ago, soothed the aching, empty place inside her as nothing else could.

"Secrets," she murmured. "So many deep secrets, so much damage. My father, Ty and Kylie..." She let out a long sigh. Then she leaned back in his arms to look at him. "You look like... you've been through hell yourself."

He knew it was true—his eyes were more red than gray, he hadn't shaved in two days, and he'd been in these rumpled clothes for too long.

"It's been a long week." He grimaced, shrugging it off.

"How did you find me?"

"That," he said wryly, "is a story I don't have the energy for at the moment. Let's just say you left a trail of people behind you who are quite liable to murder me if I don't treat you right."

"I did?"

"Starting with Greg and Mr. Doyle, and ending with a nurse at the hospital who didn't even remember your name. But she remembered you."

She colored. "I... How is Henry?"

"Fine. And so are Sam, Hal, John and Mrs. Kelsey." He stifled a yawn; now that he'd finally come to a halt, his body was making its need for rest known.

She stared at him. "You saw them all?"

"Yes." He yawned helplessly again. "Plus one monster dog who had designs on my backside."

She giggled; he'd never thought such a tiny little sound could make him feel so good.

"You met Wolfie!"

"Wolfie?" He gave her a sideways look. "That beast is named Wolfie?"

"He's not a beast! He's a pussycat, once you get to know him."

"That dog is a pussycat like a buzzard is a butterfly."

"Well, I can't blame him. I've had designs on your backside a time or two myself."

He stared at her. She was blushing, but there was a growing joy glowing in her eyes, and it washed over him in a warm, sweet wave.

"Lady," he said huskily, "my backside is yours anytime you want it."

Her blush deepened, then faded as concern joined the joy in her expression. "Your leg?"

He shrugged, battling yet another yawn. "It aches now and then. But nothing I can't live with. A little rest and it's fine." In the jungle with Miguel, it had done a hell of a lot more than just ache, but he wasn't about to add that to her worries.

"Rest now, then," she said softly; she clearly hadn't missed his smothered yawns. "You need it."

His arms tightened around her as he shifted on the narrow bed. "You . . . you'll be here? You won't leave?"

"No. I won't leave."

She snuggled down beside him, with utter and complete trust, and something warm and comfortable began to expand inside him. Not the fiery heat she seemed to be able to rouse in him at a touch, but a tender warmth that lapped at the edges of his mind, lulling, soothing, until he slipped gently into an exhausted sleep.

"It's beautiful," Jamie said breathlessly as she looked down over the valley. She took in a deep breath, dragging in air rich with the scent manufacturers had futilely tried to bottle for years: tangy, inimitable pine, clean and crisp.

"Yes," Trey said briefly.

Jamie watched as he pulled his duffel bag, then her two canvas bags, out of the back of the Range Rover Hank had had retrieved from the car lot in Scottsdale. The sturdy vehicle had taken the mountain road up to Hank's small cabin easily, and in a comfort that had cut Trey back to inquiring if she was all right only every fifteen minutes or so. She had tried to tell him she was fine, but he persisted in acting as if he expected her to shatter at any moment.

For the first few days Jamie enjoyed the novelty of being coddled by this fierce, strong man. She was tired; the nightmare of the miscarriage hadn't quite left her yet, and she reveled in Trey's tender care. But when her energy began to return, she realized something was missing in his treatment of her, something vital and intense.

He'd said he understood what she'd had to do, the night of that awful confrontation, but that didn't mean he'd truly forgiven her. Had she hurt him too much, this man who had been so badly hurt already? Was that why every night as he lay beside her in the one bed the small cabin had, he was so excruciatingly careful not to touch her?

Did he blame her for getting pregnant in the first place? Or for losing his baby? He wouldn't talk about it, hadn't even mentioned it since the day he'd found her. Had he not meant them at all, those words that had eased her pain? How could she tell him how much she needed him to hold her, just hold her, when the time when they should be closest was when he seemed the most distant?

It was only in her dreams that he came to her, touching her in that way she remembered so clearly, yet that seemed too incredible to have been real. So often she would awake on a soft moan, feeling his hands on her body, only to realize he was lying rigidly motionless beside her.

She clung to the dreams, not knowing how to make them real again. And each time it was harder to awaken and find that the vivid sensations, as hot as a desert mirage, were just as insubstantial. She'd lost her father, she'd lost her baby, and now it seemed she'd lost Trey, even though he was right beside her.

One morning, the wisps of the mirage lingered as she sleepily opened her eyes to look at him. He was watching her, and for an instant the old hunger was there, heating his eyes to that silvery warmth. An answering heat kicked through her, and her lips parted for a quick breath.

He moved slightly, as if involuntarily, the motion tugging at the sheet that was all that covered them on the warm spring night. Jamie glanced down, saw the undeniable evidence that he was aroused, and thought she must still be dreaming. Or else he was.

"Were you dreaming, too?" she whispered.

He sucked in a short, sharp breath, and Jamie saw the realization hit him, that she had been dreaming of him, of making love with him. His gaze fell to her breasts, seeing in the taut, hard crests pressing against the thin sheet the truth of his guess, and the effect her dream had had on her.

With a convulsive movement he pulled her to face him, one hand going to the back of her head, to tilt it for his kiss, the other going to the firm fullness of her breast. His lips were fierce, his tongue hotly probing, as his thumb pressed and rotated her rigid nipple. It rose instantly to his touch, hardening even further with a swiftness that made her moan.

She wanted him now, right now, with no preliminaries, to ease this hollow, pulsing ache whose only cure was the ready fullness of his male body. But abruptly he stopped, a low groan breaking from him as he pulled away.

"Jamie, no. We can't... you're not... well."

Lord, was that why he'd been acting so oddly? "I'm fine," she said hastily.

"But they said you'd hemorrhaged—"

"That was weeks ago. I'm fine now. The doctor said there wasn't any real damage, and as soon as I felt like it, I could..." Her blush deepened. "As long as I don't... get pregnant again for a couple of months." More color. "He put me on the pill."

He still hesitated. "Are you sure—"

"I'm sure. I've missed you so much," she whispered.

He drew her head down to him, and Jamie could hear his heart hammering in his chest. Her own was keeping pace. He loved her, she thought, even if he couldn't say the words. Her mouth searched for his, and when his lips took hers, her heart soared on wings she'd thought mangled beyond repair.

That first touch ignited a fire that consumed them both with such speed it left them breathless. They clawed at clothes, his briefs and T-shirt, her panties, discarding them as soon as they were free of them, kissing, touching, stroking with a hunger that startled them both.

When his hand slid down her body to probe into the soft, feminine folds, it was with gentle care. She felt him shudder when he reached his goal; she was hot, and slick, and she parted her legs for him with bold eagerness.

"Oh, Jamie," he groaned, his voice hoarse, "do you really want me so much?"

"Yes," she whispered, hips arching to his hand, "so much."

"How? Tell me, Jamie." She felt her cheeks flame, but he persisted. "Please, tell me what you want."

"You," she said, her voice choked with the need that overcame her shyness. "So deep there's only one of us. I want to feel you all the way to my heart."

"Jamie," he said with a shudder, moving to kneel between her legs. His hands slipped beneath her, lifting her to him. "I don't want to hurt you," he said breathlessly, "but you're so small . . . and you make me so crazy."

"You won't hurt me. I promise. Please, Trey, hurry! It's been so long."

"I know," he ground out. "It was killing me."

He eased into her, taking her in slow, teasing stages, stretching and filling her until she thought she could take no more. Then he went on, and on, showing her just how much she could take, just how much sweet fire he could give her.

The pressure of him was relentless, building, swelling, until she cried out at the beautiful fullness.

She looked up at him, in the way she'd been too shy to do before. She looked at the tangle of his thick, dark hair, the smoky gray eyes, slitted with passion and half shuttered by the fringe of soft, thick lashes. She looked at the muscles of his chest and arms, taut and corded, and the ridged flatness of his belly.

When her gaze reached his slim hips, her thighs clamped convulsively around them, and her fingers curled against the skin of his back. She felt the scars, the faint marks that made the fact that he was here now, so thoroughly and vitally alive, all the more precious to her. And at last she looked at the place where their bodies joined, where sandy curls tangled with black, where slick, eager flesh slid into welcoming heat.

She gasped in shocked surprise at the ripple of searing sensation that swept her at the sight, and in that instant she felt her body convulse, then expand, exploding into heated, glowing fragments. She heard him, heard his low guttural cry of her name, felt his body go tense, straining, and then she lost her grip on the world and went hurtling into bright, beautiful space.

When she at last settled back into the safe haven of his arms, he was still murmuring her name in a tone of wonder. And at last, when his breathing slowed and the pounding of his heart eased, he turned to his side, taking her with him.

He held her so close, so tenderly, that after a long, quiet moment, she dared the words.

"Trey? I... About the baby..." She felt him go still, felt his muscles tense against her. "You *are* angry," she said with a tiny sigh.

"No." The denial was swift enough that it eased her anxiety a little. He raised up on one elbow and looked down at her. "It's just that... God, Jamie, I don't know what to say."

She gave him a tremulous smile, a little unsteady at the corners. "It's all right. I know you must be...relieved—"

"No!" There was no denying the sincerity of it, although he looked a little startled by it himself. "I don't... I'm not sure what I feel, but it's not that." He swallowed, then went on, his unease evident in the tone of his voice. "I thought about it, all the time, after I found out you were pregnant. Then at the hospital, when they told me you'd lost the baby...I didn't think it would hit me like that. I know it must have been so much worse for you. You had more time to...get used to the idea."

"It was horrible. I couldn't believe it was happening, even when I knew, when I felt the pains start. I felt like I was losing you all over again. That was the worst part."

Trey stared at her as if she'd said something in a language he couldn't understand. He'd been frantic with worry about her, he'd cringed inside at what she'd gone through, and that she'd gone through it alone, but he'd never really thought—never considered—that, to Jamie, losing him had been the worst of it. It was such an impossible idea, but she was looking at him so intently, with such an enveloping warmth lighting her golden eyes....

He pulled her tight against him. It was a moment before he could speak again.

"God, Jamie, you don't know how many times I tried to tell myself that you'd be better off without me." She wriggled protestingly in his arms, and he hushed her with a soft kiss. "I know. Even though I hated the thought...I tried to accept it. I felt so damned guilty."

"Guilty?"

"I...never had what you had with your father. Even before my mother died. He was...more interested in gambling than being a father. That's where my name came from, did you know? He'd needed a three to fill a straight, and didn't get it. So I became Trey."

He knew he was rambling, but he'd had little experience with baring his soul like this, and it was a painful process to learn.

"I didn't know it could be like... you two were. And then because of me you lost that, you were... like my father and me. Like it was catching or something."

"Don't, Trey. It wasn't your fault." Sadness flashed across her face. "Maybe it wasn't even his fault. Maybe someday I'll even be able to face him again. But it doesn't matter now. Nothing does, except that we're together."

"Together," he repeated, a little raggedly. "Jamie?"

"What?" She snuggled closer.

"I don't know.... I mean, this together thing... I'm not much good at it."

She went very still. Trey wished she would say something—anything—but she just lay there in his arms, waiting. At last he couldn't stand it and sat up, swinging his legs over the side of the bed. He wanted to run, to burst through the door of the small cabin and out into the mountain moonlight, away from the tangled emotions that were choking him. The only thing that held him there, poised on the edge of the bed, was Jamie's too-still presence.

After a long silent moment she spoke, soft words that plowed through him the way Lucero's bullet had plowed through his flesh. "How can you be so brave, but so afraid?"

He shuddered as the truth of it hit home. He wanted to run. Again. Because he was terrified. Of trusting. Of being hurt. Or worst of all, hurting her, when she'd been so hurt already. But in the face of her quiet, deadly accurate assessment, he somehow found the nerve to turn back to her. When at last he spoke, his voice was a rough, husky thing.

"I don't know anything about . . . what we have together, Jamie. I know what you should have, what you deserve, but I don't know if I have it to give. I don't know how."

Jamie sat up slowly, her eyes wide and troubled, as if she knew how very difficult this was for him. He made himself look at her steadily.

"I . . . care about you. More than I've ever cared for anyone." He looked away then, hearing the worthlessness of his own words, expecting her to throw them back at him with the rejection they deserved. But he couldn't lie to her. Not after the hell she'd gone through because of him.

"I know it's not . . ." His voice trailed off. He let out a compressed breath as he stared at the old-fashioned chenille bedspread now knotted up in his fists. He unclenched his fingers. He smoothed down the crumpled fabric. At last he made himself look at her again.

"I'll try, Jamie," he whispered. "That's all I can do. It's up to you . . . whether it's enough."

It seemed as if it would be enough. Days faded into brisk spring nights, darkness coming later and later each evening as summer grew closer. They had settled into a peaceful, comfortable routine, something Trey had never known in his life. They only occasionally let the outside world in, turning on the radio just long enough to catch the weather report for the mountains, and usually turning if off before anything else could intrude.

Jamie seemed to ask so little of him, merely to be there, to take long, strengthening walks with her through the woods, to hold her and love her sweetly in the night. It shook him a little to realize that these things, things he wanted to do so badly, anyway, were all she wanted, all she needed to make her content.

Content. It was a word he'd never really thought about before. He'd always thought himself relatively content with his life since he'd gone to work for Hank. He was produc-

tive, doing someone some good, living by his own unyield-
ing code, and it was enough. But the way he felt each
morning, waking to the feel of Jamie in his arms, rousing to
the sweet, willing touch of her hands and mouth on his
body, the way he felt in the peaceful hours spent together,
doing nothing more than trying to tease a laugh out of her,
or watching the sunlight, dappled by the trees, light up the
honey gold in her hair, the molten gold in her eyes, had
given him an altogether new definition of the word.

Something in him had changed. He could feel the loos-
ening, the relaxing. He could sense the lessening of tension
in himself, the unwinding. On one level he welcomed it,
welcomed the incredible relief, as if he'd let himself truly
relax for the first time in his life. Yet at the same time his old
instincts nagged at him, warned him against getting too soft,
reminded him he still had a task to do.

Lucero. The name still glowed in his mind, but it was with
a dulled anger now, not the fierce, fiery rage he'd felt before. In long, quiet moments out under the towering pines,
he tried to plan, to plot the course he would take when word
came from Miguel, but it was difficult to do when Jamie was
beside him, and impossible to remember when she looked
at him with a tenderness like he'd never known on her face.

And one day, as he and Jamie were walking through the
trees to a high ledge they had found, a spot where they could
see for miles, and where they had once wound up making
hot, feverish love back out of sight beneath the trees, he
found himself wondering if Lucero wouldn't be better left
to his countrymen, who had their own bloody debt to collect on.

He stopped dead in his tracks, making Jamie halt her own
steps to stare at him. Leaving his revenge to others was an
idea totally foreign to Trey. It ran counter to the creed he'd
lived by all his life, and his fighter's soul rejected it instantly. But then he looked at Jamie and remembered what
had happened to her—and his child—the last time he'd

taken off on his quest for vengeance. Guilt clawed at him, tugging one way, while the code so deeply ingrained in him pulled him the other way.

"Trey?" Her voice was touched with worry. "Are you all right? You look so... strained."

"I'm fine," he answered automatically. But it was a lie, and he knew it. And there was a desperation in his touch when, once more in the secluded spot they'd found, he turned to her hungrily.

The chill wind that kicked up later sent them scrambling for their clothes, and the clouds that were building on the horizon sent them straight to the radio when they got back to the cabin. As the weather report confirmed their suspicions about a fast-moving spring storm, Jamie went to the kitchen to get out the fixings for hot chocolate, and Trey began to load the fireplace with wood.

He stacked the logs carefully, an image of other nights they'd spent before a crackling fire here heating his blood before he'd ever struck a match to the kindling. He tensed his muscles against a shudder; he'd never known such sweetness was possible, never realized how much he had missed what he'd never had. But Jamie had taught him these last spring days, had taught him so much—

"—international news, the Central American country of La Selva is once more being torn by civil war as the renegade faction of the military has begun to move again. Two villages were overrun and destroyed by the fanatic sect led by former army general Rodolfo Lucero. Sources say the legitimate army will be taking quick action—"

Trey didn't hear the rest. He sat, hunkered down on his heels, holding a match in nerveless fingers. A tiny sound drew his gaze, and he looked up to see Jamie standing in the doorway, her face pale and her eyes wide with fear as she glanced from the radio to his face.

Chapter 14

Trey knew he'd been as wild as the spring thunderstorm that had swept over the mountains. As he lay panting, still clutching at Jamie's naked shoulders, his body still buried to the hilt inside her, he was afraid to look at her; half because he was afraid he'd hurt her, and half because he knew he'd see that look in her eyes, the look he'd seen ever since the day they'd heard that radio broadcast, the look of a person who wasn't sure anymore if the tiger she'd trusted was truly tame at all.

He knew he hadn't satisfied her. He'd been too frantic, too close to shattering long before she'd reached for his aching flesh to guide him home. It was as if all the confusion, all the agitation of the last two days had condensed into this moment, and his body had responded as if the answer to his dilemma was in the oblivion of the sweet satiation only Jamie had ever given him.

At last he lifted his head. "I... Did I hurt you?"

Jamie shook her head, but the look he'd feared was there in the amber depths. He wanted to soothe it away, to tell her

everything would be all right, but he wasn't sure if he believed it himself. He'd spent the last two days trying to act
as if nothing had changed, while underneath, the cool, logical side of him was telling him it was time, that the revenge
he'd lived for was at hand. But logic was now doing battle
with emotions he'd never felt before, and for the first time
in his life, he was questioning the convictions he lived by.

"I'm sorry," he whispered, not sure if he was apologiz-
ing for the hunger of her body, or that look in her eyes.
Slowly, as if gentleness now could make up for his wildness
before, he withdrew from her and slid his hand down between their sweat-slicked bodies to touch her, to caress the
flesh he'd aroused so fiercely then left wanting. She let him,
responded to him, but even as she later convulsed in his
arms, Trey could sense her fear.

It was the next morning that the message came. Miguel's
words on the telegram were simple: The rain is gone. And
with those words, the delusion he'd been harboring that he
had a choice to make vanished. And if some fragment of his
heart was screaming that this was not the choice he would
have finally made, he quashed the protest with a flurry of
preparation.

Jamie was safe now, he told himself. She was recovered,
and she could stay here until she was ready to face her father; Hank had made that clear. She wasn't pregnant this
time. She would be fine, and Trey could do what he had to
do. Soldiers had left women behind for centuries, and if he
wasn't exactly a soldier anymore, he still lived by his own
code, and he owed Miguel Cárdenas.

He was slipping the zippered case holding his .45 into his
duffel bag when Jamie came out of the bedroom, her eyes
sexily drowsy, her hair tousled from his fingers, her slender
body looking incredibly fragile in the shirt that hung loosely
down to midthigh. His shirt.

Something kicked him in the gut, hard and deep and breath stealing. How could he do this? How the hell could he walk away from her?

The sleepy look vanished the instant she saw what he was doing. "You're going back," she said, sounding stunned, her gaze fastened on the gun case.

"Yes," he said simply, not knowing what else to say.

She lifted her head, and Trey thought he'd rather be back chained to that post in Lucero's stronghold than know he'd put that expression on her face. But he had. He smothered the sound that tried to rise up from his chest, knowing it would be a begging plea for her to understand.

"I have to," he said when he was sure he could control his voice.

She just looked at him.

"Jamie, thinking about this, planning this, was the only thing that got me through back in the jungle. I made a vow then, and I have to keep it. For weeks, knowing that some- day he'd pay was the only thing that kept me alive."

"I know that." Her voice was tiny. She swallowed with a visible effort and then went on. "Do you think I don't hate him, too, for what he did to you? But they said the govern- ment is going after him. He'll get what he deserves. Let them handle it. Don't give him another chance at you."

"I intend to let them handle it. If Lucero cooperates, I'll hand him over to Miguel. But I have to do this, Jamie. Can you understand that?"

"What I understand," she said tightly, "is that if he *doesn't* cooperate, which seems pretty damn likely, the al- ternative is killing him. Or getting yourself killed. Is that what you want?"

No, that tiny part of him cried out fervently. He'd al- ways accepted the possibility of his own death as part of the risk he took. But now, when he'd just discovered how sweet life could be, that risk seemed suddenly unpalatable.

Jamie was staring at him, looking as if she could read his every thought, as if she knew he was torn, not convinced by his own reasoning. But there was one thing that was unchangeable, immutable.

"I have to go, Jamie," he said softly. "If it hadn't been for Miguel, I would have died. He found me staggering around in the jungle, already more than half dead. He compromised a mission that might have taken Lucero out for good to save my life. They had Lucero nearly pinned down when Miguel called in a helicopter to get me to a hospital. It gave away their location, and Lucero escaped. He escaped to murder more people. I owe Miguel, Jamie. I owe him my life."

For a long time Jamie just looked at him. Trey waited for the inevitable question: What about what he owed to her? But it didn't come. When at last she spoke, he told himself he should have known; he should have realized that, with Jamie, this had been his trey to fill the straight.

"At least that's a debt I can understand," she said, her voice barely above a whisper. Then she drew herself up straight, and her voice steadied. "And I know honoring that kind of debt is part of what makes you the man you are. But don't expect me to be happy about the fact that you're giving a madman another shot at you."

She turned away and walked out of the room, her back as stiff as if she still wore the brace that had once caged her.

Jamie stood staring down the narrow mountain road until the Rover was out of sight. Even after it was gone, she stood there, so still and quiet that the tiny animals of the forest came out and went about their business. A squirrel watched her with bright eyes, then began to search for food among the leaves and needles just a few yards from her feet.

Jamie wasn't surprised; there surely was nothing left of her to frighten the creature. She had never felt so hollow. The empty ache she'd felt when she'd lost the baby had eased with Trey's presence; now he'd left an emptiness in her heart that seemed to meld with the emptiness of her womb until there was nothing left but a fragile shell.

Sisyphus and his rock, she thought dazedly. Just as he'd been doomed to forever push it up the mountain only to watch it roll back down, she seemed forever doomed to watch the man she loved leave her.

She'd been wrong when she'd thought he loved her. She realized that now, realized she should have believed what he'd said. That grudging admission that he cared for her was all she was ever going to get, perhaps truly all he was capable of giving.

But he had come after her, hadn't he? Searched for her for days, to the point of exhaustion.

She smothered the tiny voice of protest. He'd known she was pregnant, and he'd felt responsible. And now that the baby was dead—she used the word purposefully, trying to jab herself into some sort of feeling—he'd probably stayed as long as he had only out of guilt. Or worse, she thought as she remembered his exquisite but impersonal care of her when they'd first arrived, out of pity.

At last she turned and went back into the cabin. She felt as if she was moving underwater, against a drag that slowed everything to half speed. One day passed into the next, but she barely noticed the change from daylight to dark and back again, or the cycle repeated again and yet again.

On that third day she heard the car approaching as she sat in the porch swing in front of the cabin, where she had been rocking herself for hours in a way she suspected wasn't healthy but was helpless to stop.

She felt no jump of anticipation at the sound of the vehicle—she could tell it wasn't the Rover. When Hank's racy little silver coupe came to a halt on the gravel drive, she didn't move, just watched as her uncle got out of the car and started toward her, a newspaper folded under his arm. The closer he got, the more his brow furrowed, until he came to a halt before her.

"Jamie? What's wrong?"

"Nothing." She saw that he didn't believe her, and knowing her uncle's tenacity, she amended it to "Nothing you can help, Uncle Hank."

She saw discomfiture in her uncle's usually composed features and knew he thought she meant the baby. She was relieved enough to let it stay that way.

"Where's Trey?" He gestured with the newspaper. "I want to show him this."

Jamie looked at him, startled. He didn't know? Trey hadn't told him? Then she saw the headline of the article Hank had folded the paper back to reveal: Renegade General Assassinated, and then in smaller print, La Selva Civil War Abating.

Jamie shivered despite the mildness of the afternoon. He'd done it. He'd succeeded in his deadly, self-set mission.

"Where is he, anyway?" Hank repeated.

"You've got the answer in your hand," Jamie said, thinking her voice sounded as numb as she felt.

"What?"

"He left three days ago. To go after Lucero."

Hank gasped at her. "He left you alone?"

Another time, Jamie might have appreciated his outrage. But she couldn't seem to feel anything through this numbness that had settled on her. She glanced again at the article. It said nothing specific about the assassin, only that the operation had been directed by the government. She wondered if Trey had escaped, or fallen perhaps into the hands of the lieutenant who had whipped him. Then she wondered at how little she felt at all. The numbness was deepening.

She barely managed to stir herself to tell Hank to leave; peace was what she needed now, she told him. He was reluctant, but at last she convinced him she needed to be alone, and that his well-meaning concern was only making things worse. She loved her uncle, but nothing he could do would change a thing.

She was still on the porch that evening when, unexpectedly, the sound of the Rover sent the squirrels off, chattering, and the birds flitting off in search of a more peaceful place.

So he was alive, she thought, wondering, with a curiosity as blunted as everything else, how he'd gotten back so quickly.

She watched him walk toward her, exhaustion evident in his every step. When he moved into the light cast from the fire she'd barely remembered to light inside the cabin, she saw the dark, weary circles beneath his eyes, the tired lines grooved into his face. It reminded her of the first time she'd seen him. After he'd survived that hell, he'd insisted on walking right back into it for some crazy male notion of honor.

When she didn't move, but just sat staring at him, her knees drawn up before her and her arms wrapped around them, he stopped at the foot of the porch steps.

"Hi," he said awkwardly after a moment.

Her expression never flickered.

"I…" His voice trailed away in the face of her silence. He let out a long breath and lowered his gaze, staring at the hand-hewn logs that served as steps.

"You'd better get some rest," she said abruptly.

His head shot up. "I… Yes. It was a long trip."

"I'm sure it was, but if you don't mind, I'd rather not hear about it."

He looked a little puzzled. "Jamie, I—"

"I'm glad you're safe."

Trey winced at her cool tone. "You don't sound—"

"Enthusiastic? Maybe not. Welcoming home a victorious soldier is one thing. I'm not sure what kind of welcome an assassin is supposed to get."

Trey gaped at her. "A . . . what?"

His unmistakably genuine puzzlement blasted through her numbness. "What would you call it? I told you how I felt. Did you expect it to change because—" she stopped for a gulp of air, afraid that now that her emotions had come rocketing back, she was going to break down "—you managed to survive after killing him?"

"Killing . . . He's dead?"

He must think her so isolated here that she didn't know yet, Jamie thought tiredly. She picked up the folded newspaper and handed it to him. He tilted it to read the headline in the flickering light.

"He pulled it off," Trey murmured softly. Then his gaze snapped back to her face. "Jamie, I didn't," he said urgently.

"Oh?"

"No. Oh, I meant to," he admitted, his voice earnest. "I packed my gear. I got on the plane. When I got to Jardín, I tried to reach Miguel. He was on a recon patrol, so it took a while. I sat there in the hotel bar, waiting. Waiting, and watching the results of that damned war parade by . . ."

He shuddered, and Jamie could only imagine what he'd seen. Just as she could only imagine what it had taken for him to go back to that place.

"The longer I sat there, the more I realized . . ." He hesitated, then came up the steps and knelt before her. "Jamie, I thought I couldn't live with myself if I didn't go. But the longer I waited there, the more I started to think that I couldn't live with myself if I *did it*—not if I lost *you.*" He sucked in a quick, harsh breath. "Then Miguel sent word. They were deep in the jungle, hot on Lucero's trail, and he couldn't spare anyone to lead me to them. He told me to go home. To you."

Jamie's breath caught. "He said that?"

Trey nodded. "Miguel told me once about his fiancée. She was killed early in the war. I didn't understand why he was telling me—not then. But when I was sitting there in that bar, thinking about...losing you forever, like Miguel lost Lupita...I finally understood. So I sent a message back to him. And I left."

Jamie heard a tiny sound, realized it had come from her. She bit her lip. His hands were over hers now, where they were clenched around her knees.

"I never meant to hurt you, Jamie. It's just that...I never...mattered enough to anyone that my dying would make a ripple in their life. I never considered that...if I died..."

"Part of me would die, too," Jamie whispered.

He nodded. She saw him clench his jaw and look away, saw the dark, thick lashes move as he blinked rapidly. She felt the unsteadiness in his hands over hers. Then his head came up again, and she saw the moist sheen in his eyes.

"I love you, Jamie," he said hoarsely. "I've never said that to a woman. I didn't think...I could ever love anyone, but I love you." He looked down at his trembling hands and made a disgusted sound. "Look at me. I'm shaking like a green G.I. on his first mission."

"Oh, Trey." In a flurry of motion she was in his arms, hugging him fiercely. "I love you. God, I love you. I tried to understand, really I did, but I was so scared, it was like I...shut down or something."

"I know," he murmured against her hair, a world of relief in his voice now that he was holding her. "I think that's what shook me the most. The idea of taking care of myself...for someone else's sake...it just never occurred to me."

"You'd better get used to the idea," Jamie said, sounding a little fierce but unable to help it. She felt him chuckle an instant before she heard it.

"I have a feeling I'm going to have to get used to a lot of things."

Jamie tilted her head back, knowing all the love she was feeling was glowing in her face, and not caring. "Let's start with this," she whispered, and reached up to kiss him.

It was much later, when the forgotten newspaper again crinkled noisily under Trey's naked back, that he thought to read the rest of the article. When he got to the end, he let out a relieved sigh.

"Miguel's the spokesman quoted in the press release, so he got away clean." He gave her a sideways look. "He's a good man, Jamie."

"I know. He sent you home to me."

Trey smiled crookedly. "So he did."

Something occurred to her then, and she lifted a brow at him. "You said you sent him a message. What was it?"

His smile softened. "It was short. Just 'Thanks.' But I know he'll understand."

He sounded so certain that she had to ask. "How?"

"I wrote it on the back of your picture," he said simply.

A warmth and joy far beyond that which his body brought her exploded inside Jamie. He was truly gone, that cold, lonely man who had lived his life thinking his death would matter to no one. And when he spoke a moment later, she saw the future roll out before them.

"Do you think . . . Hank would be my best man?"

Jamie bit her lip a moment before she could trust her voice. "Is this a proposal, Mr. Logan?"

She saw him flush, and couldn't help the smile that curved her mouth.

"I've been dropped into unfamiliar territory before," he said wryly, "but nothing like this." He raised himself up on one elbow to look at her. "I know I'm going at this all wrong—"

"Yes."

He looked at her uncertainly. "Yes, I'm going about this all wrong, or yes, you'll—" he swallowed tightly "—marry me?"

"Both."

At his expression, she couldn't help herself—she giggled. He grinned suddenly, an unshadowed, blissful grin that turned her giggle into a joyous laugh. He pulled her into his arms again.

"But, Trey?"

"Hmm?" It was muffled as he pressed a kiss against her hair.

"No secrets. Not like my father. Not between us."

He lifted his head then to look at her. "No secrets," he agreed. "They can hurt too much."

She hugged him, tightly. And he lowered his head once more to press a trail of feather-light kisses over her cheek to her ear.

"I think," she said a little breathlessly, "we'd better go inside. I think we've pushed our luck a bit, out here on the porch. We're not *that* remote."

Trey growled something that sounded like "eat their hearts out," but he picked her up and carried her inside by the fire.

"Jamie?" he said when they once more lay quietly.

"Mmm?"

"Not now, but sometime, later, when...you feel better about it, would you want to...try again?"

"Try...?"

"I know it would be hard, after this time, and I keep thinking of Chuckie..."

She pulled back to look at him, her eyes wide. "You mean...a baby?"

He nodded.

"Your baby?" Her voice had gone soft and warm, and she knew her answer rang in the sweet tone of it. She saw the recognition of it in his face—he was looking as if he'd never heard a more positive "yes." And as if he, too, was feeling so much joy that even the sadness of children lost couldn' darken it completely.

"I'm not rich, Jamie. But I haven't spent much since I'v worked for your uncle, either. Maybe...maybe we could bu a place. Like the Kelsey place, maybe, with lots of space and a place for horses, and kids, if you want. And room t grow tiger lilies."

And without walls to close in on you, she thought, un derstanding instantly. And then her heart quivered at th realization that this tough, fierce man had noticed her fa vorite flower.

"I'd love that." She whispered. Then the corners of he mouth twitched. "On one condition."

His brows lowered. "What?"

"I want a dog."

He looked startled. "Well, sure. Why not?"

"Good. I'll tell Maggie to save a puppy for me."

"Okay, but—" His brows shot up then. "Wait a minute are those puppies by any chance related to that overly car nivorous beast I met?"

"Only by blood," she said sweetly.

"Oh, no, you don't. I'm not spending the rest of my lif watching my backside. The first part was bad enough."

"Well, since I enjoy it so much, anyway, I'll watch it fo you," she said agreeably, "if you'll tell me how you *do* pla to spend the rest of your life."

His eyes turned a soft, smoky gray so quickly it left he breathless. And then he showed her, in great detail, exactl what his plans were for the rest of their lives together.

*   *   *   *   *

HE'S AN

AMERICAN HERO

He's a man's man, and every woman's dream. Strong, sensitive and so irresistible—he's an American Hero.

For April: KEEPER, by Patricia Gardner Evans: From the moment Cleese Starrett encountered Laurel Drew fishing in his river, he was hooked. But reeling in this lovely lady might prove harder than he thought.

For May: MICHAEL'S FATHER, by Dallas Schulze: Kel Bryan needed a housekeeper—fast. And Megan Roarke did more than fit the bill; she fit snugly into his open arms. Then she told him her news....

For June: SIMPLE GIFTS, by Kathleen Korbel: For too long Rock O'Connor had fought the good fight to no avail. Then Lee Kendall entered his jaded world, her zest for life rekindling his former passion—as well as a new one.

AMERICAN HEROES: Men who give all they've got for their country, their work—the women they love.

Only from

Take 4 bestselling love stories FREE

Plus get a FREE surprise gift!

ROMANTIC TRADITIONS continues in April with Carla Cassidy's sexy spin on the amnesia plot line in TRY TO REMEMBER (IM #560).

"Jane Smith's" memory had vanished, so when Frank Longford offered her a safe haven and a strong shoulder, she accepted. Then the nightmares began, with memory proving scarier than amnesia, as Jane began to fear losing the one man she truly loved.

As always, ROMANTIC TRADITIONS doesn't stop there! July will feature Barbara Faith's DESERT MAN, which spotlights the sheikh story line. And future months hold more exciting twists on classic plot lines from some of your favorite authors, so don't miss them—only in ◆ INTIMATE MOMENTS *Silhouette*®

THE WILD WEST

by Linda Turner

Out in **The Wild West**, life is rough, tough and dangerous, but the Rawlings family can handle anything that comes their way—well, *almost* anything!

American Hero Cooper Rawlings didn't know what hit him when he met Susannah Patterson, daughter of the man who'd shot his brother in the back. He *should* have hated her on sight. But he didn't. Instead he found himself saddling up and riding to her rescue when someone began sabotaging her ranch and threatening her life. Suddenly lassoing this beautiful but stubborn little lady into his arms was the only thing he could think about.

Don't miss COOPER (IM #553), available in March. And look for the rest of the clan's stories—Flynn and Kat's—as Linda Turner's exciting saga continues in

THE WILD WEST

Coming to you throughout 1994...only from Silhouette Intimate Moments.

The price of paradise...

New York Times Bestselling Author

previously published under
the pseudonym Erin St. Claire

Lost in paradise, they began a fantasy affair.

Through hot Jamaican days and steamy nights, Caren Blakemore
and Derek Allen shared half-truths and careless passion...

But as reality came crashing in, Caren learned the price. And she was
left with only one way out....

Available in April at your favorite retail outlet.

Only from ᐁ *Silhouette*

where passion lives

SBTP

COMING NEXT MONTH

#559 KEEPER—Patricia Gardner Evans
American Hero
From the moment American Hero Cleese Starrett encountered
Laurel Drew fishing in his river, he was hooked. But this alluring woman
had a tortured past and a threatened future, a future that Cleese wanted to
share—at any cost.

#560 TRY TO REMEMBER—Carla Cassidy
Romantic Traditions
"Jane Smith's" memory had vanished, so when Frank Longford offered
her a safe haven and a strong shoulder, she accepted. Then the nightmares
began, with remembrance proving scarier than amnesia, and Jane feared
losing the one man she truly loved.

#561 FULL OF SURPRISES—Maura Seger
Chas Howell's life changed irrevocably the day he laid eyes on
Annalise Johannsen. This feisty lady rancher needed help and protection,
and Chas knew the job would suit him just fine—and so would
the employer....

#562 STRANGER IN TOWN—Laura Parker
Jo Spencer thought she'd seen a ghost, so strongly did Gus Thornton
resemble the forbidden love of her past. But even though Gus claimed to
be new to town, Jo swore she glimpsed familiar desire—and haunted
memories—in this stranger's eyes.

#563 LAWYERS, GUNS AND MONEY—Rebecca Daniels
With the conviction of a major crime boss to her credit, federal prosecu-
tor Gillian Hughes became a red-hot target. Undercover agent Ash Cain
vowed to keep her safe. Yet soon he found himself in over his head,
because tough-guy Ash had fallen head over heels....

#564 HARD EVIDENCE—Laurie Walker
Pursuing the evidence that would clear her of a manslaughter charge,
Sergeant Laurel Tanner found herself with an unlikely ally, the dead
man's brother. But she soon feared that Scott Delany's helpful intentions
stemmed not from desire—but from double cross.

SPRING
fancy
'94

**They're sexy, single...
and about to get snagged!**

Passion is in full bloom as love catches
the fancy of three brash bachelors. You won't
want to miss these stories by three of
Silhouette's hottest authors:

CAIT LONDON
DIXIE BROWNING
PEPPER ADAMS

Spring fever is in the air this March—
and there's no avoiding it!

Only from

Silhouette®

where passion lives.

As seen on TV!
Free Gift Offer

With a Free Gift proof-of-purchase from any Silhouette® book, you can receive a beautiful cubic zirconia pendant.

This gorgeous marquise-shaped stone is a genuine cubic zirconia—accented by an 18" gold tone necklace.

(Approximate retail value $19.95)

Send for yours today...
compliments of ▼ *Silhouette*®
TM

To receive your free gift, a cubic zirconia pendant, send us one original proof-of-purchase, photocopies not accepted, from the back of any Silhouette Romance™, Silhouette Desire®, Silhouette Special Edition®, Silhouette Intimate Moments® or Silhouette Shadows™ title for January, February or March 1994 at your favorite retail outlet, together with the Free Gift Certificate, plus a check or money order for $2.50 (do not send cash) to cover postage and handling, payable to Silhouette Free Gift Offer. We will send you the specified gift. Allow 6 to 8 weeks for delivery. Offer good until March 31st, 1994 or while quantities last. Offer valid in the U.S. and Canada only.

Free Gift Certificate

Name: _____

Address: _____

City: _____ State/Province: _____ Zip/Postal Code: _____

Mail this certificate, one proof-of-purchase and a check or money order for postage and handling to: SILHOUETTE FREE GIFT OFFER 1994. In the U.S.: 3010 Walden Avenue, P.O. Box 9057, Buffalo NY 14269-9057. In Canada: P.O. Box 622, Fort Erie, Ontario L2Z 5X3

FREE GIFT OFFER   079-KBZ

ONE PROOF-OF-PURCHASE

To collect your fabulous FREE GIFT, a cubic zirconia pendant, you must include this original proof-of-purchase for each gift with the properly completed Free Gift Certificate.

079-KBZ